A Tale of Three Women

A Tale of Three Women

A Novel

by Eustace Palmer

AFRICA WORLD PRESS
TRENTON | LONDON | CAPE TOWN | NAIROBI | ADDIS ABABA | ASMARA | IBADAN

AFRICA WORLD PRESS
541 West Ingham Avenue | Suite B
Trenton, New Jersey 08638

Book design: Saverance Publishing Services
Cover design: Nii Okai Djarbeng

This work is pure fiction and any resemblance to actual persons is coincidental

Library of Congress Cataloging-in-Publication Data

Palmer, Eustace.
 A tale of three women : a novel / by Eustace Palmer.
    p. cm.
 ISBN 1-59221-736-2 (cloth) -- ISBN 1-59221-737-0 (pbk.)
 1. Female friendship--Fiction. 2. Sierra Leone--Fiction. I.
Title.
 PR9393.9.P35T35 2011
 823'.92--dc22

                          2010054292

Dedicated to the memory of my late mother

Comfort Thelma Palmer

and to my sisters: Eustacia, Monica, and Cecilia.

PROLOGUE

My friend, Adekunle, is always so punctual. I remember telling her that if, after she died, her funeral was set to begin, the mourners were already in the church, but the minister was not, she would rise from the dead, burst open her coffin, and walk out.

I suppose she must have got her punctuality from her father, the late Mr. Adetokumbo Decker, a one-time head-master of a leading boys' school and choirmaster of his church. Both Mr. Decker and his daughter were sticklers for correctness and punctuality.

So, naturally, I was surprised when Kunle kept me waiting at this restaurant at Rawdon Street for over forty-five minutes. Knowing her and what her reaction would be if I arrived late, I'd got there at fifteen minutes to twelve for our twelve o'clock appointment. I went to our usual table where I could get a good view of the street, sat down comfortably, and ordered a pint of Heineken to sip while I waited. At a quarter to one, she was still not there, and the waiter, a very handsome young boy of about twenty-one, must have started wondering what was going on with this middle-aged woman who came to a restaurant alone and would not order a meal until her friend arrived, but whose friend did not seem to materialize. Was this just a ruse to sit down and gaze at him, as quite a few women of her age were now fond of doing?

I gazed onto the lively, active street. Hawkers of all kinds were selling all kinds of wares. One fifteen-year old boy was selling small bags of cold water to anyone who felt thirsty and was willing to risk contamination. A young woman was selling corn on the cob from a basket that she balanced on her head delicately and with utmost efficiency. A baby of about nine months was strapped to her back; his feet were showing, as was his head, which hung back rather danger- ously, though he was sound asleep. I felt like rushing out and telling her that she needed to adjust the baby's head, for that young neck was hanging back in such a way that it could soon snap. Some women simply did not know how to strap young babies on their backs.

My god! What on Earth could have happened to Kunle? We had so much to discuss. We were both in the Old Girls Association of our former high school and needed to plan for the next annual dance. We had to report to the next meeting of the committee, and it did not look as if we were off to a good start. I was about to call over that sweet waiter and order a second Heineken when she breezed in, all five feet six inches of her. She was wearing a blue dress and black shoes and was carrying a large brown handbag.

"I am so very sorry, Beatrice, to have kept you waiting," she chimed, plopping her plump self onto the chair oppo- site me and putting her handbag on the floor.

"About time too," I said rather coldly, pretending to be offended, though it was impossible to be offended by the exuberant and inordinately jovial Kunle.

"You would not believe it," she said, "but I have had the most amazing experience."

"I dare say," I replied. "It had to be amazing to make you late for an important appointment. What is it? Have you met a new boyfriend?"

"What a one-track mind you have," she said. "No, this is not about men at all. It is about women. I have just met the most remarkable woman I have ever met in my fifty years of existence. Believe me a truly remarkable woman. You know that I am currently interviewing some women, old and not so old, for a research project I am conducting."

"Yes," I answered. I knew of Kunle's research project; she would talk about it whenever she got the chance. She was a Senior Lecturer in Sociology at the University in Freetown, having obtained a Ph.D. from Temple University in the United States. She was very good at what she did and had been able to obtain a sizeable grant from UNESCO to conduct some research that will, doubtlessly, result in a groundbreaking study of the attitudes, backgrounds and development of women in the Western area of Sierra Leone.

"Well," she continued, "I was introduced to this woman who lives at Murray Town, in a lovely house overlooking the estuary of the Sierra Leone River. Mrs. Priscilla Thompson is ninety years old and blind, but, believe me, she has the finest mind of any woman I have ever met and she has the most remarkable memory."

Kunle's talk about this old woman with the finest mind she had ever met aroused my curiosity tremendously, for, exuberant though she was, Kunle was not given to exaggeration. Her discipline and her training over the years, not to mention her ardent desire to be an effective teacher, had produced in her a penchant for accuracy. So I was sure she was speaking the truth. Besides, she had a very fine mind herself, and if anyone was in a position to judge the quality of others' minds, it was the brilliant Kunle. Small wonder that her male colleagues at the university were always in awe of her, in fact, were scared of her, and one of the reasons why she had never got married. Naturally, I was already beside myself with curiosity and itching to meet this Priscilla Thompson myself, this woman who had aroused the unqualified admiration of my brilliant and highly educated friend.

"I sat talking to Mama Thompson for two hours this morning," she continued. "What am I saying? Listening is more like it. I had hoped it would be an interview, and that I would be asking most of the questions. Instead, she did almost all the talking during those two hours, and I sat spellbound, hanging on her every word, while this woman, who still exudes tremendous zest for life, poured out her reminiscences. Believe me, it was the most educative two hours I have ever had in my life."

"She must surely be a most remarkable woman if she had that impact on YOU," I said. I would myself very much like to meet this woman who gave my highly educated friend such an educational experience.

"Yes," Kunle replied. "You must come with me the next time I go to interview her. You will be in for an unforgettable treat."

"Surely, I will" I said.

The following Wednesday, at nine thirty in the morning, I found myself in my friend Kunle's car being driven toward Murray Town, on the Western outskirts of Freetown. We left early, because we knew the traffic would be horrible. We had to contend with, among other things, the machismo of taxi drivers who thought that being in control of a car gave them an opportunity to demonstrate their masculine potency, and who would stop whenever they were hailed by a would be passenger, or try to overtake you or cut in ahead of you, thinking that your female timidity would force you to yield them right of way. If they thought so, they were hopelessly deceived in my friend Kunle. She was more than a match for them. With a determined glare she would press on ahead and dare them to come hit her car. Ultimately, they had to give in to defeat, no doubt cursing under their breaths. As we turned right into Wilkinson Road, we passed the fountain on the left that, instead of water, spouted mounds of garbage that someone had failed to collect. There was a badly executed statue of someone on top of it and a madman lying naked at its feet. Vehicles of every kind tried to merge into the traffic from Congo Town Road, and one needed to be the kind of skilled and determined driver my friend Kunle was to avoid being hit by them. Pedestrians walked on both sides of the road, mostly shabbily dressed and hungry looking. Some children were still making their way to school, despair rather than hope largely scrawled on their faces. A man dressed in rags was selling jelly coconuts to whoever wished to buy them. He deftly cut open the large fruits with a dirty looking cutlass that seemed specially designed to infect the purchaser with typhoid, cholera or some kind of dysentery. But these consumers must have been tough and immune; they always kept coming for more.

We turned right into Murray Town Road that had once been beautifully surfaced and macadamized, but was pockmarked all over with potholes that posed a challenge to any driver. However, my friend, Kunle, was as practiced a driver as any, and knew how to negotiate her way around them. In a few minutes we turned left onto the equally rugged but unbelievably vibrant street along which Mama Thompson's house stood. It was a magnificent pink and white building. It had been built a few decades ago, but was well maintained and still looked strong. We parked along the street and rattled the steel gate. In a few minutes we were ushered into Mama Thompson's parlor by a strong-looking young boy, obviously a servant of hers. The old woman sat majestically in a well- appointed chair slowly fanning herself. After some introductions and pleasantries were exchanged, she began her fascinating tale.

CHAPTER 1

I was born in 1910. You don't believe me? Well, I probably look much younger than I really am. It runs in the family. You should have seen how young my father looked in his coffin when he died at the age of 70. One of my friends told me that she could not believe he was a day older than sixty. I still have my birth certificate to prove that I am 90. I have other ways of proving it to you. You see, I still have a very good memory, and I can remember things that happened over eighty years ago. I can certainly remember the influenza epidemic that happened in 1918. Two of my aunts, my mother's younger sisters, Aunty Nancy and Aunty Sabina, died in that terrible scourge. Aunty Nancy could not have been more than twenty-one. She was my favorite aunt because whenever she went out she used to bring back all kinds of delicious eatables for us children such as coco-nut and ginger cakes. She would also tell us the most amusing stories.

Then, one day, we were told not to make a lot of noise because Aunty Nancy was ill. The house we lived in was a two-storied wooden house in typical Maroon town style along Bathurst Street, and we children were shunted upstairs one morning and commanded to stay there. I knew at once that something strange was afoot. The preparations for the burial must have been very hastily done. I suppose they did not want us to come face to face with the presence of death.

Although we could not go downstairs, we could look through the window at what was happening in the street. What I saw coming toward the house was unmistakable. It was an eight-foot long, black hearse with black feathers on the roof and glass panels on all the sides. Then it stopped right in front. The two men who had been pulling it opened the glass-paneled door of the hearse and pulled out a long brown box such as I had seen often during funeral processions. They proceeded to bring the box into our yard.

About half an hour later, I heard the piercing screams of women weeping bitterly and the authoritative tone of the men, ordering them to keep quiet and giving instructions:

"Pull it toward your own end so that it will be slack and there will be enough space for the head."

"That's right! Cross the hands across the chest. That's it."

Then, I heard the unmistakable sounds of hammering. Before long, I saw that the long brown box was being taken out and was followed by my mother and father, a stream of people walking behind them. It was placed securely into the hearse. The glass-paneled door was shut, and the procession moved up the street.

That was what I remember of my Aunty Nancy's death. The next day, of course, Aunty Nancy was not there. Aunty Sabina followed Aunty Nancy. She had, in fact, attended Aunty Nancy's funeral but fell ill a week after that. Soon, she too had died, and I saw the whole mysterious spectacle repeated. In a sense, both Aunty Nancy and Aunty Sabina were lucky, if one could call that luck. At least, they had a funeral where crowds of mourners accompanied their corpses to the church and cemetery. Some unfortunate people did not even have the honor of a funeral during that disastrous period. People were dropping like flies, and

everyone was afraid of venturing out, lest they became sick themselves.

I believe the government even forbade gatherings of any kind. Schools were closed down, and church services could not be held. The scourge took its toll on all kinds of people: old and young, male and female. Someone would be strong and healthy-looking one day and the next day, they would suddenly come down with severe fever and then die within three days. After a while, People even got scared of looking after the sick or handling the dead. There was no time to arrange funerals, and no carpenters even went to work to build coffins. Instead, once every day, everyone heard the lugubrious calls of the sanitary men as they made their rounds, ringing bells rhythmically and mournfully.

"Bring out your dead! Bring out your dead," they chanted.

The air was pregnant with death and the scarcely muffled sounds of women sobbing. We children stealthily sneaked out from under the beds where our parents had ordered us to hide and saw bodies being taken out and thrown on to the piles already on the carts that stopped outside of every house for its contribution.

Then as suddenly as it had started, the epidemic stopped. When we went back to school, we saw that quite a few of our friends were no longer there. All the children in my family survived.

My mother, Mrs. Druscilla Peters, was of proud settler stock. Her parents were direct descendants of the Maroons and Nova Scotians who came over from the West Indies and America toward the end of the eighteenth century. You can see some of their memorial tablets on the walls of Zion on the Level, Wilberforce Street, and College Chapel, Rawdon Street.

On my father's side, however, I am descended from liberated Africans. I remember my father, Thomas Peters, telling me that his grandfather was one of two young brothers who had been snatched from Yorubaland in the late eighteen twenties and were being taken as slaves to work on the plantations in America when their ship was surprised by British warships. The British eventually won the battle, rescued the slaves, and took them to Lumley village or Pasande as it was then called. My grandfather and his brother were both baptized and given the name of Peters. They both became very ardent church-goers after that, and started the two branches of the Peters family, which achieved some prominence in the rural area surrounding Freetown.

Although secondary schools had been established in Freetown by the time I was born, my father, who had himself attended the Sierra Leone Grammar School and was a highly respected Civil Servant earning the princely sum of sixteen pounds, thirteen shillings and four pence a month, and could easily have afforded to send me to secondary school, had some very strange views about the education of girls. To be fair to him, most men of his generation and class shared his views. He thought it was a waste of time and good money to invest in the education of girls who, at that time, were only destined for marriage and motherhood. Strangely, my mother had similar ideas.

She used to say: "The important thing is for you to comport yourself in such a manner that some day a 'broko-foot man' will see you and come ask us for your hand in marriage." A 'broko-foot man' is literally a man with a broken foot, but in reality a good, serious man. Then, she would continue: "you will marry him, have his children and look after his home. You will be very well provided for. But the important thing is to prepare yourself for that kind of life."

So, while my younger brother was given the privilege of a secondary education at the Sierra Leone Grammar School, we girls were educated only up to the primary school standard. But, believe me, the kind of education we had then was much more solid than the education received nowadays, and I am not exaggerating. I know of boys and girls who are currently in form four and even form five, who cannot tell you what twelve multiplied by twelve is. They simply do not know their multiplication tables. They also do not use the English language properly; you hear them saying things like "my brother and me" while we were taught to say "my brother and I." Nor can they tell you how many books there are in the old and New Testaments, or in what year Queen Victoria ascended the throne. I know of fifth formers who cannot tell you how many days Christ fasted in the wilderness, or when the British declared parts of Sierra Leone a protectorate. We knew all those things, although we had only a primary education. Our teachers knew what they were doing. Furthermore, if you were not destined for secondary school, and the teachers thought it was too early for you to leave school, they even suggested to your parents that you should spend an extra year in standard six, sometimes as a kind of assistant teacher; so you learnt a lot more. Moreover, we had manners, which is a lot more than can be said for the younger generation these days.

So I left school at about the age of sixteen, but that does not mean that I embarked on a life of idleness. Not a bit of it! From Monday to Friday, after doing my chores and having breakfast, I left our house at Bathurst Street and went to the house of my sewing mistress, Sissy Dinah. And I had to arrive punctually, as if I were still going to school. In fact, going to Sissy Dinah's from Monday to Friday was like going to a kind of finishing school. It was a kind of apprenticeship system whereby one was apprenticed to the sewing mistress for a number of years, but one learnt much more than merely how to sew. It was part of what you might call an informal educational system for girls. Most Krio girls, no matter what their class was, had to have a sewing mistress.

Of course, she taught them how to sew, so that when they got married and moved into their husbands' houses, they could sew the clothes for their family, and also make their own window and door curtains, cushion covers, and bed linen. One of the first things a husband bought his new wife was a sewing machine, and woe betide her if she did not know how to use it.

But the sewing mistress taught us much more than how to sew. She taught us how to cook and prepare all kinds of dishes. This was particularly useful if your own mother was an indifferent cook. My mother, being of settler stock, was very good at cooking stews, but she was not particularly good at cooking things like palava sauce, cassava leaves sauce, or potato leaves sauce. I perfected my skills at cooking those things during my apprenticeship with my sewing mistress. By the time the average Krio girl graduated from her apprenticeship, she was an accomplished cook who could be trusted to sustain her husband's health by preparing the most succulent dishes. She would also have learnt how to prepare things like ginger beer, rice bread and pap, which would be important for her children. The sewing mistress made a special point of sending us to market for her, so that we learnt how to buy the best goods and avoid the shoddy ones, and, most importantly, how to bargain. In fact, we spent more time learning how to cook and shop than we spent learning how to sew. It was a veritable education in home economics, as you would now call it.

At any given time, there may have been as many as ten young girls apprenticed to one sewing mistress, so we ended up learning how to interact with people of different temperaments and backgrounds. The friendships made here lasted for the rest of our lives.

I spent about four years with Sissy Dinah. My stay with her came suddenly to an end in the most unexpected of ways. She was about forty-five years old and was quite a good-looking woman, though she was still unmarried. However, with her sewing business and ten or so young girls apprenticed to her, she made a very good living. She rented the lower floor of a very nice two-storied house along Pa Demba Road, and her home was always luxuriously appointed. Of course the house had to be luxuriously appointed; she was an excellent seamstress and made the most wonderful window curtains, door curtains and cushion covers. Although she was financially comfortable and didn't need a husband to support her, we knew that she was receiving the attentions of quite a few men.

There was one man in particular who seemed to be her regular beau. He was tall, about fifty years old, and very handsome. He had a very good job at the Cable and Wireless Department, as we called it in those days, and he made enough money to masquerade as the handsome beau around town. He was always dressed in white: white gabardine trousers, white shoes, white shirt, and even a white coat. In fact, we all called him Mr. White. We never got to know his real name. He knew he was handsome and that the ladies ogled him, and you should have seen how he strutted about, erect and head held high, sending his long legs ahead of him like a marionette. How we young apprentices secretly giggled whenever he came to visit Sissy Dinah and they went inside the house and locked themselves securely for about two hours in Sissy Dinah's inner room, the holy of holies, as we used to call it!

The trouble about their relationship, though, was that Mr. White was married with a wife and five children. In my innocence, I often wondered whether or not it bothered Sissy Dinah that she was carrying on with someone else's husband. It would have been one thing were it a clandestine relationship. But the whole street seemed to know about it. Indeed, Sissy Dinah seemed rather proud of the fact that she was the special girlfriend or 'sweetheart' of the desirable

Mr. White. I later realized that that sort of thing did not bother people much in those days; it was almost accepted that handsome married men who earned a lot of money would have sweethearts, as they were called, outside the home, some of whom would even bear children for them.

For all intents and purposes they were polygamists although they had only one legally married wife that the law and the church recognized. For some odd reason, the wives did not mind the 'sweethearts' who bore children for their husbands as much as they minded those who did not. I suppose they saw those sweethearts who bore no children as loose women, whereas those who had children had a sense of responsibility toward the children and would elicit an equal responsibility in the men. I once heard a woman say, "I do not mind how much time my husband spends outside our home, as long as he supports our children and brings me mine when he comes back home."

Mr. White certainly seemed to spend most of his time at Sissy Dinah's, but in his case, his wife, Sarian, seemed to object very strongly. One fine Friday morning, we had all settled down to the sewing chores Sissy Dinah had given us when a tall, thin, dark woman strutted confidently into the compound.

"Young girls, good morning," she said in a sweet calm voice.

"Good morning Ma," we all chimed in respectful response.

"Is your mistress in?" she asked.

"Yes, Ma," answered one of the apprentices. "Priscilla, go and tell Sissy Dinah that someone has come to see her."

When I went inside, Sissy Dinah was giving instructions on how to make a particular kind of skirt.

"Sissy Dinah," I said, "there is a lady outside who has come to see you Ma."

My mistress left what she was doing and came outside to see who this visitor was.

"Good morning," she greeted the visitor affably.

"Good morning," the visitor replied in a voice that was still calm. "Are you Dinah?"

"Yes. I am Dinah."

Then all hell broke loose. The woman who had appeared so calm and had spoken in such civil tones suddenly placed her arms akimbo and shouted at the top of her voice for the whole neighborhood to hear:

"So you are the 'senjago' who is trying to take my husband away from me! You are the filthy 'raray' girl who is incapable of finding her own man but has to steal other women's husbands!"

She then turned toward the street and shouted, "Pa Demba Road people please come and see the slut who has stolen my husband and keeps him here in her nasty house, preventing him every day from going home to his wife and family! Come and see the senjago!"

She then picked up a small tin bucket and a nearby stone and started beating the bucket with the stone, making such a racket that the very dead must have woken up.

"Well today will be a day for the two of us," she continued. "This yard will not be big enough to hold the two of us if you do not swear immediately that you will have nothing further to do with my husband."

There was nothing that Freetown then loved, as it does now, like a good quarrel between two women, especially if it was over a man. A crowd had already started to gather outside the gate and I could see the more respectable women peeping from behind the blinds of their houses to watch the fray. This was certainly the effect that Mama Sarian intended, and she was gratified by the response. She raised her voice even louder and beat the bucket with even greater intensity.

9

"I say leave my husband alone! Leave my husband alone and go find your own man."

You may easily believe that my sewing mistress was taken aback by this onslaught that had suddenly materialized out of nowhere. When the woman had entered, Sissy Dinah must have thought Sarian was some new customer come to place an order for a new dress; instead, here was her rival humiliating her to the entertainment of the entire neighborhood. She was open-mouthed with astonishment; however, she soon recovered her composure and started giving back as good as she got.

"Who are you," she shouted, "who are you to come into my compound and accuse me of keeping your husband?" She started clapping her hands: "Neighbors, please come and see my trouble. I was here this blessed God's morning minding my own business when this good-for-nothing woman whom I have never seen before came into my compound and started accusing me of taking her husband. Come and see my trouble oh!"

"Do you deny it?" continued Sarian, "Do you have the gall to deny that my lawfully married husband has been spending almost every evening after work here locked in your room with you? What have you been doing in there? Have you been teaching him to sew? Do you think I do not have my spies? They have seen him coming here every day to visit you, you Jezebel! Well let me tell you, Senjago, if you don't leave my husband alone, dogs will lick your blood, just like they did to Jezebel in the Bible. Mark my words!"

"Ibosio!" shouted my sewing mistress, who now realized that there was no point in denying the accusation. "So you are the dried up witch who cannot satisfy her husband so that he comes looking to other women for comfort and enjoyment. Just look at you! You are old and skinny and ugly. What man would want you? Are you surprised that he comes here looking for what you are unable to give him?

Look at you and look at me? You are a pot of dried up beans. So, you must not complain that your husband goes around looking for the fresh, succulent stuff. I can give him what he wants. I am young. I am beautiful. You are an old withered plantain tree."

"I may be skinny," Sarian replied, "but at least, I am not barren. I have given him five children. Five! You are shriveled up inside and sterile and barren. You are a witch who has eaten up all the children inside you. Or maybe you have sacrificed them for your medicine so that you can keep on attracting young men. It is your bad life that is following you wherever you go."

"Do you dare call me barren?" shouted my mistress. "Look, I am still young. I can still have children. It is you who are barren. You are like a dead palm tree that is just waiting to fall down. You can have no more children even if your husband were to sleep with you every day of the year, twenty-four hours a day. And now I challenge you. Just you leave your husband with me for one more month and I swear to God I will bear him male twins."

"You bear male twins?" replied Sarian. "Where will you keep them in that stick-like body of yours? You will die childless in your old age like a dog, without any one to take care of you, and you will be buried in the king's highway. But I am warning you. I am warning you in the presence of your apprentices and the whole of Pa Demba Road, leave my husband alone and let him come back to his wife and family. Or else, I swear to God that when I have finished with you, I will make you curse the day you were born and the useless mother who gave you birth."

With that, the wife marched out of the compound, slamming the gate behind her and still shouting recriminations for the benefit of the neighbors.

"Do you dare insult my mother?" shouted my mistress as she tried to dash after Sarian. "It is your own mother who is useless and who gave birth to such a useless daughter. Do you dare threaten me? Do you dare threaten me you useless old witch?" She was spoiling for a physical confrontation. However, some of the other occupants of the compound managed to restrain her. As much as they enjoyed the verbal fisticuffs between the two female rivals, they did not want the argument to degenerate into a physical fight in the open street. Everyone knew that although our mistress had put on a very brave face, she would prove no match for the strong and furious Sarian who would have fought with obvious right on her side.

My mistress allowed herself to be restrained, but she went on:

"Imagine that foul-mouthed witch coming into my compound this God's morning and insulting me, when she is to blame for her husband going after other women! But it was just as well that you held me, friends. I would have showed her pepper. If I had gotten hold of her, I would have ground her teeth into the dust and made her eat grass. The nincompoop!"

She strutted into the house.

We apprentices looked meaningfully at each other as if to say "this was bound to happen someday," but we did not utter our thoughts aloud and we went back to our work. Everything returned to normal after that. I say "normal" because the confrontation did not result in Mr. White's ceasing his visits to Sissy Dinah. In fact, from what I could gather, it seemed as if the row had given a tremendous boost to his ego. I heard he even bragged to Sissy Dinah that when news of the confrontation reached him that day at his work, he went home immediately and beat his wife within an inch of her life. How dare she raise a scandal and question his male privilege of having as many women as he wished? Did he not provide adequately for her and her five children? Had he not graced her with his name? Did she not go about calling herself Mrs.? Did she not wear his ring? Did they not go to church together every Sunday and sit in the same pew and wasn't their family treated as such by all and sundry? What more could she want?

My mistress for her part seemed to bask in the glow of being the preferred woman of the dashing Mr. White, to the full knowledge of the entire neighborhood. She even seemed to think it was good for her business. A month went by, and she seemed to have put all thoughts of Sarian and her threats completely out of her mind. One Thursday, however, she was reminded of it all. That's when an old man who, from the big country- cloth gown that he wore, seemed to have come originally from up country, came into the compound and asked for her. The man looked very mysterious and all-knowing. He had broad tribal marks on his dark lean face. His hands were gnarled, and he was barefoot. His eyes were sharp and reddish. Just looking at him sent a chill down my spine. Had I been old enough to give advice to grown-ups I would have warned Sissy Dinah not to meddle with such a man. But I kept my thoughts to myself, while remaining alert, as did all the other apprentices, for this old man had aroused our curiosity, and even though Sissy Dinah invited him into her parlor and we apprentices were outside in the yard, we could not help overhearing the main details of the conversation:

"I am Pa Alimamy," the man said. "I am a murray man, a medicine man. Please, my sister, don't think it strange that I have come to you, instead of the other way round. Usually, it is people who come to me to help them solve their problems: to cure them of their sicknesses or, in some cases, to get rid of their enemies. I can do that. I can see far. I can see into the distance and I can see into the future. But you must not think, my sister, that we murray men are all wicked. More often than not, we help people, and in my case, in particular, if I see any evil threatening someone, I warn the person, even though the person may not have come to consult me."

By this time my mistress was not only curious, she was shivering with dread.

"God forbid," she said, "that anyone should wish to harm me. I have done no harm to anyone; I have no enemies. When I go to church on Sunday I pray for everyone, even for those who might wish to harm me without a cause."

"Yes, my sister, but the world is bad. Are you sure that you have no enemies? Look deep into your heart and consider. Think deeply. These days you do not have to be bad for someone to wish to harm you. You would not believe the number of good people who have been killed by wicked men and women. Sometimes for position, sometimes for money or property... sometimes for beauty... sometimes for the men..."

At those words, my mistress gave an involuntary shudder and looked down.

"Yes," continued Pa Alimamy. "I can see that you remember now. You are a very beautiful woman, and your beauty gives you enemies. I felt it one day this week when I passed by your gate. After I went home, I was ill throughout the day. I consulted my spirits who told me that Dinah, in this house, was in very grave danger from her enemies. I consulted them further and they gave me all the details. Hm! Hm! Hm! The world is bad."

By this time my mistress was beside herself with anxiety and curiosity.

"What is the danger, Pa Alimamy? Please tell me."

"You have a handsome lover, no? And his wife would like to have him all to herself. Many women do not mind sharing their men, but there are some selfish women who would rather have their men all to themselves and they will do anything to bring this about. They will kill for their men. Believe me, the world is so bad."

"Lord have mercy! Lord have mercy!" shouted my mistress. "So they want to kill me for my man. But God will not allow them. The great God above will not allow them."

"Ishallai!" exclaimed Pa Alimamy, religious solemnity and devotion written all over his face. "That is why the spirits revealed your danger to me, so that I could warn you and let you know what you must do to triumph over your enemies. Look for yourself."

He reached into a large pocket in his dirty gown and brought out a cluster of cowries. He rattled them for a while in his gnarled, tightly shut hand, while muttering incomprehensible incantations. Beads of perspiration started running down his aged face. Then, his whole body suddenly convulsed with an ecstatic "ah" and he dropped the cowries. For a while, he remained in deep concentration, eyes firmly closed. Then, he suddenly seemed to wake out of his stupor and as if seeing them for the first time, looked at the arrangement of cowries on the floor.

"Allahamdudilai! It's Just as the spirits revealed to me. My cowries never lie. Do you see those three cowries over there? That small one is you; the bigger one in the middle is the man; that one, the biggest of all, is the other woman. You see how the sharp edge of the cowrie is turned toward you? It means she intends to kill you. See how menacing she looks? And see how dark the area around your own cowrie looks? It means darkness is about to engulf you, the darkness of death. I am sorry for you my sister. Believe me, I am sorry for you."

At this Pa Alimamy actually started shedding tears. Perhaps, if my mistress had not had the confrontation with Sarian, Mr. White's wife, she might have doubted the truth of Pa Alimamy's divination. But hadn't Sarian publicly sworn that she would deal with her, that she would make her curse the day she was born? Hadn't Sarian threatened her? And here was this murray man confirming it all, although he obviously knew more than he was prepared to say. He must be speaking the truth. She had a deadly enemy who was after her life. But the ways of God, the great Jehovah, are inscrutable. He really works in mysterious ways. He had ensured that this aged sage got wind of Sarian's evil intentions and had bid him come to warn her of the threatened catastrophe.

"Aye, Papa God tenke! Pa Alimamy, tenke tenke, sir," my mistress blurted out in sincere gratitude for her timely deliverance from that evil witch Sarian. "I don't know how to thank you for what you have done. It is God himself who has brought you to me. Yes, you are right. I have a handsome lover whose wife came here not more than a month ago. She threatened to kill me if I did not leave her husband alone. When her husband came home and found out, he gave her a sound beating; now she wants to take it all out on me. It is God himself who has brought you to me. Please tell me what I must do to get rid of this threat."

"It will not be easy; this woman is really dangerous and deadly," Pa Alimamy said. "Remember, she is the wife, and her husband gave her a very good beating. She does not only want her husband all to herself, she wants to take revenge on you completely. She wants to kill you. She is already working on it. But the spirits will not allow it, if you do as I say. You will have to carry out a sacrifice. You must perform the sacrifice early on Sunday morning before everyone wakes up. It must be done with a white cock, four white kola nuts, four red ones, and a cup of white uncooked rice. You must take the whole lot to the junction of Westmoreland Street and Bathurst Street and leave them where the four roads meet. I will then boil some special leaves and bring the brew to you in a bottle. Every day for seven days, beginning with the Sunday following the sacrifice, you must put a cup of the brew into a bucket of cold water and wash your whole body thoroughly, from head to toe. Don't use

any soap. It will be a foul-smelling brew, but it would not be effective if it did not smell. That way we will get rid of the threat completely and you will live long to prosper and enjoy your lover."

"Pa Alimamy, Tenke, tenke, tenke, sir," said my mistress, clasping her hands. She then knelt before the scruffy old man and almost wiped his dirty feet with her beautiful hair.

Pa Alimamy was true to his word. Within a week he brought my mistress the brew he had promised. My mistress also played her part. That Monday morning, as I walked along Westmoreland Street on my way to Krootown Road Market to purchase a few items for my mother before going to Sissy Dinah's, I saw the body of a large white cock in the middle of the road. It was surrounded by grains of uncooked rice and several lobes of kola nuts. We did not have motorcars in those days, so the cock was not mashed to a pulp as it would be nowadays. I shuddered as I looked into its large glazed eyes that looked accusingly at the world. I knew that Sissy Dinah had performed the sacrifice that Pa Alimamy stipulated.

A few days later, some of us were settled down at our sewing machines, assiduously performing the tasks our mistress had assigned us that morning, when we saw her coming out of the back door of the house. It was a beautiful morning in the month of May. The sun was already shining brightly in a cloudless, blue sky, though it was not yet hot, as it was still morning. Sissy Dinah had a small garden to the side of the house where she cultivated some rose and jasmine plants. The plants were out in full blossom, the jasmines standing out in beautiful contrast to the pink and red roses, and the air was fragrant with lush scent. As Sissy Dinah came out of the house, her beautiful face shone with radiance. Dark people can be so much more beautiful than lighter people, particularly when they are happy. She was bare from the shoulders upwards and had a blue lappah tightly draped around the rest of her body. As she made her way to the outhouse that served as a bathroom, she exuded health and happiness, which was no doubt due to her conviction that she was taking the essential steps to ensure her continued health and prosperity and the discomfiture of the evil forces that threatened her life. She walked elegantly on the paved stones, holding in her right hand a large bottle with a very dark liquid in it. Almost immediately, the fragrance that we had enjoyed so far was transformed into the foulest-smelling aroma. It was as if a corpse that had lain rotting in the earth for weeks was suddenly dug up, or as if mounds of feces from a nearby lavatory had been hauled up and scattered all over the length and breadth of the compound.

We all held our breaths and started sniffing. "Hnm! Hnm! Hnm!" rang through the air that had hitherto been perfectly pure. When we realized the source of the foul-smelling aroma, our sniffing was replaced by poorly muffled giggles.

"You are laughing at me, aren't you?" said Sissy Dinah. "My daughters, please don't mind me. I am trying my best for my body. I am trying to stay healthy and protect myself from the wiles of wicked women. When you get to my age, you will know that the world is bad, and you must do whatever it takes to protect your beauty and your life. So go on and laugh at me, but you will probably be doing the same thing twenty years from now."

From the bathroom we could hear the "splash" "splash" of the water as Sissy Dinah bathed herself thoroughly. She was so happy, she sang as she bathed. Her singing was infectious, and in spite of the disgusting aroma that filled the air for the rest of that day, some of us could not help joining in the popular ditty that came from the bathroom in melodious tones.

"Akpa ooman doyah, buy you roboh rum,
Akpa ooman doyah, buy you roboh rum.

Buy you penny ginger, buy you one cup sugar.
Make you ginger beer sweet
Tangains boy go buy am."

Then, suddenly, that beautiful May day was completely transformed. Dark clouds appeared out of nowhere and obscured the erstwhile bright sun. A heavy breeze started to blow.

"It's going to be a tornado," yelled one of my mates as we scampered indoors for safety. Within a few minutes, the heaviest downpour I have ever experienced was drenching the earth. As the lightning sparked, we screamed with fear, whistled for protection, and covered our ears against the expected thunder. Sissy Dinah, who was still trapped in the bathroom, shouted to us to bring her an umbrella, so that she could run into the safety of the house. But so heavy was the downpour, and so loud the thunder that most of the girls were terrified to do so. However, I revved up my courage, grabbed an umbrella that was rolled up in a corner, and rushed out to her as she cowered beneath the eaves. As we both rushed into the house under totally inadequate cover, I was almost stifled by the disgusting smell that exuded from her body. It was as if I was standing next to a decomposing corpse. Normally, a bath should cleanse a person and make her fragrant, but Sissy Dinah, to my offended nostrils and young imagination, seemed truly polluted by her bath that day.

The storm did not last long; nonetheless, we all stayed indoors for the rest of the day. No matter where we were, though, that disgusting smell persisted. It was as if death itself and corruption were in the air. We knew that since Pa Alimamy had instructed Sissy Dinah to bathe with the disgusting lotion for seven days, we had to endure that stench for a whole week and more. Some of the girls even feigned illness and did not come to work for a few days. Josephine, one of my closest friends, said that the smell clung to her even after she got home. Her mother sniffed it on her and asked her, rather snottily, where she'd been. She had to bathe herself thoroughly and use the most fragrant perfume to get rid of it.

Two weeks later when we went to Sissy Dinah's as usual, we discovered that she was ill and was confined to her bed. We had to go into her bedroom to be given our instructions for the day. I was shocked by what I saw before me. Her formerly beautiful and lustrous face was ashy gray and seemed to lack any life. Wrinkles had developed within a few days, and the once brilliant eyes were dazed. The soft melodious voice was now hoarse and her whole body was listless.

Later, she called me into the room and I saw that she was shivering horribly. She asked me to get more blankets from a nearby cupboard and cover her with them. When I did as she asked, I discovered that her body was actually very hot. I simply could not believe there could be such a change in a person's bodily wellbeing within just a few hours. We apprentices looked at each other, hardly daring to utter our fears. When we did speak, it was in muffled tones and whispers. As the day progressed, Sissy Dinah got much worse, and her relations had to be summoned. They decided to take her to the hospital immediately. She had to be put into one of those lorries that we used to call "bone-shakers" because they were poorly constructed and had next to no suspension. You should have heard Sissy Dinah howling. Whenever any part of her body was touched, she was in the most excruciating pain. She screamed as if she was being touched with burning torches. Some said that she howled all the way to the hospital as the bone-shaker shook and her body and decaying bones rattled.

Of course, we apprentices had to suspend going to her house because there was no one to give us instructions. Then one dull morning, the gate of our house at Bathurst Street opened, and my friend Josephine walked into our yard.

"Sissy Dinah is dead," she announced.

We hugged each other and gave vent to our grief. She had been a very good sewing mistress, but also a kind of mother to all of us. It was like losing a very close relation. How could she be dead? Less than three weeks ago, she was young, healthy and vibrant. And now, she was as dead as a doornail. She had been mightily deceived by that evil ogre, Pa Alimamy. He had cunningly tricked her by telling her things, seventy five percent of which were true. Yes, it was true that she had a handsome lover; it was true that she had a deadly rival in love, and that this rival was determined to have her life. But Pa Alimamy did not come as her savior to protect her from the wiles of her fierce antagonist; he was actually the agent of that antagonist and had employed his skills and deadly, foul-smelling brew to end her life. When she bathed with that filthy concoction, she was not cleansing and fortifying her body; she was actually polluting it and dooming it to destruction. Yes, the world is bad.

As her apprentices, we were expected to be on hand that day to help sew Sissy Dinah's shroud. In those days there was no refrigeration, and funerals had to be held within twenty-four hours of the person's death. Sissy Dinah's funeral was fixed for four in the afternoon that day. It was the first time that I had actually helped to sew a shroud. Of course, Sissy Dinah had sewn shrouds before, but she had done them herself and, according to tradition, had started at midnight, so that by morning when we apprentices arrived for work, she was already finished. Now we actually had to help shape those yards and yards of immaculate lace and satin materials into the beautiful, wide-skirted shroud that would drape the body of our sewing mistress. I shuddered as I sat down at my sewing machine. Some of the girls even burst into tears.

We worked fast, and there were many of us. So, although the shroud was elaborate, trimmed with all kinds of beads, bows, and frills, we finished it just after midday. Some of us had also sewn the white lace curtains that, according to tradition, had to be hung on the windows. When they brought the body of poor Sissy Dinah home from the mortuary at about one o'clock in the afternoon, we all burst into tears and shouts of lamentation. Four sturdy men struggled to get the body, wrapped in a red hospital blanket and laid on a stretcher, through the door of the house and into the bedroom, where it would be prepared for burial. Our grief would have been great in any case, but it was intensified by our shock when we saw the condition of the corpse. The once beautiful face now looked old, wrinkled and coal black, and poor Sissy Dinah's body was bloated to about twice its usual size. When some of her male relations saw the corpse, they had to rush to the undertakers to let them know that they had to make a much bigger coffin than the one they had been working on. The inevitable delay caused the funeral to be rescheduled for four-thirty instead of four o'clock.

In the meantime, the female relations washed and dressed the body in the lovely white lace and satin shroud, a shroud truly befitting a sewing mistress, and Sissy Dinah was laid out in the parlor on a bed that had been brought there for the purpose. I am sure I was not the only one who remarked on the stark contrast between the ugliness of that once beautiful face, now unnaturally aged, winkled, and contorted in death agony in spite of the skilful efforts of those who prepared the body (some say she had died howling) and the loveliness of that elegant shroud, lovelier and more elaborate than anything Sissy Dinah had ever worn during her lifetime. I kept thinking to myself, "what, after all, is man? Everything, including beauty, will pass away. All is but vanity."

The coffin was so enormous, that the men who were struggling to take it out could not get it through the door. They had to get it through one of the windows by first

22

resting it on the ledge, while some other men received it outside. Word had spread rapidly through Freetown about the mysterious and baffling death, and hundreds of people turned up for the funeral. Some came out of curiosity, but Sissy Dinah also had many friends, relations and customers, and they all came out to pay their last respects. So it was a very long procession that followed the corpse to Buxton Church and from there, to King Tom cemetery.

That was the end of Sissy Dinah. Of course, news spread like wildfire throughout Freetown that it was Sarian, Mr. White's wife, who had killed her. Sarian strenuously denied it. I once saw her loudly defending herself at Kissy Road Market to a group of stone-faced women, who, I am sure, did not believe a word of what she said. Mr. White obviously believed the rumors and, in great anger, gave her a sound beating and then, kicked her out of his house without a penny to her name. Apparently, he shouted after her that if she was capable of killing her rival out of jealousy, he could have no guarantee that she would not kill him by poisoning his food. He could not allow such a woman to continue cooking for him and his children.

They had been married for over twenty years and had got five children together, but the only things she was allowed to take with her were her clothes. Mr.White installed one of his many female admirers in the house to replace his wife and look after him and the children. Sarian went to live with one of her relations at Krootown Road and was obliged to eke out a harsh living by selling plantains and fried akara and abobo. She died in great misery a few years later. From what I heard, Mr. White did not even turn up for the funeral, and he forbade any of the children to do so.

CHAPTER 2

That was the end of my sojourn at Sissy Dinah's establishment. The sewing school was disbanded, and we went our separate ways. However, the friendships we had formed there were to last. Some of us are still very good friends. There were three of us who shared a particularly close bond, though we were very different from one another. Josephine Freeman was a high-spirited girl, though not especially beautiful. Nonetheless, she had several advantages that ensured that, in spite of her plain looks, she would make a very good marriage. Her parents were aristos, as we used to call them, Freetown people who belonged to the social elite. They looked down rather snobbishly at the less fortunate members of the community and used to boast that they were of pure settler stock, totally unadulterated by liberated African blood. Indeed, I believe they spoke nothing but English at home. Josephine's father, Columbus Freeman, had even gone to Fourah Bay College and was a Bachelor of Arts. He was one of the few indigenous Sierra Leoneans to hold a senior position in the Sierra Leone Civil Service, the upper cadres of which were almost entirely occupied by Englishmen. I believe he was Colonial Secretary, and he and his wife hobnobbed with doctors, lawyers, and Englishmen and went to garden parties at Government House. They lived in a big stone house along Circular Road.

As a young girl, Josephine had attended the Annie Walsh Memorial School, but in those days there was no preferable occupation open to her after school. She certainly did not wish to be a teacher, and she could not go to College. It was the 1920s, remember. Though fairly well-educated, marriage and motherhood were all she could look forward to. Her parents wanted her to be well prepared for this life, so she had to be apprenticed to a sewing mistress. That was how she came to be apprenticed to Sissy Dinah.

At first, we the other girls were repelled by her high and mighty airs. For the first few days she refused to speak in Krio, always turning up her nose whenever anyone spoke to her and pretending that she did not understand a word of what we said. How we laughed at her behind her back and made up songs to mock her! All this, however, came to an end one fine day, when she was forced to blend in with the rest of us.

Sissy Dinah called her in and told her it was her turn to go to market and shop for some fish and foofoo.

"I do not know how to shop for foofoo," she replied. "In our house, the nurse and the servants shop for things like foofoo."

"Well, while you are here, you will do like all the other girls and learn how to shop and cook," Sissy Dinah replied. "That is why you are here."

With great reluctance, she grabbed the basket and money that the courageous Sissy Dinah thrust into her hands and made her way to Krootown Road Market. Actually, I believe she did quite well with the bargaining, for when she returned, Sissy Dinah complimented her on her shopping. We all then happily joined in with pounding and straining the foofoo. About an hour later, Sissy Dinah said, "Josephine, you will now have to cook the foofoo."

"Yes, Sissy Dinah," Josephine replied.

About half an hour later, Sissy Dinah saw Josephine joking and horsing around with all the other girls in the compound and she shouted out, "Josephine, have you finished cooking the foofoo? Why are you not in the kitchen cooking it?"

To our great astonishment Josephine replied, "That is alright, Sissy Dinah. The foofoo is boiling"

"Lord, have mercy," shouted Sissy Dinah. "What do you mean, the foofoo is boiling?"

We all burst into the most uproarious laughter at Josephine's expense. It was quite clear that in her kind of home, she had never seen foofoo being cooked. She thought you were supposed to cook it like rice: pour some water on it, put it on to the fire and leave it to boil. Our laughter at her was curative, though. After that, Josephine mellowed out. She came off her high horse and became one of the group.

The other member of our little trio was Annie Macauley. She was of much humbler stock, both of her parents having descended from liberated Africans. They occupied a small one-story house at the lower end of Circular Road. She was a very pretty girl, with a fair complexion, dark brown eyes, lovely rings on her neck, and a beautiful gap between her two front very white teeth. She had long, black, glossy hair that she was constantly having plaited. When she smiled or laughed the whole world seemed to be a pleasant place to live in, and she was always laughing. Very few things seemed to annoy or disturb her, and she always seemed to look for the silver lining behind every cloud. Although she was so pretty, she was far from being arrogant, maybe because of her humble origins. She was always repeating the favorite adage of our mothers: that all she was hoping for was for a "broko-foot man" to turn up some day, marry her, and father eight children.

Well, when we all left Sissy Dinah's establishment, marriage was about the only thing on our minds. We were all about twenty years old at the time.

I remember one morning, I had just returned from Krootown road market where I had been shopping for the usual ingredients in order to cook the day's meals, when my mother called me into the parlor and said:

"Come here for a minute, Priscilla, I have something to say to you."

"Yes, Mama," I replied, putting down the basket of fish I had in my hands, and sat down opposite my mother in the parlor. There was a look of joy on her simple face, although she was trying to look stern at the same time.

"Well, our God is a good God," she said. "You will now see why I have always told you to comport yourself decently and properly. A man has come forward to marry you, and your father has agreed."

This sudden news produced a mixture of alarm and joy in me. Who would not be overjoyed at the prospect of marriage at such an early age? In those days, it was what all girls were destined for. I knew of several women who were in their thirties before they got married; some had even got one or two children before they got married, at times not to the men with whom they had the children; some got children and never got married; some simply never got married at all and never had any children. Those were the most pitiful of all. And here was I, twenty years old and fresh from my sewing mistress's school, and someone had already come forward to marry me. I would have my own home, my own husband, and my own children. It would be a beautiful life, the life for which I had been so carefully prepared. And yet, I was alarmed because I did not know who the man was. Suppose he was in his forties and already getting gray! Suppose he was ugly or fat or very poor and we had to live in the poorest areas of the town! How my friends would laugh at me! I can just imagine what Josephine would say. But I had no choice. In those days, marriages were arranged, and once my father said yes to the marriage proposal, I would have to go along dutifully.

Whatever were my real thoughts, I pretended to be satisfied and happy, as my mother went on.

"He is a decent and respectable and hardworking young man. He is about twenty-seven."

At this, my heart leapt with joy. At least my husband-to-be was young, not someone on the verge of middle age.

"He is called Bernard Thompson. He is quite educated and is a third grade clerk in the Public Works Department, where he earns a decent salary and will be able to keep you in a good home. Besides he is ambitious and will go very far. He is a good Christian and a chorister at Holy Trinity Church. He is the son of the late Patrick Thompson, who died some years ago, but his mother, Millicent Thompson, is still alive and they live at Guard Street. They are very decent people and it will be good for us to be connected with such a family. We have looked into the family's entire history. Both his mother's and his father's people originally came from York village, and there is no history of madness, or strange diseases, or witchcraft in the family. It will be a very good marriage."

I smiled radiantly. If my parents were pleased, I had to be pleased as well. My smile expressed not just my happiness, but also my gratitude to my parents for helping to make such wonderful provision for me. I would have a husband to provide for me and look after me, and, God willing, children to provide for me in my old age. What more could a woman want?

"You can see now," my mother continued, "the importance of comporting yourself decently. If you had not done so, do you think a good man would have come forward to marry you?"

"No Mama," I said, "I am happy and grateful."

"You can go now and continue with your cooking. Your intended will come to the house this evening to talk to your Pa and have his first conversation with you. You must prepare yourself."

Dutifully, I went back to the pantry to continue my preparations for cooking. I still had mixed feelings about the marriage. There was still one problem, which, apparently, was of no importance to my mother. Was my husband-to-be handsome? I almost shut my eyes and prayed to God that he would be.

Fortunately, he turned out to be quite good-looking, in his way. He was not overly handsome, but he had a very pleasant and attractive face. He was of lighter complexion than I was, about five-foot nine, and he walked erect and with great dignity. He was also quite slim, though broad in the shoulders.

He also showed tremendous respect to my mother and father when he came to visit us that evening, and he was quite considerate toward me. I was extremely pleased with my "catch" and considered myself very lucky. This was not a "broko-foot man" at all; this was an extremely eligible young man.

My friends Annie and Josephine were ecstatic when I told them later that week.

"You lucky so-and-so!" exclaimed Josephine. "What medicine did you and your mother have to work in order to catch him? Young men of his kind are rare to come by these days. If they show any attentions toward you, it is because they want you-know- what from you. Then, after they have ruined you they go and marry someone else with wealthy parents. Annie, when do you think our own turn will come?"

"With God's help," Annie replied, "we too will soon be lucky. I pray for it every day. I am very happy for you, Priscilla. I suppose you will want Josephine and I to be your chief bridesmaids, won't you? Please, please, please! I have never been a chief bridesmaid before, and they say that if you are a chief bridesmaid, your own turn to marry will soon come."

"Of course," I replied happily. "You two will be my chief bridesmaids. Who knows, some dashing young men might see you at the wedding and ask their parents to approach yours for your hands in marriage. God moves in mysterious ways."

My happiness was almost complete. The usual pre-marriage ceremonies were undertaken. One day, my would-be-husband's family duly came to our house and, during an elaborate engagement ceremony, formally asked my father to allow their son to marry me. They promised to nurture and take care of me, and to help foster good relations between the two families.

I say "almost complete", because there was one major problem, and that was my would-be-husband's mother.

Mrs. Millicent Thompson was a very domineering woman. She was rather short, quite stout, and had a voice like a man's. In fact, it was generally rumored that she had worn the trousers in the Thompson house since day one, and that her husband's fatal heart attack was caused by her continual harassment. She was a sides-woman at Holy Trinity Church, and I myself know for a fact that whenever it was time to take up the collection, she always insisted on leading the group of four sides-women. She would hold her head erect, clutch the collection plate in her right hand, and march to the front row in a stately and very dignified fashion, thumping the carpeted aisle with her high-heeled shoes. And after the collection was taken, she would march up again to the high altar in a most majestic fashion, as if she were Queen Victoria herself. When she got to the steps before the choir stalls and high altar, she would look down before raising first her right leg, and then her left. Then,

in an even more pompous manner, she would march with short, dignified steps to present the offerings to the priest. It was quite a performance.

It seemed that, even after her son's marriage, she expected to have, not just a daughter-in-law, but a menial and slave who would be programmed to do her every bidding. She fully expected that her son and his wife would continue to stay in her house, that she would continue to rule his life and even cook his meals, and that his young wife would merely be a kind of unpaid servant. Up to this point, Bernard Thompson had allowed his life to be run by his mother. I believe that she had even arranged his very nice job at the Public Works Department by making very skilful use of her church connections. In fact, strange as it might sound, it was she who found me out, and suggested me as a suitable wife for him. She had been a client and very close friend of Sissy Dinah's, whom she had visited on several occasions. It was during these visits that she saw me, observed my rather pliant behavior, and decided that I would make a good wife for her son and an excellent daughter-in-law for her. Without my knowing it, she had also gone to our church, Zion on the Level, to see how I dressed to church and observe me further. After she decided that I would make a suitable wife, she told her son about the woman she had found for him and advised him to go to Zion on the Level one Sunday and observe me himself.

"Did you see her," she asked him when he returned home that Sunday afternoon.

"Yes Mama," he replied.

"Do you like her?" she asked.

"Yes," he replied. "I liked her. She looks very pleasant, quiet and unspoiled."

"I can vouch for that," replied his mother. "I'm sure she does not yet know anything about man's business. And she is not one of those young women who will talk back at her husband. You need a wife whose nose you can thrust your finger down. I know she is an excellent cook, and she will help me keep your home nice for you. Whatever she does not know, I will teach her. I am sure we can train her. Since you like her, I will now approach her family. I am sure there will be no problems."

I don't know whether or not it was this statement that his new wife would help her keep his home nice for him that started to engender some resistance in the hitherto pliable young man. I do know that he mentioned it to two of his friends as he was having drinks with them one day, after work.

"My mother has found a nice-looking girl to be my wife," he said to Eugene Pratt and Ade Smith. "She says she will help her keep my home nice for me."

"Do you mean," said Eugene, "that you intend to stay in your mother's house after you get married?"

"Well, what's wrong with that?" asked Bernard. "A lot of young married couples do that, these days. It's cheaper and it keeps the family together."

"I would not advise it," said Ade. "Besides, no offense, but you know your mother. She will still want to rule the roost, and that might not make for good relations between her and your wife."

"It will be a recipe for disaster," said Eugene. "You are now earning a decent salary. I advise you to rent a good house and move into it after your marriage. I'm not saying you won't have your own problems. But at least, you can solve them between the two of you, without the interference of a mother."

It seems that Bernard had also been thinking along these lines, so it did not take much to persuade him. Whenever he had thought of marriage in the past, he had imagined himself, his wife, and their children in their own home, con-

stituting a nice happy family. His mother had never been part of the picture.

Before the wedding, therefore, Bernard secretly went around looking for a suitable house for himself and his new wife. Eventually, with his friends' help, he was able to get the bottom floor of a nice two-storied building along lower Bathurst Street, not too far, in fact, from where my parents and I lived. You can just imagine Mrs. Millicent Thompson's shock and sense of outrage when her beloved son calmly told her one Sunday morning, after church, that he had found a house for himself and his wife-to-be. She literally exploded.

"What, in God's name, do you mean?" she shouted at the top of her voice. "Are you saying, you will be moving out of this house once you are married? Isn't this house good enough for you anymore, the house that your father left to us, that his own father left to him? Isn't there enough space here? How many rooms do you and your new wife want to occupy?"

"Mama, please don't be angry," replied Bernard. "It is not that the house is not good enough for me. You know that I love it and that I am not high-minded. I just think that my wife and I should start out our new life in new circumstances and in a different environment."

"I see, so it is the environment. Is it? You no longer like our east-end environment; you want to live with the aristos in the central area. I know what it is. Your new wife and her upstart settler people have poisoned your mind and convinced you that the east-end environment is no longer good enough for you, because it is not good enough for their daughter. Who are they anyway? Do you think I do not know that some of their ancestors were shoemakers, while my father was a minister of religion in the Anglican church? And now they think that the eastern environment is not good enough for their daughter and son-in-law!"

"Mama, you are being unfair. Mr. And Mrs. Peters are quiet, unassuming people who respect you and have the highest opinion of you. They are not, by any means, what you call aristos, and they do not look down on people living in the east-end of Freetown. In fact, they have a number of relations living in the east-end and even at Kissy village. It's just that I feel that my wife and I ought to be independent and shape our life together."

Then, Mrs. Thompson tried another tactic. She tried playing the role of the about-to-be- abandoned and helpless female, and she broke into tears.

"So you want to leave me here, alone, in this big house, now that your father is dead. This is the gratitude I get for all my labor. I carried you in my belly for nine months, changed your nappies, and nursed you when you were ill, and this is the thanks I get. Now that you are about to have a wife, you wish to abandon me. Suppose I fall ill in the night? Who will know? Who will take me to the hospital? Alright, go! One day, they'll tell you and your new wife that I died in the night alone, without anyone to hold my hand, that they had to break down the door to find me dead on my bedroom floor. If that's what you want, go away with your new wife, ungrateful wretch!"

Of course it was simply not true that she would be left alone. She had two teenage youngsters living with her: indigent children of close relations, one male and one female. They did all the chores and ran all her errands.

Bernard Thompson had hitherto been a very obedient and quiet young man, doing whatever his domineering mother wanted him to. Now that he was about to get married, he had suddenly grown up and acquired a commendable presence of mind. So, in spite of his mother's ranting and tears, he stood his ground and his determination remained unshaken.

You see, his mother blamed poor me and my family for a decision that Bernard had made on his own. From that day onward she refused to talk to my mother or to have anything to do with her. Instead, she started to spread all kinds of foul rumors about our family, claiming, among other things, that my mother's sisters had died of unnamable diseases they had contracted from loose living, and that I was no better. She refused to have anything to do with the wedding and ordered some of her close relatives not to attend.

To complicate matters, my own father, Thomas Peters, died suddenly. Mrs. Thompson saw this as God's judgment of us for our wicked ways. My father passed away in his sleep one Saturday at the respectable age of seventy, which was very old in those days. He had been very well known in Freetown, having attended the Sierra Leone Grammar School, and having been, as I have said, a leading civil servant in town. He was not a member of any of the lodges, but he had once served as a Society Steward at Zion on the Level. Naturally, the choir was in attendance at his funeral and, since he had a large family and wide circle of acquaintances, the church was quite filled with mourners. He was buried in a family vault at Ascension Town cemetery.

Under the circumstances, Bernard decided that we should have a quiet wedding, not the big and sumptuous ceremony we had originally planned. My mother also agreed. It would not be fitting to have a loud wedding, as she called it, only a few months after my father's death, when we were even supposed to be still in mourning. Besides, a loud wedding would allow people to talk a lot and repeat all Mrs. Thompson's unsavory rumors.

I was slightly disappointed, because, like any other young girl, I had always dreamed of having my own elaborate wedding with a long elegant gown, long white veil and flowers, a church full of guests, and my father giving away his eldest daughter. We would have a gorgeous wedding cake, a cake and wine ceremony, lovely bridesmaids, many women in beautiful aso-ebi doing the goombay dance to their hearts' content, and my mother proudly prancing as the mother of the bride. However, I understood Bernard's decision and decided to make the best of it. I knew it was the right thing to do. My husband, then and always, had an uncanny way of making the right decisions. Isn't it glorious when you have a husband on whose judgment you can depend? I always felt that I could leave the most important decisions to him. He always thought and acted accordingly. God rest his soul!

Unfortunately, my two friends Annie and Josephine, were deprived of the opportunity they had so looked forward to: of being my chief bridesmaids. Bernard (from now on I will call him Mr. T, because that was what I always called him, since he was seven years older than I was) and I had a simple wedding with very few witnesses. In fact, the wedding took place on a Sunday after the morning service, so it could not have been a loud wedding anyway. Who would have dreamt of dancing the goombay on God's holy Sunday?

I wore a simple white dress, white shoes, and a white hat, and I carried a nice white handbag instead of flowers. After the ceremony, my mother entertained a few relatives and friends with the traditional rice bread, ginger beer and jollof rice. In the evening, Mr. T came for me and took me to our new home at lower Bathurst Street.

Thus, my married life began, a life that was to last for fifty glorious and eventful years. I was proud and happy when I moved into my home. I was scarcely twenty-one years of age, and I had my own home. I took great pride in decorating it and making it comfortable for my beloved Mr. T. He bought a lot of new furniture, and I sewed the loveliest cushion covers and tablecloths for them. One of his distant relations, Joseph, came to stay with us. He helped with the more laborious chores, such as pounding rice and foofoo, getting water at the street tap, and polishing the immaculate wooden floor.

I felt so grown-up planning the week's menu, going to market and trying to ensure that the money Mr. T gave me every month lasted until the next month. I did not have a job outside the home as young wives have today, but I really felt that I had a full- time job, taking care of Mr. T's home. It called forth all my energy and resources. You can imagine my pride on our first New Year's Sunday together, when Mr. T brought home his friends for drinks after morning service, and they complimented me on the loveliness of my home and the deliciousness of the fare I served them!

"Bernard," said Eugene, "Indeed, you have indeed got an excellent wife. A good wife who can keep your home nice and beautiful, and cook delicious meals is the greatest blessing that a man can hope for."

Mr. T smiled with satisfaction and went on contentedly smoking his pipe and exchanging banter with his two friends.

For my own part, I could see that I was the object of envy for all my young friends and acquaintances. My new husband always came home straight after work. Then, after having the dinner I laid out for him on our nicely decorated dining table, he would go off to choir practice, go fishing with his friends at Government wharf, chat with visitors, or just sit around, smoke his pipe and converse with me. He was very musical and had acquired a small pedal organ from a friend. He had taught himself to play when he was young, and he now spent quite a lot of his time playing hymns and chants on that beautiful instrument. You can imagine how proud I was to have such an accomplished husband. Moreover, Mr. T did not drink like some other husbands and never gave me any problems in that regard. Eugene had said that a good wife is the greatest blessing a man can hope for. I also believe that a good husband who has the fear of God in him, works hard to provide for his wife and family, and does not go lusting after other women, is the greatest blessing a woman can have.

My happiness was greatly enhanced when I discovered, only one month after we got married, that I was pregnant. I had made sure that no man touched me before I moved into my husband's house, and I was rather innocent about such matters, unlike some of my friends. It was my mother who confirmed it after I told her how I had been feeling and what had been happening to me. Mr. T was overjoyed when I told him.

"Mr. T," I said to him one evening after he returned home from work, "I think I am expecting."

"Are you sure?" he asked.

"Yes," I replied. "I told mama about what was happening and she has confirmed it."

"God be praised. To think I will now have my own child, that I will be a father! I am sure it will be a boy. The first child has to be a boy."

I smiled. I also wanted a boy. Our people are always happy when the first child is a boy, men in particular. It's as if it were a proof of their virility.

"Now look," Mr. T went on, "you must be careful from now on, and not exert yourself too much. Let Joseph do more of the work. We don't want any accidents to happen."

In about three months there was visible proof that I was pregnant, and all my friends and relations were delighted. The only fly in the ointment, as it were, was my indomitable mother-in-law. Mrs. Thompson had never said a word to me since the wedding. I know that some parents who've objected to their children's marriage still visit them after the event and try to be reconciled. Not so Mrs. Thompson! She was a very vindictive woman. Mr. T dutifully called on her a few days after we got married, hoping that she would have mellowed out, but she barely spoke a word to him and coldly went on with her piece of embroidery. As I have said, my Mr. T had grown up and had become very strong-minded himself. He just said that if she wanted to continue to be hostile he would let her be hostile, and he forbade me to go and visit her. He knew his mother, he said, and he did not want any unseemly scenes.

You would have thought that, even if Mrs. Thompson were still angry, she would have been delighted at the thought of having a grandchild to continue her husband's line. Nothing of the sort! Instead, that inventive and resourceful woman went around spreading a rumor that I was not pregnant. According to her, girls like me were incapable of bearing children, and she said that I had padded my belly with old clothes to make it appear that I was pregnant. She was gleefully looking forward to what I would tell my husband when I did not deliver a baby, after all. I myself heard the rumor one Saturday when I went to market and heard two women whom I barely knew giggling near me.

"So Mrs. Thompson's daughter-in-law is expecting," said the one.

"Noh oh!" replied the other. "Let me tell you word. My friend Tabitha said that Mrs. Thompson told her that her daughter-in-law is merely pretending. She has stuffed her belly with old clothes to make it look like she is pregnant, but there is nothing in there."

"Talk word!" said the other.

I could have died with shame and embarrassment. However, the encounter seemed to put new strength into me and I went home and prayed to God to give me a safe delivery, so that all my enemies would be ashamed.

CHAPTER 3

I was very much looking forward to the arrival of my baby, but I was also very scared. Childbirth in those days was not what it is now, though even today we hear of tragedies. The doctors and the nurses were not as skilled as they are now, and many women preferred to have their babies at home, attended by native midwives, who, in some cases, had more knowledge than the Western-type midwives in the hospitals. Mr. T, however, was determined that I should have the best care, as he termed it. My anxiety was heightened even more when, on one occasion before the birth, our doctor gave us a prescription, and we took it to the dispensary to obtain the medicine. We had gone to the hospital in a hurry, and I had only a simple pair of slippers on my feet, which were therefore inadequately protected.

"How many months gone are you," asked the stern-looking dispenser, his fierce bespectacled eyes glued to my almost bare feet.

"Seven months, sir," I replied respectfully.

"Seven months," he shouted, "and you come out in this cold weather without anything on your feet? I can see you from afar." He meant, "I don't think you have much longer in this world."

"She is a young wife sir," Mr. T put in apologetically. "This is our first child."

"Hunhn" grunted the dispenser, unmollified . "The children, these days!"

Believe me,that scared me. For the next two months, I was a bundle of nerves in spite of Mr. T's loving efforts to reassure and convince me that all would be well. I knew of several women, young and not so young, who had died in childbirth. In fact, childbirth was generally called "the woman's war," because there was no certainty that one would come out of it alive. I remember one woman in particular: Mrs. Benjamin, I think her name was. She was in her late thirties and already had six children. So she was an experienced woman who had already gone through six pregnancies. She was one of my mother's friends, and her daughter, Cordelia, was also one of my close friends. At the age of thirty-seven, she became pregnant again. You see, we did not practice much birth control in those days and, in any case, the overall feeling was that children were a gift from God and one should accept them whenever they came. If God gave Abraham's wife, Sarah, a child at the age of ninety, why should one be sad if God gives one a child at thirty-seven, especially when there were so many other women longing in vain for children? Children were God's gift and an insurance against old age. Besides, in those days, one did not know how many of one's children would survive into adulthood. God does everything for a purpose.

Anyway, Mrs. Benjamin became pregnant again at the age of thirty-seven. She used to be a very sturdy and energetic woman who was always doing something about the house. Moreover, she was a good trader, selling all kinds of things from the comfort of her own house. However, one day when I visited her daughter, I saw how slow she had become. She was slow because the pregnancy had caused her to be bloated, about three times her usual size. And

41

then, one day as I was going to market, I saw her daughter rushing along the street going in the opposite direction.

"My mother has gone into the hospital," she hastily gasped, anxiety written all over her face. "She should be giving birth any time now."

"Don't worry," I said. "There is a God above. I am sure all will be well."

You can imagine how devastated I felt when I heard later that day that Mrs. Benjamin had died without actually giving birth. She had gone into convulsions while still in labor and had not regained consciousness. They said that she would have given birth to triplets, but the three unborn children also apparently died. The whole town was in shock. I remember going to the funeral at St. John's Church. A funeral is, in most cases, a sad affair, but this was one of the saddest I had ever attended. The church was packed full with mourners. As we started singing the withdrawal hymn, the eight men who were handling the coffin lifted it off the stand and tried to turn it around, to start bringing it out of the church. But then, there was a tremendous noise. "Patatras!" The men had dropped it. It must have been too heavy for them. Or maybe one of them was not up to the task. Just imagine the noise made by such a heavy burden falling to the floor! The church was in immediate uproar, but the minister did his best to maintain order and to get us all to compose ourselves.

"There must be someone handling the coffin that she does not want to touch her," said one woman in the row in front of mine.

In the end, order was restored, and we proceeded to Ascension Town cemetery to bury the unfortunate Mrs. Benjamin. That incident will always remain stamped on my mind.

So, you see, childbirth was no child's play in those days. Fortunately for me, everything went well and I gave birth to a healthy boy. My Mr. T was beside himself with Joy. He had a son to carry on his name and line. My dear mother came to stay with us for a while to put me through the paces of handling a young baby. Believe me, that was no easy matter. I had to bathe him in water of the right temperature; see that he was properly exercised every morning; know when to feed him and when to give him water; change his nappies and keep them clean. But he was my pride and joy, and I learned fast. Imagine my joy on the Sunday he was christened at Holy Trinity Church! I wore my simple white wedding dress for the occasion. It was the first time I had worn it since our wedding, and it seemed to send a message to all those who saw us that day. The message was that I was now a truly married woman who had given her husband that precious gift of a son and all my enemies could go and drown themselves in the ocean.

So, what about my vicious mother-in-law, Mrs. Thompson, who had been spreading the rumors that I was padding my belly with old clothes to appear pregnant? To be frank with you, I never held a grudge against her, and I was secretly afraid of her and what she was capable of doing. I realized that marriage involved the union of two families, and that her antagonism had caused an estrangement between members of my family and several members of hers. In fact, I looked forward to the day when the two families would really come together. My mother was much less compromising. She saw my mother-in-law as a witch who was determined to do anything in her power to destroy me, and she was determined that should not happen. That's why when she came to see me and my baby at the Cottage hospital before we were discharged, she could not help shouting out aloud:

"God be praised! My daughter has given birth to a baby boy. All her enemies will now be ashamed."

"Be careful Mama," I told her. "You know what Freetown is like. People will go and tell Mrs. Thompson that you called her an enemy."

"I do not care," replied my mother. "I know that God is with us. The same God who protected you during pregnancy and has given you a boy will defend you. Just trust in God."

And as if to reinforce her point, my mother recited the words of the twenty-first psalm then and there, asking me to join her. She then brought out a small new Bible, opened it at psalm ninety-one, placed it under the baby's pillow, and ordered me to keep it there constantly. As she placed it she recited the first verse: "He that dwelleth in the secret place of the most High shall abide under the shadow of the Almighty." Oh, the great faith of our fathers and mothers! It went a long way and stood them in good stead.

However, the birth of the baby effected a great miracle. It brought about a reconciliation between me, Mr. T and his domineering mother. What our people say is true. There is nothing like the birth of a baby for bringing out the best in people, just as other things can bring out the worst in people. Remember that! If you have a baby, be suspicious of those who do not come to wish you joy. I don't know whether it was a desire to adhere to the common custom or simply her pride in having a grandchild, her first grandchild and a boy at that, but my mother-in-law suddenly appeared at our doorstep one Sunday, two weeks after the baby was born. She was dressed in her Sunday best and had obviously come straight from church.

"Good morning Mr. Thompson! Good morning Mrs. Thompson," she said rather sarcastically, laying the stress on the Mr. and Mrs. "So, you did not think it fit to come in person and tell me about the birth of my grandson. You had to send someone to tell me," she said, as she marched in and ensconced herself in our best chair. "But I am determined

to do what is right. I have come to see my grandson. Where is he?"

I could see that her son, Mr. T, was obviously relieved that she had changed her attitude, and I was very pleased at the possibility of a reconciliation.

"He is in the bedroom in his cot," I said, "but I will bring him out."

So I brought young Bernard Jr. out and handed him to his grandmother. The child woke up and bawled out immediately, as if he did not like the hands into which he had been placed.

"So they have taught you also to be against me, have they?" said Mrs. Thompson. "Well, whether they like it or not, you are my flesh and blood. I can see my late father's eyes in your eyes. Don't you mind them; we will live long in this world and enjoy rice and foofoo, bitter leaf and jollof rice. All our enemies will be ashamed."

By this time Mr. T was himself beaming quite happily and so was I. He had been quite fond of his mother in his way, and though he had grown up significantly since his marriage and valued his independence, the estrangement had taken its toll on him. I, too, was happy that Mrs. Thompson had come round at last. It meant we would finally be reconciled with other members of the Thompson family.

"Have you decided on his names as yet?" asked my mother-in-law.

"We have decided on only one," said Mr. T. "He will be called Bernard after me. We still have to decide on two other names."

"Well, one of them has to be Onesimus, after my father," his mother said.

"Onesimus it will be, then."

"He must have an African name, an aku name. I suggest Babatunde, which means 'Papa has come back.' Papa could

45

refer to your late father or my late father. In fact, it could refer to both."

"Bernard Onesimus Babatunde," said Mr. T. "B.O.B. Bob for short. That sounds nice."

So, my son was christened Bernard Onesimus Babatunde; the names were called out loudly by Eugene, one of his godfathers, at that happy christening ceremony at Trinity Church. My happiness was complete.

My mother came over quite often to help me look after the baby, but so did Mrs. Thompson. She came all the way from Guard Street to help me. She was quite proud of her grandson, who seemed to be growing very fast. Within six months he was such a heavy boy, and was already sitting upright. By the time he was eight months old, he was crawling all over the place. He was the main cause of our moving back to my mother-in-law's house at Guard Street. Could you believe it? Our landlady, Mrs. Virtue Smith, decided that she wanted the lower floor of her house back for one of her own relatives who would soon be married, and she gave us one month's notice to move. I suspect, though, that the real reason was that she did not like the idea of my mother-in-law coming over so frequently to her house. They had been acquaintances at one time, but had fallen out at a Mothers' Union meeting. I do not know what the real cause of the quarrel was, but, knowing my mother-in-law, I was not surprised that she had fallen out with anyone, so I did not go into the reason.

I suppose that Mr. T could have found another house for us to move into, but it would have been difficult to find a suitable one within a month. In any case, as I have said, something happened to Bernard Jr. that caused Mr. T to decide that, for the time being, at any rate, we should move in with his mother.

One day, Junior suddenly fell ill and went into convulsions. Mr. T was away at work, so I was alone at the time and did not know what to do. Was my only son, the pride and joy of my life, going to die on me like so many other young babies? In tears, I quickly bundled him on to my back and rushed to my mother at upper Bathurst Street. She tried everything she knew but to no avail. We were obliged to rush him to the hospital.

The doctor gave him an enema and did something else to him. I was so confused at the time that I can't even remember what else he did. Then, he gave us some medicines and asked us to take him home, assuring us that he would be all right. Junior seemed much better when his father came home from work that evening, but I told Mr. T what had happened. You could see concern all over his face. Within an hour, though, the convulsions started all over again and I started crying again.

"I know what I will do," said Mr. T. "I will go and get your mother to come and stay with you, while I go and get my own mother. She will know what to do."

My mother came and started trying all she knew. In the meantime, Mr. T went to get his own mother. He must have run all the way, for in about an hour and a half he came back with his mother. But they were accompanied by an old man called Pa Rose. Apparently, his mother had known immediately that in this kind of situation, a traditional herbalist ought to be summoned. So, they had both run all the way to his place at Kissy Village and asked him to come.

Pa Rose immediately started his ministrations and incantations. He slapped Junior on his buttocks, rubbed all kinds of things on him, then asked my mother for some stinking weed. She hastily got it from her own backyard, and Pa Rose rubbed the herb and its juice on to Junior's face, back and arms, and did all kinds of things that I cannot now remember. Within a short time, the convulsions had stopped and Junior was sleeping soundly and smiling in his sleep.

"I don't think it will happen again," said Pa Rose, "but if it does, just rub this on him, and put this into his nostrils. There are lots of evil spirits about, but these medicines will stop them.

Junior never had convulsions after that, but Mr. T was so scared that he decided it would be unwise for me, an inexperienced mother, to be left alone with the baby. It would be good to have someone around who would know what to do or who to summon should anything serious happen. That was why he decided that we should move back into his mother's house. Seeing the splendid role Mrs. Thompson had played during Junior's illness, I myself was not disposed to object. I also knew that Mr. T had clearly let his mother know that he intended to be the master in his own family. So, we moved to Guard Street and occupied the lower floor of the Thompson family house.

For a while, we didn't have any problems with my mother-in-law. She seemed to be quite satisfied with helping to look after her grandson. She would come down every morning after Mr. T had gone to work and ask me how Junior was. She would take him in her arms and cuddle and sing to him. She seemed to have been able to channel her bossy energies into looking after and helping with her grandson. That left me with more time to look after my home and take care of my cooking. Whenever I had to go to market I would leave Junior with his grandmother, instead of strapping him to my back as I used to do when we lived at Lower Bathurst Street. I would return to find her delightfully playing with the baby. I would then attend to my cooking and leave the two of them together.

Mrs. Thompson and I, in fact, became quite close and she used to regale me with stories of her younger days and events that happened in Freetown before my time. She told me about the opening of the railway and the Bai Bureh Hut Tax rebellion. At times, she tried to order her son around, but he firmly let her realize that he was now his own man and he would only take her words as advice.

One day, Pa Rose returned. He said he had come to see how the young man, as he called Junior, was doing. He was delighted to see that the baby was doing well and was now a toddler, having just started to walk.

"But my young sister," he said to me as Mrs. Thompson sat there listening, "the world is still a bad place. There are lots of evil spirits about, and you must protect yourself and your baby. Look, I am going to give you this," he said, producing something out of the pocket of his brown gown. What he brought out looked like the tail of a small bush animal. It was about four inches long, with beads and some red tafti material cleverly sewn into it. "I shall hang this over your mantelpiece. It will protect you and your baby."

"Thank you, Pa Rose," my mother-in-law said effusively. "God will bless you."

Then, Pa Rose took his leave.

I will not say that I am not superstitious, nor will I say, after witnessing what happened to my sewing mistress, that I do not believe that there is such a thing as African science. Some of our people are highly skilled at harnessing the forces of nature and using herbs to bring about the destruction or discomfiture of others. I did believe Pa Rose when he said that the world is bad and that I must protect my baby from evil. Also, I had never forgotten my misery at Junior's recent mysterious illness. I certainly did not wish to repeat the experience. So, even though this object that Pa Rose hung above our mantelpiece sent a chill through my spine whenever I looked at it, I let it stay there. Besides, I received encouragement from my mother-in-law regarding the object.

"Pa Rose certainly knows his trade. He is one of the most powerful and effective herbalists around, and he has been able to spare many lives that I know of," she said.

When Mr. T returned home from work, I told him about Pa Rose's visit and showed him the strange thing he had hung over the mantelpiece. Mr. T tended to be less superstitious than I was, but even he just shrugged at it.

"Let it stay there," he said. "Pa Rose knows what he is doing. After all, he saved our baby. This thing can do no harm, even if it does not do any good."

So, we forgot about the object and our lives continued as before. I soon became pregnant again. This time, however, it was a very difficult pregnancy, and I was glad that my mother-in-law was there to help out. I was confined to my bed almost throughout, and she had to help with the cooking and with Junior who was growing rapidly and was a healthy, troublesome two year old, rampaging all over the house. How was he to know that his mother, who was lying there almost helpless on the couch, was feeling quite sick, was expecting another baby, and could not play with him?

My feet were swollen to about twice their normal size. This is, of course, not very unusual during a pregnancy, but a bigger problem was that my blood pressure seemed to be constantly elevated. This also happens, at times, during a pregnancy. My greatest problem, though, was that I had suddenly developed constant palpitation and irregular heartbeats. There were times when I could hear my heart pounding away within my chest. The doctors tried all kinds of medicines, but to no avail. My mother consulted several traditional healers, each of whom provided his own odd concoctions, some to drink and some to rub, but there was still no improvement. Why, you might ask, did we not try Pa Rose on this occasion? The answer is that the great Pa Rose had himself succumbed to the fate that must overcome us all. He died at the ripe old age of eighty-four, soon after I became pregnant.

So I languished through my second pregnancy. The time came for the delivery. Astonishingly, the delivery itself

went very smoothly, and I had another boy. Mr. T was again beside himself with Joy. His line and his name were now confirmed.

My mother-in-law continued to relish her position as grandmother. She took charge of the second baby, because I still continued to be quite ill, in spite of the relatively smooth delivery. With my mother-in-law more or less in charge, my own mother did not have to come as often as she did when I had had my first baby. There was not much public transport in those days, and it is a fairly long walk from Bathurst Street to Guard Street. And besides, my mother-in-law seemed quite competent to look after things. She was completely in her element. So, there I was, more or less still immobilized on the couch, only propping myself up occasionally to breastfeed the baby, while Mrs. Thompson went about giving orders to the young relatives who were helping us. She also did most of the cooking, hummed to the baby when he was upset, and shouted at Junior, telling him that he must learn to behave, now that he had a younger brother.

And so, time went on and our lives went on, but my condition did not improve. The second Baby's christening was much quieter than the first because I was ailing. In fact, I could barely walk to Holy Trinity Church for the christening. When we returned home, I was so weak that I merely flopped down on the couch. And still no one could tell precisely what was causing the irregular heartbeats and the palpitation. In spite of my condition, I still had to suckle the baby, and this left me even weaker. One week, my condition was so poor, that Mr. T got really scared. I believe he thought I would not make it, that I was going to die. And to be quite honest with you, I myself started to think that my days in this world were already numbered and that I would die and leave my husband a young widower with two young children.

I remember overhearing a conversation that my husband had with his mother one Monday, after he returned home from work.

"Bernard," she said, "have you made sure that you and Priscilla are not in arrears with your church dues?"

"I have been paying mine," he replied. "Since we are in different adult classes we pay separately. I am sure that she has not kept up her payments, since she has been so sick recently and has not been going to class or to church. I will check with the Vicar."

You must understand that in those days adults, as well as children, attended Bible classes regularly. Women generally went on Wednesday or Friday mornings, and men on Friday evenings. And of course, going to class meant that you kept up your class dues, or class pence, as we called them. If you did not pay these dues, the dues that supported the Church, you might not be given a funeral service when you died. To die and be taken straight from the house to the cemetery, by direct boat, as we used to call it, was the height of disgrace for the family. It meant that you were not a regular churchgoer. What scared me so much was the implication of the conversation between my husband and my mother-in-law. It sounded like they expected me to die soon and did not want the family to be disgraced through my not having a funeral service in the church. So they were going to ensure that my class pence were paid up to date.

Imagine my consternation when, two days later, I again overheard my husband saying to my mother-in-law:

"Mama, I found out that Priscilla was very much in arrears with her class pence, but I am going to the church right now and I am going to pay what she owes."

"That is the right thing to do, my son," she said.

And without saying anything to me, Mr. T left, presumably for the church, to bring my class pence up to date and ensure that if I died I would have a funeral service in the

church. But what surprised and alarmed me even more, was that my mother-in-law showed no emotion at this. She spoke in a very practical down-to-earth way about all of it, and then went on cooing to her grandson.

"Yes," I thought. "Yours is yours and mine is mine. If I were her own daughter, she would show more emotion if I was going to die."

As it was, I did not die, as you can see. I lingered on in the same condition for another fifteen months, while my mother-in-law, the indomitable Mrs. Thompson, continued, more or less, to take charge of everything that I should have been doing in the house.

It was a visit by my friend, Annie Macauley, that brought things to a head. She had continued to be a great friend of mine after we all left Sissy Dinah's. In fact, she was godmother for my elder son, while Josephine was godmother for my younger son. In those days, a boy had one godmother and two godfathers; a girl had two godmothers and one godfather. Anyway, one day, Annie visited me and was shocked by my condition.

"Priscilla," she said, "I cannot allow things to continue like this. What is your mother doing? By now, she should be consulting all the medicine men in this town."

"She has been doing her best," I replied. "She has consulted several, and they have given me all kinds of concoctions and ointments, but none of it has worked."

"Well," said Annie. "I know a particularly good herbalist who lives in the heart of Grassfield. He is from Guinea. Those Guinea herbalists are very good. I will go consult him and let you know what he says."

Annie was as good as her word. A week later, she came to visit me again and what she said surprised me in a sense; in another sense, it did not.

"Listen Priscilla," she said. "Are you prepared to believe what the medicine man told me, what I am going to tell you?"

"You know that I trust you, Annie," I said. "And in any case my condition is such that I am prepared to believe anything."

"It is your mother-in-law who is responsible for your illness. That is what the Pa said. It is not that she really wants you to die, although she would not mind if you did. She wants you to be a kind of permanent invalid so that she could be in charge of the house and continue to run things."

At first, I opened my mouth in disbelief, but when I considered what had been happening in the house ever since the early days of my second pregnancy and also my mother-in-law's attitude just before Mr. T and I got married, everything seemed to fall into place.

"Oh the wickedness of this world!" I said. "So, this woman would not mind if her daughter-in-law, the mother of her grandsons, died and left her husband a young widower. Why? Why? Why?"

"Power," said Annie. "She loves power. She exercised power over her husband when he was alive. She exercised power over her son before he got married, and she still wants that power. Some women just love power. They can never be satisfied with taking a back seat. That is why she is constantly quarrelling with all her friends in the Mothers' Union and the Sideswomen's Union. She always wants to be first. But that is not all."

"What more is there?" I asked.

"Did she bring an old man to you, and did he hang an animal's tail over your mantelpiece?" Annie asked.

"Yes," I said. "It was the late Pa Rose. Mrs. Thompson brought him over to cure Junior when he was seriously ill. A few months later, he came back to find out how Junior was getting on, but he also told me that the world was bad, and

although Junior now seemed healthy, I had to take steps to protect my family. He gave me the strange thing to hang over my mantelpiece and said that as long as it was there, no one would harm us. There it is," I said, pointing to the strange and fearful looking object over the mantelpiece.

"Ibosio!" shouted Annie. "You mean you forgot what happened to our sewing mistress? The medicine man I have just consulted told me that your mother-in-law employed a powerful herbalist to hang a 'sebeh' in your house. As long as the thing is there, you will always be ill. It was a clever device. It was not meant to protect you. It was meant to destroy you and protect her interest. Like a fool, you did what she wanted."

"Lord, have mercy!" I shouted. "The world is indeed bad. Who can be trusted?"

"You must remove that thing," Annie said, "otherwise you will never get well."

"But what shall I tell Mr. T? Can I make him believe that it is his mother who has caused my illness?"

"Well, you do not have to tell him all the details. Just remove the nasty object. He might not even notice that it has been removed. Men hardly notice these things. I assure you, you will get well, after doing that. Once you get well, you can persuade him to move back to your own house."

I was quite convinced by what Annie told me. How could I not be convinced? She did not know about Pa Rose's second visit and how he hung the fearsome looking object over the mantelpiece. She had not known about the sebeh over the mantelpiece at all before the medicine man told her. And yet she, or the medicine man she had consulted, had divined it exactly. Moreover, the object was supposed to protect my family and me, but it had patently failed to protect me. Removing it could do no harm when I was almost on the point of death. So, without consulting anyone, I removed the animal's tail with its beads and red tafti. And would you believe it? I immediately started to improve, and in a month's time I was perfectly well again. It was then that my mother-in-law noticed that it had been removed. She raved and ranted when I told her that I was the one who did it. My husband was so disgusted by her conduct, that he decided, without my suggesting it, that it was time we moved back to our own house. Within a month we had found a decent one-story house along Wellington Street and moved into it. I was mistress in my house once more.

CHAPTER 4

So far, continued Mrs. Priscilla Thompson, I have talked only about myself. However, this story is essentially about three women. It has to do with my friends Annie Macauley and Josephine Freeman as much as it does with me. We were still, as I've told you, great friends, after Sissy Dinah's. I was the first to be married, and the others were, of course, looking forward to the day when they too would be married.

I always thought that Annie was the more likely to get married first, because she was very beautiful. Some young man or some young man's family was bound to notice her sooner, rather than later. Besides, she was quite a nice girl. She was very friendly and had a bubbly, outgoing personality, though she was not the domineering, masterful type. But that, I thought, should endear her all the more to young men, who, for the most part, did not really like very bossy wives. They preferred quiet wives into whose noses they could poke their fingers, as the saying goes. Well, Annie was just such a personality.

She first met Eugene, Mr. T's bosom friend, at Junior's Christening. She was Junior's godmother, so she was carrying the baby most of the time. She was the one who carried him to church and handed him over to the minister, before the latter asked Eugene, as the baby's godfather, to name the child. But Eugene was not paying attention to the minister or to anyone else. His eyes were glued to Annie who was looking radiant that day in a blue chiffon dress, white shoes, and a white hat.

"Name this child," the minister had said.

But there was silence. The minister looked around at everyone with a puzzled expression.

"I said name this child," the minister repeated.

Mr. T gave Eugene a pinch on the arm to bring him back to consciousness. Eugene suddenly came to himself with an "oh" and proceeded to recite Junior's three names to the accompaniment of giggles from all and sundry.

We all had a tremendous laugh at Eugene's expense when the ceremony was over and we had all left the church.

"What was the matter with you, man," Mr. T said to him. "Had you been drinking beforehand? You mean you could not wait for the ceremony to be over before getting on to the booze?"

"Booze was not the problem," said Ade Smith, Mr. T's other friend. "It was that mermaid that you contrived to get as Junior's godmother that blew his mind off."

"I see," said Mr. T. "So you have taken a fancy to Annie Macauley. I do not blame you. She is a very beautiful girl and is, as far as I am unaware, unattached. But let me warn you. I know you, and I will not have you trifling with the affections of such a nice girl as Annie. She deserves to have a nice man who will marry her and give her a stable home."

"Oh, I have the very best of intentions for her. If I can get her to look in my direction, I will marry her one day and make her the queen of my castle."

You see, Mr. T's friend, Eugene, had developed an unenviable reputation of being an unstable ladies' man who broke all the girls' hearts and then ditched them. He was the same age as Mr. T, but he showed not the slightest sign of wishing to marry and settle down. He had gone down on record as saying that he wished to enjoy himself first, because once he

was married he would be tied to one woman, and his enjoyment would be curtailed.

"I have been trying to get godmother Annie Macauley to look at me and just give me a smile," he said to Mr. T, soon after we returned to the house, "but she pretends to be busy with Junior. Why on Earth must she carry the baby all the time and not lay him down to sleep? If she wants a baby, she can easily get one of her own. I can certainly help her with that."

"I have warned you," cut in Mr. T, "not to trifle with the peace of mind of that nice, innocent girl. I will not have it."

"But she is determined not to look at me, and I am determined that she shall. Why should she not, like all other women, find me irresistible? But you wait, she will come round."

I was also beginning to be anxious for my friend Annie Macauley, because I knew of Eugene's reputation. Tall, dark, and extremely handsome, he thought he was God's gift to womankind and every woman who saw him was bound to fall for him. He had already ruined two young girls who had had babies by him and, of course, had remained unmarried. At that time, having a child before marriage was a kind of stigma. It was all right if the young man married you after the fact, and made an honest woman of you, but if he did not, you stood a very good chance of being left on the shelf. I did not want such a destiny for my very good friend Annie, and I hoped that she would continue to have the presence of mind to resist Eugene.

During the sumptuous entertainment that we put on at our home after the christening ceremony, I could see that our friend Eugene was putting on his charm. He looked particularly dashing in his fawn suit and white and brown shoes. There he stood, smoking a cigar he held elegantly in his left hand, and helping himself quite generously to Mr. T's supplies of rum and whiskey that at that time were extremely cheap. This helped to raise his spirits tremendously.

I saw him approach my friend Annie with a swagger and a smile and sit down on the chair next to her, as she still held Junior.

"And who is this beautiful angel that Priscilla and Bernard found to be Junior's godmother?" he said. His face glowed with admiration.

Now my friend Annie, like me, had not had the benefit of a secondary school education, although our primary education, as I have said, was quite respectable and had taught us many things that a lot of children at secondary school today do not know. Still, her English was not very good, but since the dashing Eugene had spoken to her in English, she felt she also had to reply in English. She probably thought that would raise his estimation of her. So, she said rather coyly, adopting a tone of haughtiness:

"Your betters have come; I don't yarns. You totes yourself and comes to yarns? I yarns!"

With a curl of her lip, suggesting the utmost disdain, she turned herself away from the indomitable Eugene. She had meant to say, "your betters have come to flirt with me and I gave them no encouragement; what makes you think I am going to encourage you?" Of course, she was merely putting on an act, trying to dictate the terms on which she was to be won. But others had heard the grammatical and stylistic boo-boo. Guffaws and giggles exploded throughout the room. I was quite embarrassed for my friend Annie, and I thought that Eugene would now realize that she was not highly educated and, therefore, not worth the effort of courting.

However, after an initial expression of amazement on his handsome face, the irrepressible Eugene showed that he understood the game and was not to be deterred. So he pressed on with his attentions. For the rest of the afternoon

and evening, he hardly spoke to anyone else and by the time the festivities came to an end, it was quite clear that he and Annie were firm friends, if not yet lovers.

"I could see that she was playing hard to get," he said to Mr. T just before he left. "But I have subdued more beautiful and haughtier girls than her, and I will get her yet."

"I have warned you not to trifle with her feelings," Mr. T said to him, once more. "She is a particular friend of ours and I would not like to see her come to any harm."

"How do you know my intentions are not honorable?" Eugene asked. "After all, I am still a bachelor. She might yet succeed in getting me to the altar."

"Just be careful with her," Mr. T warned, finally.

Well, where women were concerned, Eugene was nothing if not determined. He was very determined to get Annie, and he persevered. In the end, he completely won her heart.

"Oh Priscilla," she said to me one day when she visited me, "I am sure he is the man for me. I have found my man at last. He is so handsome, so nice and sweet. He makes me laugh so much, and he buys me all sorts of things. Do you see this beautiful bracelet on my arm? He bought it for me. He also brings my mother all kinds of gifts."

Eugene was an up-and-coming accounts clerk in the United African Company and had access to all kinds of goods sold at a discount to the employees, like foodstuffs, drinks, and crockery. Whenever these items were up for sale, he did not hesitate to buy anything for his sweetheart and her mother. Annie's mother took to him very readily and already saw him as a future son-in-law.

"Has he said he wants to marry you?" I asked Annie.

"No, but I am sure he will quite soon. My mother has already started making plans for the wedding. Oh Priscilla!" she said, her eyes glistening with pure happiness, "I was sure I would get married not too long after you did. I felt it in my bones."

"Well, do be careful," I said. "You can never be too sure."

"Oh, I know his family will soon come to request my hand. My mother expects it any day now."

Annie's mother, Admire Macauley, was, like Annie herself, a very simple soul with great confidence in the goodness of human nature. Her husband had died many years ago, leaving her to care for two children, a boy and a girl. She did her best, eking out a meager living as a trader in all sorts of goods. She had many contacts up country, who sent her plantains, potatoes, and cassava, that she regularly collected from the station and resold wholesale to other traders, or at retail prices outside her own small house at the lower end of Circular Road, just by Victoria Park. She did not have many relatives, but she plied a good trade, and her family managed to survive. She was looking forward very much to her daughter's marriage to help mend the family's fortunes. Obviously, in the debonair Eugene she saw just the man to do that.

One afternoon, I was sitting down in our parlor in our new home at Wellington Street, mending some clothes, when I looked out of the window and saw Annie walking toward the house. Mr. T had gone to his evening choir practice, and the children were asleep. So I was alone in the house. The affair between Annie and Eugene had now been going on for the best part of two years, but they were still not married. In the meantime, I had not only had a second child, but my husband and I had moved to our new home all by ourselves.

I could sense immediately that all was not well. As I have said, Annie usually exuded an ebullient and outgoing personality, so it was easy to tell when she was in distress.

"What is the matter Annie?" I said after the usual courtesies. "You do not look like yourself. Is your mother ill?"

"Hm! It is not my mother, Priscilla, it is me. I am in deep trouble," she groaned, as she lounged on my best chair.

I sensed almost immediately what must have been the matter, but I let her tell it herself.

"What is it, Annie? Tell me."

"I am sure I am pregnant, Priscilla," she blurted out and burst into tears.

The sight of that ebullient body wracked with sobs was too much for me, and I tried to comfort her as best as I could, although I was also stunned by what she told me.

"My God !" I said. "But still, these things can be mended. It is not the end of the world. Are you sure?"

"I am absolutely sure," she replied. "There can be no doubt about it."

"Well, have you told Eugene? Surely this is the time for him to come forward, step up to the plate, do the right thing, and marry you. Then all will be well."

"No," she said," I have not told him yet. I'm not sure how he will react."

"What do you mean, you're not sure how he will react? Aren't you sure that the child is his."

"Of course, I am sure. There has been no one else. But haven't you heard what Eugene has always said about marrying women who are pregnant? One day I overheard him say to your Mr. T: 'If any woman comes and tells me that she is pregnant and I am the father I will put a knife to her throat. The last time a girl came and told me that she could not see her period, I told her to go and look for it where she left it. How can I be sure that the child is mine? If we were married and she became pregnant, that would be a different story. But I am not marrying any woman who already has a bun in the oven. She must be empty and light when we walk down the aisle. I will not have my friends laugh at me and say that I was forced to marry against my will. No sir! Not this Eugene Pratt! I will marry at a time of my own choosing, when I have had as much fun as I want to have, not because anyone forces me to.' Oh," Annie moaned, "what am I going to do?"

So here was a problem. I could have said to Annie, "I warned you to be careful," but that would have been almost cruel in the circumstances. I could also have said, "but you must tell him, you will have to tell him." However, I, like so many other people, was painfully aware of the girls Eugene had got pregnant and then ditched. How could I be sure that if Annie told him of her condition he would not ditch her like the others? Even if he accepted the fatherhood of the child, there was absolutely no guarantee that he would marry Annie, and marriage, above everything else, was what Annie wanted. So I could see the problem.

"Have you told your mother?" I asked.

"Of course not," she replied. "If I told my mother, the first thing she would do is accuse me of being a slut, of not having enough pride and self-esteem to preserve my chastity until marriage. Then, she would burst into tears and wonder what she could have done for God to punish her by first depriving her of her husband, and then giving her a daughter who could not maintain her pride. She would march to Eugene's house and confront him, accusing him of ruining her child, and she'd demand that he marry me. That would just throw everything into total confusion. It would put Eugene's back up like a threatened cat's, and he would ditch me then and there. No! I have not told my mother and I don't intend to tell her. You are the only person I have told, because you are my best friend, and you must not tell anyone, not even your Mr. T."

"So what do you intend to do?" I persisted.

"I will have to abort the pregnancy, "she coolly replied.

"Good God, Annie," I said, "you are not seriously thinking of that. That would be murder. Children are a gift from God, and we must not destroy God's gift. Who knows what

the child will grow up to become? He might become the most distinguished citizen in Sierra Leone in fifty years time. He might become a doctor or a lawyer and the comfort of your old age."

"Fat chance of that happening," she said. "Even if Eugene accepts the fatherhood, do you think he will marry me? Don't you know what our society thinks of outside children, children born out of wedlock? My child will not have a proper education. How then can he become a doctor or a lawyer or a distinguished citizen? No, I will have to get rid of the pregnancy."

I was genuinely horrified at what my friend Annie was proposing to do. Maybe I am traditional and conservative, but I do still believe, as I did then, that children are a gift from God, and we must not destroy them. Besides, it would mean taking a life, and it could be dangerous. So I said to my friend Annie:

"But that sort of thing could be dangerous, Annie. How are you going to have it done? Have you not heard of several women who tried to abort pregnancies and who died in the process? Would it not be better to live and have your child, even if you were to remain unmarried for the rest of your life, than to die and go your grave before your time? Of course, everyone would know what you died of and your family would be disgraced."

"I have thought of all that," she said. "But some of those women who died in the process were already far gone with their pregnancies. That is why they died."

"How far gone are you?" I asked.

"Only two months," she said."

Still, I was not convinced. I thought my friend was seriously underestimating the danger. I would never have thought of doing that sort of thing myself, and I can't imagine how any sane person could. I remember a particularly tragic case that happened just before this, sometime in the early

1930s. This woman was a friend of my father's sister. Her name was Cordelia Cromanty, and she was an exceptionally beautiful woman in her late thirties, who already had three children, two boys and a girl. She had had a happy marriage, until things began to turn sour. Some people say that her husband's people turned him against her, claiming that she was a witch who wanted to destroy his manhood. How could people believe such nonsense? If she had wanted to destroy his manhood, would she not have done so long ago before they had three children? Which woman would want to destroy her husband's manhood? Apparently, the relatives said she wanted to do that in order to stop him chasing other women. Is that the way to prevent your husband chasing other women? By destroying his manhood? What sense is there in that?

Anyway, the husband apparently believed his relatives, and he accepted their suggestion, which was also the suggestion of some medicine men, apparently, that he should have nothing to do with his wife, sexually. Can you believe that? Some men are not only stupid. They are also irresponsible. Now, he really started chasing other women and completely neglected his wife. He went for months, years, without touching her. One could see the effect of this on Cordelia Cromanty. Well, a woman also has needs, you know. It is not just men who have these desires. There she was, a married woman, and her husband had not touched her for years. So, her beautiful face became long and drawn, and she lost weight. Strange enough, the thinner she became, the more convinced her husband and his family were that she was a witch.

In desperation, she also took a lover. As fate would have it, she became pregnant, and it was clear that her husband was not the father. What was she to do? She confided in my aunt and said she had decided to abort the pregnancy. My aunt strongly advised her against it, especially since, at the time, she had been pregnant for about five months. However, Cordelia Cromanty said she had no alternative. She could not have another child in her husband's house. She thought her husband had not yet detected the truth, and merely assumed that she had started putting on weight again. He did know, however, but decided not to say a word. He thought he would wait until she delivered the baby, then disgrace her and throw her out of his house.

So, having decided to abort the pregnancy, Cordelia Cromanty asked my aunt to accompany her to the house of an herbalist, who would give her some potion that would achieve the desired effect. At first, my aunt was reluctant to go, but Cordelia was her best friend and she was distressed to see her in such a terrible fix. So, she accompanied her to the herbalist who gave her the potion. She proceeded to drink all of it, and then disaster struck. Within a week of her visit, she started having horrible stomach pains. She vomited and passed a lot of blood. When she was eventually taken to the hospital, the whole truth came out. By then, it was too late for the doctors to do anything to save her. She died in the most horrible anguish, cursing her husband, her lover, and the herbalist who gave her the concoction to drink. Of course, the whole town now knew what had happened. And would you believe it? Most people sympathized with the husband, whose wife had not only committed adultery and gotten pregnant by another man, but had actually tried to destroy the child. The town claimed that her death was a punishment from God, and the husband was free at last from the machinations of such a witch. My aunt was sick for a whole month afterward, from all the stress of that episode.

So, now that my friend Annie had taken me into her confidence and told me what she intended to do, I remembered this story about Cordelia Cromanty and the role my aunt had played. Annie was determined, however, to go ahead with her plan. Fortunately, she did not actually ask me to accompany her to the herbalist, and I took some comfort from the fact that she, unlike Cordelia Cromanty, was only two months gone. There would be much less danger involved.

So, Annie did as she had planned. She too became horribly ill, afterwards. I remember visiting her at the time, and her unsuspecting mother told me that she was suffering from stomach-ache because of something she had eaten. Her beautiful face looked sad and tired, but I was sure she would not die, and she did not die. She recovered after about three weeks although she had lost a good deal of weight. I never told my husband, and, apparently, Eugene knew nothing of the incident. He carried on his affair with Annie as though nothing had happened.

CHAPTER 5

Years went by.

Mr. T and I continued to reside happily at our home on Wellington Street. He was a very serious, hardworking young man, and a devoted husband and father. He made progress at his work and received a well-deserved promotion. This meant that we were able to buy some nice things for our home: new furniture, for example, among other things. I never had any problems with him, as far as other women were concerned. Not that I would have minded a lot if, every now and then, his eyes strayed and admired other beautiful women. I honestly feel that some women fuss too much over their husbands casting glances, or even occasionally flirting with other women. I think men are by nature promiscuous. It is their nature to flirt, and marriage was invented partly to keep them rooted down to one woman. What does it matter if their eyes roam now and then? The important thing is that they come home to us the truly married wives, maintain us in dignity, and maintain their homes and families. What about those societies that practice polygamy? What are the wives supposed to do? Fight each other every day? Wasn't it similar in our culture, where it was the customary norm to have lots of sweethearts? To behave as Sarian did is ultimately to bring about the destruction of everyone. One has to behave sensibly about these matters.

Mr. T, however, gave me no cause for concern. He continued to come home punctually every day, after work. He ostensibly enjoyed his meals, went to choir practice, or out fishing with his friends. He never went to the bars, or anything of that sort. He did not waste his money. He was also very fond of his children, although he did not play very much with them. He left that to me. In those days, fathers were supposed to demonstrate authority; they didn't have much time for playing around.

By this time I had birthed four children. My third pregnancy resulted in a pair of twins, a boy and a girl. My friends, Annie and Josephine, were still unmarried. After her traumatic experience, Annie had not become pregnant again, to my knowledge, but the affair with Eugene still went on. I was beginning to get worried about her. Eugene was rapidly rising in the Accounts Department of the United African Company. He ought to have been thinking of marriage. He still had not proposed to Annie, though, or asked his family to approach hers. Moreover, Annie was now in her late twenties. It was time she got married and started raising a family.

Then, one afternoon, to my great surprise, Annie breezed into my parlor and announced:

"Eugene and I are going to be married, Priscilla."

"Glory alleluia," I shouted. "So he is going to marry you at last. Please sit down. When will it be? How did it come about? Are you engaged?"

"No," she replied. "We are not engaged yet. But that will happen soon."

"So you have finally got him, you clever girl! I am sure you will be very, very happy. You deserve to be, after all that has happened."

"God moves in mysterious ways. I trust in him. I know that as long as I put my trust in him, everything will end well. Some of my friends had advised me to use 'atefor' on Eugene, to bring him round, but I don't believe in that sort of thing. I believe in God, and now God has worked his wonders. It happened like this: My mother, seeing that Eugene was not serious about marriage, and that I was getting on in years, decided to take the bull by the horns when, one day, Eugene visited."

" 'Annie' she said, 'let me disturb you for a minute. Please go round to Mrs. Chambers and ask her to send the dishes she wanted me to take a look at.' "

"Dutifully, I obeyed. I knew that she was not really in a hurry to see Mrs. Chambers' dishes, and that her real motive was to get me out of the way, so that she could talk to Eugene privately. She told me all about it later."

" 'Eugene, please don't think I want to interfere,' she said, 'but as a mother, I must be concerned about my daughter's future. You have been seeing her now for several years, and she is advancing in age. Several young men have come to me to ask for her hand in marriage, but I've told them all that it was out of the question. You seem to be the man of her choice. Now I must ask you seriously, what are your intentions for Annie?' "

" 'Mama Macauley,' he replied, 'you need not be concerned. I have very serious intentions for her. I intend to marry her. She is the woman of my choice. I was only waiting for some promotion at my job before making any serious proposals. Fortunately, that has happened now. I've been assured a promotion that ensures that my position in the company is secure, and that I will be making enough money to support a family. So I intend to become engaged to Annie quite soon.' "

" 'God be praised,' my mother replied. 'I knew you were a serious young man at heart. My family will be ready to entertain proposals as soon as your family is ready.' "

"So you see," Annie continued, "Eugene has come round at last. I knew he was just waiting till his position with the UAC was secure. The engagement ceremony is set for a month from today, when representatives from Eugene's family will come to mine and ask for my hand. I want you and Bernard to be there."

"Of course we will be there," I replied. "This is a day I have often dreamed of, and I will not miss it for the world."

I was genuinely happy for my friend Annie's good fortune. To think, she will be married at last to the young man she loves! Mr. T and I arranged for his mother to come spend a few hours with the children, while we both went off to the ceremony at Annie's house. There were quite a few people there, mostly relatives and friends of the Macauleys. As we took our seats in the parlor, Annie's mother whispered to me:

"Priscilla, you must come into the bedroom with me. You are to be one of the 'roses' brought out for inspection by Eugene's family before Annie comes out."

"But Mrs. Macauley," I said, "don't you think I am too old for that sort of thing? Besides, I am already married. You need young, unmarried girls for that."

"Nonsense," she replied. "You are still quite young, and you are very beautiful. This family is short of young girls, and we want to bring out five before Annie comes out."

So I went into Mrs. Macauley's bedroom where there were four other young women assembled, and we waited for the distinguished suitors.

At precisely seven o'clock, we heard shouts of "they are coming, they are coming, shut the door." The door was shut, but from the bedroom where we 'roses' were kept, I could see that the delegation consisted of five men and two women, ranging in age from about forty to about sixty-five. They knocked on the door three times.

"Who has come to disturb my peace, this glorious God's Friday evening, when my family and I are relaxing in my house?" shouted Pa Desmond Smythe, in a stentorian voice. He was Mrs. Macauley's first cousin, and was about sixty years of age. He had been chosen by Annie's family to be their spokesman. As was the custom, the bride-to-be's mother never said anything, She spoke through a spokesperson, usually an elderly male relative.

"It is a group of friends, Pa," replied Pa Benoni Pratt, Eugene's sixty-five-year-old uncle. Also, according to tradition, the groom never went himself to ask for the hand of the woman he wanted to marry, but his family elected a spokesman as well. It was understood that it was the bridegroom's family that was going to ask the parents of the bride to give their daughter to their young male relative and their family. In fact, the marriage would not only be a union of husband and wife, but also a union of two families.

"We have come on a very pleasant mission," continued Pa Pratt. "We have very good intentions toward you and your family. Please let us in and we will discuss the nature of our business. You too will be pleased."

"I don't know," Pa Smythe pretended to muse. "For all I know you may be thieves who have come to burgle my house, or maybe even murderers intent on murdering me and my family."

"As God himself is our witness," reassured Pa Pratt, "we are not thieves or murderers. Our mission is the exact opposite of theft and murder. You will find out why we've come if you let us in. We, too, know that the world is bad and everyone has to be careful these days. We understand your caution, but we want to assure you that we are decent people who have come on a very pleasant errand."

"That is exactly so," one of the members of the delegation chimed in.

"Well," said Pa Smythe, pretending to be mollified, "I will have to consult the other members of my family, before I let you in. We are a very good and respectable family, and we'd have a lot to lose if thieves should take it into their heads to rob us."

Pa Smythe receded from the door and feigned deep consultation with the other members of his family. After a few moments, he came back to the door and said, "Well, you are lucky; the other members of the family think that I should trust you, and they've convinced me that I should let you in. If it turns out that your intentions are not honorable, on their heads be it. And if you mean any harm, please know that there are a lot of knives and cutlasses around here that we could use to defend ourselves."

With that, Pa Smythe proceeded to unbolt the door and let the delegation in. After the welcoming pleasantries and introductions, the seven members sat down in comfortable chairs and Pa Smythe proceeded:

"So, Mr. Benoni Pratt, what is your mission?"

"Well, good friends, I was passing by one Sunday, after church, when I looked into your beautiful garden with its lovely flowers. In particular, I saw one that took my breath away. It was the most beautiful and radiant rose in the garden. Believe me, I stood there for several minutes, lost in admiration, and wondering how there could be such a pretty thing in God's creation. It had obviously been well nurtured and groomed. It was the very picture of innocence and love. I was so attracted by it, that I was determined to have it as a present for my son, Eugene Pratt. And so I got together this delegation of respectable friends and relatives to come ask you to kindly give us that magnificent rose for our son."

Of course, the beauty of an engagement ceremony in those days is that one always spoke indirectly. You did not use the name of the girl. You called her a flower or a gem: a rose, jasmine, diamond or pearl. This was what was going on to the extreme delight of all who were there. Also, the engagement ceremony involved a contest of sorts between the spokesmen of the two camps, as they sought to outdo each other in this delicate negotiation. So, you can understand if, instead of being pleased that he had such an admirable rose, Pa Smythe broke into a tremendous tantrum and hurled words of defiance at Benoni Pratt.

"I knew that your intentions were not honorable. My instinct told me. I should not have let you into my house. You mean that, after I opened my doors to you and welcomed you in the presence of all these good people, you intend to come and steal something that I possess? You have the audacity to ask me to give you one of my roses? Do you know how much care and attention I devote to my flowers to make them all bloom as they are doing? Do you know how much expense and love I put into their nurturing? And now you come, after our gracious welcome, to ask me, just like that, to give you my most precious rose to give to your son? I was mistaken about you. Perhaps you should leave, after all. Come on, get out!"

"Please, please, Mr. Smythe, do not be angry," Pa Pratt pleaded. "We know that it is difficult to let go of something that you attach great value to, particularly a flower that has been so carefully nurtured. By giving that rose to our son, you will not lose it; you will always remain close to it. You will be welcome to come to our home and see how carefully we too will be nurturing it. That beautiful rose will bring the two families together in unity and amity, and the rose will blossom all the more.

"Well, I believe your words. But do you promise to take good care of it, as good care as we have taken of it? Indeed, you will have to pay more attention to it than we have, because it will be growing in an alien environment. Has your family the resources and the patience to take good care of my precious rose, to ensure that it does not wither?

Have you good soil? Are the air and atmosphere around your home healthy and conducive to good nurturing?"

"Absolutely," replied Pa Pratt. "The soil around our home and the atmosphere are among the best in this blessed God's country: the air as well. If you give us this rose for our son, we promise, in God's name, to water it every day, nourish it with good fertilizers, and keep it in good sunlight. It will continue to grow and flourish and be just as outstanding as it has been in your garden."

"Will you protect it from thieves who might come in the night to steal it? Do you give me your word that you will not get fed up with it and turn your attention from this rose to other flowers like disgusting yellow bells?"

"I give you my word," replied Pa Pratt. "This rose will always be the center of attention in our compound. How can it but be, since it is so beautiful? We will protect it from prying eyes and dirty hands that might wish to uproot it. It will be the centerpiece of our garden"

"All right," I believe you," said Pa Smythe. "Let us bring the rose out. "Admire," he called out to Annie's mother, "bring the rose for these people to see."

At this moment, I was asked to come out of the bedroom and go into the parlor. Although I was now about twenty-seven and a married woman with four children, I still looked quite beautiful and even younger than I was. On this occasion, I had on a beautiful pink dress. I marched into the parlor and turned myself around for everyone to see and admire my beautiful figure. I could see that the members of the delegation were impressed, and those who did not know me might have thought that I was indeed the 'rose' in question.

"Mr. Smythe," Pa Pratt went on after taking a good look at me. "I can see that you indeed have some extremely beautiful flowers in your garden. This one is also radiant and beautiful, but it is not the one I have in mind."

"I see, you can't be satisfied," said Pa Smythe. "You not only want a beautiful rose from my garden, you also want to deprive me of my most beautiful rose. I am beginning to regret that I let you in. However, I have let you in, and I've promised to give you a rose. Admire, bring out the rose."

Another beautiful young girl was produced, a cousin of Annie. She was only about eighteen, and many young men would have loved to have her hand in marriage. But she was not Annie, so again, Pa Pratt went through the ritual of praising her beauty but said, in the end, that she was not the rose he had in mind. The merry dance went on and on, until Annie finally came out of the bedroom. She looked absolutely radiant in a blue dress and wearing a coy smile. Pa Pratt went into raptures:

"This is indeed my rose; see how beautiful she is? This is the rose I saw."

Everyone laughed and clapped as Pa Pratt hugged Anne to his bosom, welcoming her into his family and showing how well they were prepared to care for her.

After the raptures were over, Pa Pratt went on to say, "As an earnest of our good intentions and of the way we will care for this beautiful rose, we have brought you this small gift. Please receive it as a token of the high esteem in which we hold your family in general, and this rose in particular."

He then handed over a packet to Pa Smythe, who then went into the bedroom with Mrs. Admire Macauley and another male relative to check on the contents of the packet. In the meantime, drinks and refreshments were served to all present. Before long, Pa Smythe and the others came out to say that they were satisfied with the token that was in the packet, and would gladly give their rose to Pa Pratt and the delegation, for their son Eugene. Cheers and hurrahs rang through the small confines of that house. Pa Pratt went on to say that within a short time, Eugene would come for his rose, and the final ceremonies would be conducted that would unite the two families. There were further cheers and the women in the group burst into song:

"Yawo Mammy don answer yes oh! Yes oh! Yes Oh! Yawo Mammy don answer yes oh! Yes oh! Yes oh!" The song meant "the bride's mother has said yes."

Then, the female members of the group danced out of the house and into the street. They continued dancing and singing for the next hour along Circular Road, so that everyone would know that Mrs. Admire Macauley had agreed for her daughter Annie to marry Eugene Pratt, and that the wedding would take place shortly. People came out of their houses or watched us dance through their windows. It was indeed a memorable and happy occasion.

Annie Macauley was engaged at last to her Eugene. Annie's mother, in particular, was beside herself with joy at the prospect of her daughter getting married. What woman would not be? The role of "Mother of the bride" at a Krio wedding is a very important and enviable one, next only to those of the bride and the groom. Every mother looks forward to her daughter's wedding day, when people will sing and dance around her as she comes home from the church:

"Yawo Mammy aybi so! Yawo Mammy aybi so!" they'll sing. That means the bride's mother is well dressed, beautiful, and respectable (literally it means she is heavy). The prospect of her daughter's imminent marriage had even further significance for Mrs. Macauley. As I have said, the family was not well off. She hoped her daughter's marriage would raise the family's financial and social status. After all, Eugene was earning a handsome salary at his respectable job in the United Africa Company. She expected some of that money and respectability to filter through to her. She even spoke quite seriously to Eugene, one occasion when they were alone together. She told him how delighted she was that he had come forward to marry her daughter, and that she was quite sure the two would make a very good marriage and have a happy family. She was delighted at having the privilege to welcome Eugene into their family, and would regard him as her own son. She confessed to him that, as he himself must have realized, there were not many men in the family; her husband had died several years ago (God rest his soul). Therefore, Eugene would virtually be the head of the family, and she was looking forward to such a handsome, earnest and respectable young man filling that role. Though they were not very well off, they were honest and decent, she continued. She had brought up her daughter well, and was sure she would be a very good wife for Eugene.

She spoke sincerely, and obviously meant every word that she said. Maybe Eugene was impressed and even flattered. After all, was it not great to be regarded as the head of any family? Maybe at the time he seriously intended to get married. After all, was he not engaged? Had he not sent a delegation of elders to Annie's people to ask for her hand and had not Annie's people agreed?

But what did engagement really mean to Eugene? It is amazing what some people think an engagement involves. Some people think it is as good as being married. They think that as long as the couple is engaged, they can even go on living together indefinitely without bothering to actually get married. I know of several couples that have remained engaged for years. It suits the men best of all, of course, because it means they have all the privileges of married life without the legal obligations. They have someone to cook for them, look after their household, even bear and look after their children, and provide comfort for their beds. But there is no legal contract, and if they like, they can turn the woman out of the house, without a penny to her name. They do not even have to go through the formalities of a divorce.

Others think engagement means that both the man and the woman should stop paying attention to anyone else apart from their betrothed from that day onward. An engagement ceremony gives notice to the world that both the man and the woman are spoken for, and that all other parties should hold off. In fact, the popular expression we used in those days to describe a betrothal was "to put stop." We did not use the word "engage." The young man's family went to "put stop" for the girl. She was supposed to cease all other romantic activities she might have been having.

Clearly, that was not how the Cassanova, Eugene Pratt, saw his engagement with Annie Macauley. That he was engaged to one of the prettiest girls in town did not put a stop to his philandering. Several months went by after the engagement, but Eugene did not seem keen to begin preparations for the wedding, even though he and his family had paid trousseau money to Annie. As the months went by and we received no news of a fixed wedding date, I became anxious for my friend and decided to confront her with my fears.

"Annie," I said to her one day as we sat in my parlor, "when are we to dance the goumbay at your wedding? When is it going to be? You must give us adequate notice so that I can begin to save some money for a special wedding outfit and for my aso-ebi."

"Don't worry my sister," she replied. "We will announce the date soon. Eugene is expecting another promotion that will give us even greater security and enable us to rent a really magnificent house in a good part of town."

I could see, however, that she was not telling me the complete story and that my fears were not without foundation.

"Are you sure Annie?" I asked. "Is there no other problem?"

She hesitated for a moment, and her face became clouded. I could see that there was something wrong. I could also see that she too must have heard some of the reports that were circulating about Eugene's other amorous activities in spite of the fact that he was engaged.

"I am not sure," Priscilla," she said. "There are times when I am so anxious that I can't sleep at night."

"Well, you have to be strong, Annie," I said to her. "You must tell Eugene to realize the seriousness of an engagement and stop fooling around with other women, or he will lose you. Tell him that you'll break off the engagement. Give him an ultimatum."

"How can I give him an ultimatum?" she said. "When one gives an ultimatum, one should be prepared to carry it out. I am in no position to carry out such an ultimatum. I am twenty eight, Priscilla, and getting on in years. What man will look at me now? The whole town knows that Eugene and I have been carrying on for the last several years. Besides, I do love him. No, that's not the matter. I don't mind his fooling around with other women, provided he marries me in the end. Once I have his ring, I will know that he is mine. I will be the rightful, legal wife, and he can even carry on as he pleases. No, his flirting with other women is not the problem. The problem is his mother. I am not so sure that she really wants this marriage."

"I see," I said. "In that case, you have a major problem, a really big problem." I immediately recalled the problems I had had with my own domineering mother-in-law, Mrs. Thompson, and realized that even if Eugene married Annie, there would be major problems ahead, if Eugene's mother was opposed to the match.

CHAPTER 6

Eugene's mother, Mrs. Susan Pratt, was a woman with an indomitable spirit, like my own mother-in-law. She was fiercely class-conscious and a veritable snob, if ever there was one, although her origins and those of her husband, Mr. Thomas Pratt, had been very humble indeed. She was the daughter of a blacksmith, a man who repaired pots and pans and also made metal railings for the wealthy. Whenever I had cause to go to his shop along Waterloo Street, I noticed he was almost always covered in soot. His job was indeed a filthy one, but that was the only trade he knew, and he made enough money out of it to keep his small family together. Susan was the eldest of his three daughters. Not surprisingly, she did not have much education and married her husband, Thomas Pratt, at a very early age.

In those days, Thomas was a shoemaker and as far as I know, his ancestors had all been shoemakers for about three generations. In other words, they did not belong to the highest echelons of society. Perhaps to compensate for this, his new wife made up her mind that her family would rise in societal status. She encouraged her husband to work as hard as he possibly could (some people say that he even worked behind closed doors on Sundays) so that they would make enough money to pretend that they belonged to a higher class.

Susan Pratt persuaded her husband to use the money he had saved to not only build their one-story wooden house along Percival Street, but also a small store that was adjacent to the house. Then, they invested some money in trade. Their little store was always full of odds and ends: such as calabashes, second-hand shoes and clothes, provisions, and other knick-knacks. At times, Susan traveled to places like Nigeria and Fernando Po and came back with all sorts of goods for the store. The store was by no means a glorious one, like some of those along Water Street or Little East Street, but it enabled Mr. and Mrs. Pratt to make some extra money. Eventually, Mr. Pratt gave up shoemaking completely and devoted himself to the store.

His wife, in particular, kept on pretending that she belonged to the higher classes. Quite often, she would refuse to use her native Krio with customers, but would speak in English instead. She was not highly educated, though, and she made numerous gaffes with her use of the language, gaffes that soon became the talk of the town. Schoolchildren used to go to her store after school and pretend that they wanted to buy something. But they merely wanted to hear her usual mistakes with the English language, to "shoot" as they called it. They'd all burst into uproarious laughter as they left her store and made their way home, and they'd tell their classmates in school the next day.

She is reported to have said one day, when the daughter of a friend entered her store, "Oh Princess, I hear your mother has another stomach. Please wish her good luck for me." What she meant was that she'd heard that the girl's mother was pregnant a second time. Needless to say, that gaffe was repeated all over Freetown the next morning, and all the school children shouted it out as they passed by her store.

Although her lack of serious education was patent, Mrs. Susan Pratt pretended that she had gone to secondary school. She spread lies around that she was an alumna of the Annie Walsh Memorial School, which had been established in 1849 and was the oldest secondary school for girls in the whole of West Africa.

On one occasion, when the school was having its annual Thanksgiving service, an occasion in which the Old girls were expected to participate, she put on a gorgeous white dress, strapped the school's hatband on to her hat, and turned up at the service with the full intention of marching through the streets of Freetown, pretending she was a respectable alumna of the reputed institution. Of course, people knew that she was a pretentious upstart, and unfortunately for her, one of the real Old girls of her generation spotted her and knew immediately that she was a fraud. At first, the woman engaged in polite and jovial conversation with Mrs. Pratt, but when the latter was off-guard, the former calmly asked her what year she entered the school.

"Oh, it was in 1900," she replied.

"Indeed," the Old girl said. "That is very strange, because I entered in that year too, and I cannot recall seeing you at all."

"Well, I was a very quiet one in those days," replied the indomitable Mrs. Pratt. "I did not call attention to myself."

By now, several other Old girls had become aware of the conversation and were keenly listening to the exchange.

"Can you remember any of the teachers who taught you, during all those years at Annie Walsh? Who was your form teacher?" asked the Old girl.

"Oh, em—emm—em," stammered Mrs. Pratt. "Let me see now. There was a Miss Gilpin and a Miss Cole. Yes, Miss Gilpin and Miss Cole."

"We did not have any Misses Gilpin and Cole at the Annie Walsh," put in another woman, who was much more blunt than the first.

"Well, maybe I've got the names wrong," retorted Mrs. Pratt and moved to another area of the parade. No one spoke to her for the rest of the afternoon, and everyone refused to march in line with her. She had been exposed as the fraud she was. For the next two weeks, Freetown was full of stories of the woman who pretended to be an Old girl of Annie Walsh, and was found out and shunned by the genuine Old girls. Mrs. Pratt had to hide her head in shame and did not appear in public again for another four weeks.

At times, when she and her husband quarreled, Mrs. Pratt would throw his "humble" origins in his face.

"I don't blame you," she would hiss. "I blame my father who handed me over to a mere shoemaker, descended from a line of shoemakers."

"And what about you?" Her husband would ask. "Wasn't your father a blacksmith, descended from a line of black-smiths, just about the filthiest people in the community?"

"Oho," she would scream. "So, now you are cursing my father. At least my father made iron railings for the wealthy and went into mighty houses. He mingled with the best in society, with aristos. You would just repair the dirty shoes they walked in, dirty shoes that had trod on all the filth of this town. So, don't you dare to say that my father was filthy."

Nothing delighted Mrs. Susan Pratt more than to be asked to be godmother at a wedding or Grand Chief Patron at a Thanksgiving service. Both meant that she was impor-tant. Whenever she was godmother, she would spend her husband's money on expensive clothes, shoes and a hat, and would make sure that she entered the church late, after the bride had gone in, so that she would attract maximum atten-tion. She would ask her neighbors to be present outside the home of the bride after the wedding, so that as she stepped out of the car, people would shout and sing, "Godmammy aybi so! Godmammy aybi so!" Then, she'd dance and prance around before entering the house. Later, she would throw a lavish party. Her friends and relations would wear the expensive 'aso-ebi' she had chosen for the occasion.

Whenever she was asked to be Grand Chief Patron, she'd wear an expensive dress, and would take her time marching up the aisle to take her position near the steps leading to the altar. Then, she would turn to face the congregation, smiling broadly and holding the grand plate in her hands, while the humbler collectors were taking up the collection.

This was Eugene's mother. Naturally, she expected great things of her son. While he was still in school, she would say to friends, "Eugene is going to be a great doctor or lawyer, someday. Nothing less." She regaled herself with this fantastic and imaginative scenario of her son as the distinguished doctor, and herself as doctor's mother organizing his social life.

It would have been helpful, of course, if her son obliged her by working diligently in school. But Eugene, though not stupid, was an indifferent student, who never quite succeeded in graduating from the Methodist Boys High School. Instead of finding his way overseas to be trained as a lawyer or doctor, he had to content himself with starting his adult life as a lowly clerk with the United Africa Company. Still, Mrs. Pratt did not give up hope. She fully expected her son to gain the favor of the white managers of the company and be given rapid promotion, so that someday he would himself become a manager. Above all, she expected him to marry into a superlative family, as she used to say. He should not, by any means, make the mistake she made by marrying into a low family. He must now set his sights on the daughter of a doctor or lawyer or one of the higher-up Krio merchants. She looked to her son to help raise her status in society.

You can imagine, therefore, that she looked on the relationship with the humble Annie Macauley with the gravest misgivings. Whenever Annie went to their house at Percival Street, Mrs. Pratt would hardly deign to speak to the young

woman. If Annie ever dared to ask whether Eugene was at home, Eugene's mother would roll her eyes and spit out her words like a venomous snake.

"How should I know whether he is at home," she would hiss. "I am not his keeper. He comes and goes as he likes." She would not say another word to Annie, but would merely nod when the latter said goodbye.

"What is the matter with you?" she asked her son, one occasion before the engagement. "Don't you know that you could do much better than marry the daughter of a nobody? That is what they are: nobodies. Her father is dead, and no one knows what he did for a living, while alive. They live in one of the poorest areas in town in a rented house. Her mother sells small things like matches and candles and kerosene for a living. I wonder how they manage to make ends meet. Do you want your friends to laugh at you? You will soon be a manager for the United Africa Company. Do you think you'll be able to present this girl to your superiors, if they invite you to parties and receptions? She cannot even speak the English language. Don't you have any pride? And what about me? After all I have done to bring you up and encourage in you a sense of self worth, do you want my friends to laugh at me and say that I am the mother-in-law of a girl like that, whose mother sells kerosene for a living?"

"But Mama," Eugene would say weakly, "Annie is a very nice girl, and she is one of the most beautiful girls in town. All my friends are envious of me for capturing the heart of such a beautiful and quiet girl. Besides, I am sure that before I met her, she had had nothing to do with any other man. She is also a good cook, and will take very good care of my children, when they come along."

"And are those the most important things? Don't you know that class is also very important? You must marry a girl who other people will not look down on. Don't you know that you must marry a girl with 'tracing'? This girl's family does not have any 'tracing.' Who was her father? Who was her grandfather? Who was her great grand- father? You must marry a girl who will help to lift you up, not one that will bring you down to her own filthy level. Do you expect me to go to parties at her mother's house and mingle with women who wear head-ties to church instead of hats, and who have never worn imported shoes in their lives?"

"What you say is true, mother. But I have gone so far with Annie that I am not sure I could go back now. We have been seeing each other for so many years now, and all our friends expect us to get married. If I do not marry her, people will blame me and say that I have wasted her time. Besides, where am I to find this high-class woman that you speak of? I have tried making advances to some, but they all look down on me as the son of a lowly shoemaker and petty trader. Also, most of them are very ugly; I cannot bear the thought of spending my life with them. That would be utter misery."

"And do you think looks are everything that matter in a marriage? If that was the case do you think I would have married your father? The most important thing is to get someone who will help raise you up in life and ensure that your children and grandchildren mingle with the people who matter."

Conversations like this had a profound influence on the shallow Eugene. This was one of the main reasons why he delayed getting engaged to and marrying Annie. Of course, he was also a philanderer and wanted to have as much fun as possible before marriage. You might wonder why, in the end, he decided to get engaged to Annie.

Well, there were several reasons. One was that he was making progress in his work and needed a wife, as some of the senior people in his company were constantly reminding him. A wife, they said, added dignity to a man. No matter how successful a man was at work, he was a nobody if he did not have a wife at home to support him and to accompany him to church and other engagements. Another reason was that he was really timid and in spite of his skill at seducing women, dared not approach the highbrow daughters of the mighty that his mother liked. Those he did approach turned their noses up at him. Then there was the influence of his friends, like my Mr. T, who kept urging him to do something about Annie, since, after all, he had been seeing her for several years. Mr. T really liked Annie and warned Eugene on several occasions that he would not be pleased if he disturbed her peace of mind. Eugene's marriage to Annie would, in fact, bind all of us friends even closer together. Finally, Eugene's father, Mr. Thomas Pratt, never forgot his own humble origins as a shoemaker, even if he had achieved some success as a trader. He did not share his wife's highfalutin notions. Besides, he used to say, as he was a father himself, he would not like any young man to treat his own daughters the way his wife was proposing: to ditch them, after several years of courtship. That was a matter of great concern to him. For these reasons, Eugene decided to set aside the objections of his mother and carry on with the proposed marriage to Annie. But even after the engagement, Mrs. Pratt remained lukewarm toward Annie and warned her son not to hurry with the wedding.

Another complication arose in the relationship, however: it concerned my other friend Josephine. I was not as close to Josephine as I was to Annie. As I've told you, Josephine's father occupied a very high and important position in the Senior British Colonial Service and was a college graduate. Therefore, she belonged to one of the highest echelons of Freetown society and did not mingle too much with us after our sewing mistress's death, although we still were friends. Remember that Josephine was godmother to my second son, and she visited Mr. T and me every now then. She was still unmarried and was still living with her parents.

As I have said, she was not a very attractive young woman, and very few men paid any attention to her. She visited me much more often than she visited Annie, even though they both lived along the same Circular Road. Josephine's house, however, was at the upper and more fashionable end. Whenever she visited Annie she didn't stay long. She told me that she couldn't stand Annie's mother. I suppose she secretly looked down on Annie's family. Quite often they would both meet at my place, and we would all three talk at great length about days gone by, about our sewing mistress, Sissy Dinah, her strange life and even stranger death.

One Sunday afternoon, Josephine visited our home at Wellington Street, and the conversation was lively and pleasant. My Mr. T was a very jovial man who certainly knew how to entertain guests. The three of us spent a pleasant afternoon together, before Josephine left. About fifteen minutes after she had gone, I realized that she had forgotten her very nicely rolled umbrella.

"Look, Mr. T," I said, "Josephine has forgotten her umbrella. Why don't you run and give it to her? It will be terrible for her if it rains."

"She must have gone quite far by now. It will be difficult for me to catch up with her. I am sure she will come back for it when she realizes she has left it. At least, she will know where she left it."

At that moment, Eugene turned up and started joking in his usual breezy way:

"And how are my fine married friends doing on this blessed Sunday?"

"Don't you worry." said Mr. T. "Soon, you will be entering this life yourself and then, we will see whether you joke about it."

"Oh, I don't expect marriage to curtail my privileges. I will have someone to cook for me and look after my house, of course, but I still expect to go out and come in when I

want. I assure you, I do not intend to be the typical married man."

"Well, we will see about that, once you get married, "Mr. T replied.

At that very moment, who should come in again but Josephine who had discovered that she had left her umbrella.

"Hallo, Miss Venus Freeman," Eugene greeted her. "It has been ages since I last had the pleasure of your delightful company."

"I am Josephine Freeman," Josephine replied rather more coyly than usual. "And let me tell you, flattery will get you nowhere with me." But Instead of leaving as soon as she had got her umbrella, she sat down once again.

"That is a very handsome suit you are wearing, Mr. Eugene. Did you get it on loan from your company?" she joked.

"No, no," replied Eugene. "This was made to measure by the most skilful tailor in town. There is none like it in the whole of Freetown. The material was brought as a gift for me from the United Kingdom, by one of the most senior British officials of our company. He thought it would look good on me. Don't you think that it does?"

"It certainly does," said Josephine. This banter between them went on for the next hour. When, at last, Josephine got up to leave, Eugene said he was leaving as well. He had a church function to prepare for that evening.

So, the two left together. And so, I am sure, began the liaison that eventually wrecked all the hopes of our good friend, Annie Macauley. Whenever I muse about all these events, I wonder at the way that chance can affect our lives for the future. If only Josephine had not forgotten her umbrella that Sunday afternoon! If only Eugene had not decided to visit us, that same Sunday! Quite a few people's lives might have taken a different turn.

You might well wonder why Josephine who came from an elite family and had demonstrated such a snobbish attitude, condescended to flirt with Eugene, whose ancestry was much humbler than hers. Her parents and Eugene's parents did not move in the same social circles, in a society that was very class-conscious. In fact, the only reason why Annie and I had even met Josephine was that we had the same sewing mistress. Otherwise, our paths would never have crossed. Her high and mighty parents certainly intended her to marry some doctor or some lawyer.

The problem was, as I have told you, that Josephine was not very pretty. Her figure was a bit on the stout side, and anyone who wanted to be uncharitable would have called her dumpy. Her legs were short and thick, and her face was broad with a large, flat nose. She tried to compensate for this by walking in a stately manner with short steps, as if she were marching all the time to the strains of some brass band. However, this merely made her look more ridiculous. Quite possibly, some parents belonging to Josephine's social circle suggested her to their sons, as a fitting object for their attentions. But I am sure that the young men objected very strongly.

Josephine was approaching thirty and still, no suitors had come forward for her hand in marriage. There was a very strong possibility that she might be left on the shelf. What was she to do? She was still dependent on her parents and had not been trained in any profession. Indeed, she was getting desperate. Although Eugene belonged to a much lower social class, he was, as we have seen, a very dashing and handsome young man, one of the most eligible bachelors in town. He was now in his early thirties and should, by all accounts, have gotten married by now. He was a smart young man who was making progress in his job with the United Africa Company. So was it any wonder that Josephine might flirt with him? And the irresponsible Eugene

was not the kind of man to decline a challenge to flirt, even though he was engaged.

It is quite likely that when they began their liaison, Eugene did not intend for it to get very far. He just wanted to have his fun, and then ditch Josephine as he had done with lots of other young women. What he hadn't bargained for was Josephine's capacity for scheming and duplicity. He did not realize that a desperate young woman like Josephine would go to any lengths to make sure of her catch. So, in a sense, Eugene was trapped in a net partly of his own making.

These were the early days of the war. I mean, the Second World War, of course. Many young men of all classes had been encouraged by the British to fight for "King and country." They'd been promised lucrative rewards and opportunities, once the war was over. That meant that young men were, in a sense, in short supply.

The Second World War! I remember that war. Freetown harbor, as you know, is a natural harbor, and a good many British warships came to berth there. I remember seeing the British sailors in their smart white and blue uniforms, as they proudly strutted through the streets of Freetown. Because of this, Freetown was often a target for German reconnaissance planes, and their heavy, droning sound was quite commonly heard. You really knew that a war was on and that, in a sense, we were part of it.

I remember one incident in particular very vividly. The twins were now about a year old, and they were quite a handful. I had four children then, and I had to do something with them all those days when I needed to go to market. I would take the two eldest children and one of the twins to my mother's at Bathurst Street, strap the other twin firmly to my back and proceed to King Jimmy or Kroo Town Road market. On this occasion, I went to King Jimmy market, went down the steep steps leading to the market, and started making my purchases. I used to enjoy the shopping, haggling with the market women and chatting with friends and relatives I met there. On this day, while we were all busy with our enjoyable shopping, we heard the sound of sirens giving the warning that enemy planes were approaching. Within a few minutes, there was total pandemonium as the market women started collecting their wares in order to flee or take shelter inside one of the concrete market buildings. Now, you know what King Jimmy Market looks like even to this day. It has some very steep steps, about one hundred altogether, leading down to the shoreline and to the buildings where the market is held. To get down to the market one has to descend all those steps, and to get back to the street one has to climb them all again. Within moments, we heard the blare of the warplanes and many of us started making for the steps. "Whirr! Whirr! Whirr!" went the planes. I looked at the sky and saw two of them. At that moment I imagined that they were coming straight for me and the baby on my back. They were flying very low and in my dismay, I even imagined that I could see one of the pilots staring down at me. There were shouts of "Lord, have mercy!" "Lord save us!" "What kind of trouble is this?" You can just imagine me running up those steps with a one-year-old baby tied to my back and a bag in my hand full of purchases. To this day, I cannot say how I found the strength or the speed to run up those steps like that. I am amazed that no one got crushed in the stampede.

I ran all the way to my mother's house at Bathurst Street. It seemed as if the planes merely intended to scare us, or they were on their way to some other place and did not really intend any harm. In any case, they did not drop any bombs, and the citizens of Freetown were spared. But it took me a good hour after I arrived at my mother's house to regain my breath and composure. Eventually, I made my way back to our own house with my four children, and who do you think I found there in the compound waiting for me?

It was Annie. At first, I thought that she too had tried to take shelter in our home from the enemy planes. She looked quite distraught and badly shaken. It was obvious that she had come to our place in a hurry, without bothering to put on decent clothes or shoes. She just had a pink print frock on, a matching head-tie, and home-made slippers on her feet.

"Oh my sister," I said when I saw her. "So you too have been scared by those enemy planes."

I began to recount my own experiences to her as we both moved into the house and into the parlor.

"My situation is hopeless, Priscilla," she said and burst into tears. "But it is not because of the enemy planes. In fact, I now wish that one of those enemy planes had thrown one of its bombs at me and ended my miserable life."

"What is the matter, my dear Annie? Is there anything wrong with your mother? I have never seen you in such a terrible condition."

"It is Eugene," she said. "He has broken our engagement." Once more, she broke into such heavy sobbing that the heart of even the most callous person would have melted.

"Oh my God! How on Earth could he do such a thing, after keeping you on tenterhooks all these years? Does he not know that an engagement is a sacred contract that should not be taken lightly? What happened?"

"He seems to have fallen for Josephine," she said. "At least, he has become involved with her to such an extent that he thought it fit to break off our engagement. Oh God! I am so ashamed. I feel so humiliated! What am I to do? I have been waiting for him all these years. I am now thirty years of age, and the whole town knew of our engagement. Who is going to marry me now? What shall I do?" She continued sobbing bitterly.

"Eugene is such a fool and a big rascal," I said. "How could he do this to a nice girl like you? We will have to get

Mr. T to talk to him. He cannot abandon you like that, after all these years. What about his mother? What did his mother say?"

"His mother is worse than he is," Annie replied. "She seems to support him wholeheartedly."

Annie then proceeded to tell me how she found out about Eugene's change of heart.

"I had not seen Eugene for over two weeks. So, yesterday, I went to their house at Percival Street to see whether all was well. It was Mrs. Pratt who answered the door, but she looked so cold and did not even invite me in. She just stood there in the doorway, glaring at me. You would not believe that I was the young woman who was engaged to her son.

" 'Is Eugene in Ma?' I asked."

" 'Well, come in and see for yourself.' "

"She walked into the parlor, and I followed her. I sat down on a chair, while she went and knocked on Eugene's door."

" 'Eugene,' she called out, 'there is someone to see you.' "

"Can you believe it? She did not say 'Annie has come to see you.' I had merely become a 'someone,' and she did not even condescend to sit with me in the parlor; she went to the pantry to busy herself with her own affairs."

" 'Tell her that I do not wish to see her. Tell her she must not come to my house any more. From this time forth she is nothing to me.' "

"I almost fainted. The man I had hoped would marry me, the man to whom I had given the best years of my life, was telling me through someone else that I was nothing to him."

" 'Do you hear that?' asked Mrs. Pratt. 'He says that from this time forth you mean nothing to him and that you must not come to see him.' "

" 'How can that be?' I asked. 'I am engaged to him; we are supposed to be getting married. What have I done? Eugene,

please come and talk to me. This is your own Annie. The Annie you are engaged to.' "

" 'Then,' Eugene said through the door, 'Mama, please tell that person that I hope she can understand Krio. After all I am not speaking English, which she barely understands. I am using the Krio language that I am sure she understands. I do not wish to see her anymore and she means nothing to me.' "

"All the while, I was crying loudly in the parlor. My whole body was shaken with sobs. Can you imagine how I felt? Up till that moment, I had thought that, one day soon, I would be walking down the aisle, hand in hand with my new husband, that we would start our married life together and have lots of children. I would have security for the future and everything to look forward to. Now, in a moment, all those hopes were dashed."

" 'Mama Pratt,' I said, 'please help me understand. What have I done? What am I to do? What has brought about this change of heart? We are engaged to marry. I have given him everything. Now, I will become the laughing stock of the whole town. What will people say? Please Eugene, please come out and talk to me. I feel I am going to die. I can't understand what is happening. Come out and make me understand.' "

"Eugene's mother had been scowling at me, and looking at me as though I was the most contemptible thing on the surface of the earth. I had hoped that as a woman, and an older person, at that, she would understand my situation and show me some sympathy. But I was wrong. I am sure that if Pa Thomas Pratt had been there, he would have sympathized with me and upbraided his son. But he had traveled up country on business. So, I was left there with those two people, Eugene and his mother."

" 'Mama,' Eugene called out from the room, 'please come here and take this to Annie. Perhaps this will convince her of how I feel, and then she will stop bothering me.' "

"Mrs. Pratt went into Eugene's bedroom and came out shortly afterwards with a piece of paper and a message on it. Without speaking, she handed it to me. The note was written in red ink. I read it with trembling hands."

" 'Annie,' it read, 'there are times when a man's eyes become blind to truth and reality, and he falls for the machinations of a wicked and scheming woman. But there are also times when his eyes become open to truth and he clearly sees that he has been living in a dream. That time has come for me. I cannot deny that I once had feelings for you, but I now realize it was because I fell for your artful and wicked schemes. You trapped me into an engagement and promise of marriage. I now realize that if I marry you, our life together will be hell. You and your disgusting mother were merely looking for a suitable man to take care of you, to raise the fortunes of your low and common family. I was the victim of this miserable scheme. If you think that I will take you into my house, give you my name, and introduce you to my superior circle of friends, you are very much mistaken. From now on, I part company with you, completely. Do not attempt to come and see me again if you value your reputation and life. Our destinies are bound to be different. From this moment on, we go our separate ways. My only regret is that it has taken so long for my eyes to be opened to the truth. Goodbye, for all eternity.' "

"I could not believe my eyes. Was this the same person I was engaged to, the person who went out of his way to woo me? Now, he was saying that my mother and I had trapped him with our evil schemes? What schemes had I used? Was he not the one who chased me? And did I not hold out for quite a while before giving in to him? By now, I was sobbing

bitterly and asking God to come to my help and have mercy on me."

" 'Mama Pratt,' I said, 'Eugene knows that none of this is true. He knows that I haven't used any schemes. Please ask him to come talk to me.' "

"The heart of any normal person would have been touched, but not those two."

" 'Okay' screamed Eugene, bursting out of the room in a towering rage. 'I have come out.' "

"The muscles on his face were literally twitching with rage and annoyance. 'Okay. I have come to tell you in person. I want nothing more to do with you. You are nothing but a cheap slut. Perhaps you think I don't know about your abortion! Do you think I am going to marry a woman who has committed murder? And whose baby was it anyway? I am sure it was not mine. Otherwise, you would have told me about it. But do you think that sort of thing can be kept hidden for long in Freetown? You got yourself pregnant by another man and aborted the baby. The father was probably a no good so-and-so who you could not bring yourself to marry, and now you want me to marry you. Do you think I intend to make myself the laughing stock of the city? You disgust me. I tell you again, you are a wicked girl and I want nothing more to do with you. I order you not to come to my house any more. That is final.' "

" 'Please, Eugene,' I pleaded. 'I confess that I aborted the child, but, as God is my witness, the child was yours. I have known no other man in my life. I did not tell you about it, because I did not know how you would react. I admit that was a serious mistake, but we can have many other children if we get married.' "

" 'So you confess to being a murderer. Even if the child was mine, what right had you to murder my child without consulting me? You are a wicked, conniving woman, and I cannot give such a woman my name. Get out of my house! Get out of my life, and never try to see me ever again.' "

"With that he went back into his room and slammed the door shut. I pleaded and pleaded with tears running down my cheeks, but he and his mother said not another word. I have not slept since, and I've hardly eaten. Tell me, Priscilla, what must I do now? I feel like killing myself."

"You will do nothing of the sort," I said to her. I tried my best to reassure her and said I would move heaven and earth, but I would get Mr. T to go and talk to Eugene, to let him know that he was in duty bound to marry Annie. Well, Mr. T tried his best. He even threatened to break up his friendship with Eugene who was his best friend and the godfather of his eldest son. Ade Smith even went to talk to him. When old Pa Thomas Pratt came back to Freetown at the end of his business trip, he also talked to his son quite seriously about the heinousness of breaking up such an engagement. Such a thing wasn't heard of, he said. But Eugene's mind was made up, and nothing could deflect him. The most important consideration, it seemed, was that Josephine was pregnant, and a young woman in her position could not afford to have a baby without getting married. Do you see the irony of the situation? While Annie had concealed her pregnancy from Eugene and had even had an abortion because she thought that Eugene would not marry her if she had a baby, Josephine was prepared to use her pregnancy as the strongest argument for Eugene's marrying her.

Eugene also had another powerful ally in his mother. You remember I have said that Mrs. Susan Pratt was an incorrigible upstart who looked to her son to help her raise her station in life. She saw her son's marriage to Josephine Freeman as a very attractive proposition. She would be allied with the Freemans, one of the most famous families in the whole Freetown community. She saw herself mingling with the high-and- mighty, visiting them in their homes, and they visiting her. She had already started trying to persuade her husband to sell the lowly one-story wooden house and build a more imposing two-story structure somewhere along Circular Road. That would be more in line with their projected rise in status. When Eugene informed her that he intended to marry Josephine Freeman, she shouted, "God be praised. I knew you would not disappoint me, my son. I knew that you would one day raise our status and achieve great things, what your unambitious father seems incapable of. A man must have ambition. He must set his sights high. I am so proud of you."

Mrs. Freeman then started spreading the word around Freetown that her son was going to marry one of the mighty Freeman family.

"Her people are very important, you know. They are also very smart people and would not allow their cherished daughter to marry into a family that was not itself important. They did a lot of searching into our family background, and eventually realized that my Mr. Thomas Pratt has become very successful with his trade. In fact, he is now building a new house that we will move into soon after the wedding. And Eugene is doing very well in his job as well, and is on very good terms with the managers at the United Africa Company. That is why they are prepared to give him their cherished daughter. Our family will gain in prominence, you know. I am sure that one of these days, my Thomas, with the help of his new in-laws, will be made an OBE, Officer of the British Empire, in recognition of his services to trade and commerce. Having the right connections is very important."

However, if Mrs. Susan Pratt thought that the Freemans would welcome the new alliance with her family she was soon to be gravely disappointed. The Freemans were, in their own subtle way, just as snobbish as Mrs. Pratt was. They were highly conscious of their own highly distinguished ancestry and thought that their eldest daughter, Josephine, was destined for the hand of some distinguished husband.

"What is this you're telling me?" Mrs. Letitia Freeman asked her daughter when Josephine told her, one afternoon, that a Mr. Eugene Pratt was to come and ask their permission to marry her.

"I said that a Mr. Eugene Pratt will be coming on Sunday to ask your and father's permission to marry me."

"Eugene Pratt?" replied the noble dame. "Who is he? Do we know his people?"

"He is the son of Mr. Thomas Pratt, who has a large shop along Percival Street. His business is doing very well. In fact, they are building a new two-story house along Circular Road, not too far from here."

"Oh," said the mother, "you mean Thomas Pratt the shoemaker. I remember he used to repair your father's shoes. Is it his son you propose to marry?"

"He is no longer a shoemaker, mother. He is now a very successful trader with good connections. His son, Eugene, is one of the handsomest young men in town and is now in charge of the provisions sections of the United Africa Company. People say that he is an up-and-coming young man who will do very well for himself. In fact, there is a lot of talk that he will be the first African to be promoted to a managerial position at the UAC. Besides, he is a Society Steward at his church, College Chapel. He has even joined the Masonic lodge. He's destined for great things."

"Hm! That may be, but we don't know the Pratts. My dear, do you really want to throw yourself away on some clerk at the United Africa Company, when you could marry a doctor or a lawyer and move in the right circles? Think of the amount of money your father and I have spent on your education and upbringing. It was to prepare you for that destiny: a woman occupying the first rank in society. Think carefully before you make such a mistake. Besides, I doubt

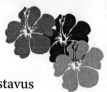

whether your father will give permission. Mr. Gustavus Wilson, of the Sawpit Wilsons, has a son about to complete his legal studies in England. He will be returning home next year. Your father was thinking of him as a suitable husband for you. Please don't throw yourself away on trash simply because you want to get married."

"But Mama I am getting on. I am no longer young. Where are the doctors and lawyers who will come forward to marry me? None has done so yet. As for Mr. Gustavus Wilson's son, I hear he's about forty-five. He is fifteen years my senior. I don't think I want to marry a man who is that old."

"A man should always be several years older than his wife, my dear. Take your father. He is eleven years older than I am, but we have had a happy marriage. An older husband will appreciate and take good care of you. Young men nowadays are totally unreliable. Their eyes tend to roam and if they marry, they have all kinds of affairs outside the family and make their wives and children miserable. Wait for Gustavus Wilson junior, and enable me to say with pride at meetings of the Mothers' Union that my daughter is going to be married to a lawyer."

In spite of her mother's entreaties, however, the equally strong-willed Josephine was determined to marry Eugene Pratt. She congratulated herself on her conquest of this dashing young man. He was one of the most eligible bachelors in town, and she'd been able to detach him, with perfect ease, from his fiancée. That, in itself was a mighty feat. To make a young man like Eugene, whom all the young women desired, fall for her and break off his engagement, was no mean feat. She would be able to hold her head high in public and put to shame all those who were saying that she was too ugly to find a husband, and would only get married if the devil himself was to condescend to come down to earth to marry her. Besides, Eugene was quite a catch. He had received two rapid promotions and was now in charge of the provisions section of the United Africa Company. There was talk that they intended to send him to Britain for further training, and that he was destined to be the first African appointed to a managerial position in that company, possibly in the whole of West Africa.

So, in spite of her mother's strong opposition, Josephine was determined to go ahead with the marriage. She might not have succeeded had her father not taken her side. Mr. Columbus Freeman was not as snobbish as his wife. His origins had not been as glorious as his wife's. He had only become successful by dint of hard work both in College and in the Colonial Civil Service. He, therefore, had great respect for the meritocracy, those men who, whatever their origins, pulled themselves up by their own bootstraps. He felt that Eugene Pratt was such a man and he was quite prepared to let his daughter marry him. Moreover, he was quite delighted to have his eldest daughter taken off his hands, a daughter who was by no means pretty and who was getting on in years. Why, she was already thirty, an age when some women were already married with four or five children.

Mrs. Letitia Freeman ranted and raved, begged and pleaded, but, in the end, realized that she would have to give in to the inevitable. She took revenge by ridiculing the Pratts whenever she had the opportunity.

"That disgusting woman thinks that because her son is going to marry my daughter, she and I will be on terms of familiarity," she said one day to a member of the Mother's Union. "It's a marriage, by the way, that would never take place if I had my way. What nerve! The wife of a shoemaker on familiar terms with me! One day, she had the gall to stop me outside Wesley Church, shouting, 'oh Letitia,' Would you believe it? She actually called me Letitia. 'Oh Letitia,' she said, 'I am glad I have met you. I was coming to spoke to you about where our children will live after they are married.' Yes, that's what she said. She said she was coming

to 'spoke' to me. Of course, she was trying to speak English, but she does not know the basic difference between 'speak' and 'spoke.' An upstart like that, who never went beyond standard four in primary school and had the impertinence to pretend she was an alumna of the Annie Walsh Memorial School, coming to 'spoke' to me! But I don't blame her. I blame my daughter who does not have a sufficient sense of self worth to realize that she mustn't throw herself away on the son of such a woman."

Mrs. Letitia Freeman certainly did not intend for there to be much intercourse between the two families, in spite of the fact that they would soon be united in marriage. Once, when Mrs. Susan Pratt had decided to visit her, she left her knocking at the gate for a good fifteen minutes before she asked the servants to let her in. Once Susan got in, Letitia pretended that she was about to go out to a meeting of her church's Ladies Guild. She was already dressed up, so there was no opportunity for the two of them to sit down and chat. Adamant though she was, Susan took the hint and did not visit the Freemans again before the wedding. Instead, she contented herself with talking about her lavish plans for the wedding.

Because of Mrs. Letitia Freeman's opposition, the engagement ceremonies were severely curtailed. Letitia certainly had no intention of having a grand wedding for her eldest daughter as would normally have been the case. Of course, as mother of the bride, she would be suitably dressed, lest people talk, but there was to be no lavish party or dancing afterwards. There was to be no goumbay dancing and no 'aso-ebi.' The reception would be held at the house at Circular Road, but only a few friends would be invited for drinks and refreshments afterwards.

Mrs. Freeman said to one of her friends about two weeks before the wedding: "You know that that disgusting woman, Susan Pratt, wants us to ask the Governor to have the reception at Government House?"

"You don't say," replied the friend in shock and disbelief.

"Yes. So far as she is concerned she will make a big splash with this wedding to show everyone that she has arrived. Columbus and I are in the position to ask the Governor, who I am sure will consent, but I am damned if I am going to do it to please that upstart Mrs. Pratt. She also wanted us to ask his Lordship the Bishop to perform the marriage ceremony and tie the knot."

"I don't believe it," said her friend.

"You may believe it. There is no telling what vulgar lengths that woman will go to show that with this marriage she is going to be well connected. A woman who is the daughter of nobody and whose husband is a shoemaker! The idea of it!"

What Mrs. Freeman reported of Mrs. Susan Pratt was quite true. Mrs. Pratt lost no opportunity of telling her friends beforehand of the splendor of the future wedding

"You will see the bride's wedding gown," she boasted. "It is made of lace and satin and embroidered with pearls. It was ordered specially from the United Kingdom. Of course, the wedding is going to take place at St. George's Cathedral. It will be at 12 noon, rather than one o'clock, when most people will be on their lunch break, so that everyone will be able to go and watch the guests as they arrive. They'll appreciate the elegance of the dresses and the beauty of the bride. There will be a lot of 'busybodies.' That is as it should be. It will be the wedding of the year."

Mr. T and I were invited to the wedding, but, as you can imagine, we were in a very difficult position. Annie was my best friend, the godmother of one of my children, and she'd been ditched through the machinations of another friend. Eugene was Mr. T's best friend and the godfather of one of our children. He had behaved in a thoroughly irresponsible

manner, though. If we went to the wedding, it would seem as if we were insensitive to the feelings of poor Annie. Yet, how could we refuse to go to the wedding? Both the bride and the groom were very good friends of ours.

I was really hurt by Josephine's behavior. She knew that Annie was engaged to Eugene and she had used all her wiles to seduce him. That was thoroughly disgraceful behavior. Someone who does that sort of thing cannot be considered a friend at all. If that's what a friend does, what would an enemy do? Some women are so unscrupulous that when it comes to finding husbands they will do anything, even betraying the best of friends. And what about Eugene? He also knew that Josephine was Annie's friend and that she was connected to all of us. And yet, he'd flirted with her and allowed himself to be drawn into a relationship that resulted in the brutal breaking off of his engagement with the trusting Annie. His behavior was really callous and unforgivable.

Mr. T was determined not to go to the wedding. He said that if he did, it would amount to an endorsement of Eugene's behavior. Quite conveniently, the Public Works Department, where he, himself, was rising fast and had been promoted to the rank of second grade clerk, required him to go up country at the time of the wedding to participate in the inspection of facilities and stock. So, he was conveniently excused. I, however, had no choice but to go, and I did so quite reluctantly. It turned out to be quite a wedding, but not the sort that Mrs. Susan Pratt had anticipated. Several hundred guests had been invited, and St. George's Cathedral was almost completely full. The choir was in attendance, and there were several clergymen officiating. I did not buy a special dress for the wedding. I had made up my mind not to do so. I wore an old though attractive fawn dress. I also sat toward the back of the church. That was my small way of showing that I was attending, but attending under protest.

The 'busybodies' turned up in force all right, but not, as Mrs. Pratt had hoped, to admire the guests and the bride. Punctually at noon, the bride's mother and father entered the church. According to tradition, the bride's mother usually arrived at the same time as the bride, because she had to ensure that everything had been properly done, and the bride had been properly dressed. With the arrival of Mrs. Freeman, we knew that the bride had also arrived and would soon walk up the long aisle.

But then, there was a tremendous commotion outside the church. As I have said, I was sitting toward the back of the church and therefore had a very good view of what was happening outside. As the bride got out of the car and started moving toward the church, on the arm of her younger brother, the huge crowd of busybodies surged toward her. For a moment I thought that they were going to attack her. There were shouts of "We want to see what the bride is wearing. We want to see it today. Allow us to come nearer and have a good look. It's been said that she would be wearing a dress the like of which has never been seen before. We want to see whether her dress is made out of human skin. We are going to touch it to see whether it is indeed made of human skin. How many human skins did they use to make that dress? We have a right to know."

And as the busybodies shouted they surged toward the bride and practically tore the veil off her head. The beautiful white dress was almost torn and became wrinkled and soiled. But for the fact that the bride's brother had the presence of mind to push her back into the car, she might have suffered grievous bodily harm. The bride's father, Mr. Columbus Freeman, had to leave his exalted position in the front row of the church and get back to the entrance to see what was the cause of the commotion. The police had to be called, and it took some time before order was restored. The crowd was eventually restrained and under the watchful

gaze of about ten policemen with batons raised, the bride was eventually able to get out of the car and make her way back to the porch for the procession. All this while, there had been uproar inside the church as well. Everyone was talking aloud and wondering what was happening outside. When the processional hymn started, few were in any mood to sing. Believe me, you cannot imagine a more dismal wedding procession. The bride, instead of smiling, was almost in tears, and it was a good while before she regained her composure. To make matters worse, when the officiating Priest asked, "Who giveth this woman to be married to this man" and Mr. Columbus Freeman came up to give his daughter away, he inadvertently stepped on her long veil. The bride's head was tugged back, and she grimaced in obvious pain. It was a good few seconds before Mr. Freeman realized what had happened and stepped off the veil. But many of the guests had seen it, and whispered to each other that this was a bad omen. By all accounts, therefore, it was a dismal wedding, and the omens for the future were not very good.

CHAPTER 7

So Josephine married her Eugene. To this day, I cannot really say whether Eugene was in love with her, whether he had merely married her for convenience's sake since she said she was pregnant, or whether he had just succumbed to his mother's ambitious drive to be connected somehow with the elite. I had a feeling it was the last. Eugene, in his own way, was as ambitious as his mother, although this ambition had not been demonstrated in school. He certainly wanted to cut a good figure in the world and be well connected. That was the way in which he hoped to get advancement. It was for this reason that he had joined the Masonic lodge.

He once said to my own husband who he was trying to persuade to join the lodge:

"Don't you know that anyone who is anybody in this city and society must be a member of the lodge? How do you expect to get on in life if you do not join the lodge? And don't you want to have a big funeral when you die, with all the members of several Masonic lodges in attendance?"

"What will it matter to me then?" replied Mr. T. "I will be quite dead. I will not know whether my funeral was big or not. It won't make any difference to me."

"But think about what people will say, think about the stories that will go around town about how elaborate the funeral was, how many ministers there were in attendance,

how many lodge members attended in full regalia. Your family would be so proud!"

"It does not matter two hoots whether I have a big funeral or not," Mr. T replied. "I do not care if only five people attend my funeral. What matters is that my soul will be right with my maker, and that I will have left enough money in the world for my widow and my children to live on, until they can fend for themselves. The chances of my doing that will be quite diminished if I join the lodge, because it is quite an expensive club."

"But it is important to you even while you are alive. The big men in the government service and the mercantile companies are members of the lodge, and if you are a member, they will have your interest at heart and make sure you get rapid promotion. Or if you have a case in court, you might find that the judge, himself, is a member of your lodge. You just have to make the secret sign to him, and you will be found not guilty, or your fine or sentence will be reduced. Believe me, it is quite impossible to make much progress, or at least, to make rapid progress in this society without being a member of the Masonic lodge. Take it from me. What you know is important, but who you know is even more important."

"Whatever progress I make in this world," replied Mr. T, "I want to make by my own honest exertions and knowledge, not by my contacts. Anything that I cannot attain by my own honest industry and abilities, I do not want to attain. It's not worth attaining at all."

There, the matter rested. Eugene realized that nothing he could say would persuade Mr. T, God rest his soul, to join the lodge. Eugene, on the other hand, seemed to have inherited such an inflated sense of status and position from his mother. And this led him to unnecessary expenses, so that until the day of his death, he was unable to save enough money to build himself a decent house, while Mr. T, as you can see, was able to save and build this magnificent house that he was able to bequeath to me and his children.

Eugene and his mother must have expected that after the wedding, Mr. and Mrs. Freeman would invite Eugene and his new bride to stay with them in their glorious mansion on Circular Road. They were sadly disappointed. Mrs. Freeman had only reluctantly consented to give the couple her blessing, and she was not likely to have a son of that contemptible woman, as she called Mrs. Susan Pratt, to stay with her in the same house. The couple would have to fend for themselves, she said. Besides, knowing the mother, there was no telling how the son might behave. She was not going to allow that under any circumstances.

So Eugene and Josephine had to find a house for themselves. They were forced to rent a lowly, one-story, wooden house along Sanders Street. It was decent enough, but it was such a come-down from what Josephine had been used to. After what she had learnt from Sissy Dinah, she was able to decorate it very nicely, and the couple got some very nice furniture from the bride's parents. It was good enough for a young couple starting life afresh, but not for Eugene or Josephine.

In the meantime, that poor girl, Annie Macauley, fell seriously ill for about a month after the wedding. I remember visiting her shortly after that and was shocked at the change in her appearance. Within a few days, she had lost quite a good deal of weight. Her mother said that she hardly ate anything and was threatening to commit suicide. She looked gaunt and thin, her face was drawn, and her eyes seemed to have sunk into her head. That lovely chocolate brown complexion seemed to have disappeared and was replaced by ash. Her cheeks were hollow.

"You must talk to her, Priscilla," her mother said to me. "Tell her that, in life, we must be prepared to meet and face disappointments. Look at me! Do you know how many

young children I buried? Three! Did I die? No! I am here. God works in mysterious ways. God is his own interpreter and he will make it plain. The Lord will surely provide. Trust in God! That is what we should do. Annie, however, refuses to listen to me. I even told her that even if Eugene had not jilted her, it would not be wise to marry a man who had gotten another woman pregnant. There is danger in that. I have known of similar cases where the pregnant woman contrived to bring about the death of the man's fiancée. So, it was just as well that Eugene broke off the engagement himself. All things work together for good. You will see."

I am not sure that I myself agreed with Mrs. Macauley's sentiments. Nevertheless, I tried to comfort my friend.

"Annie," I said, "it is not worth killing yourself over one man, especially such a man as Eugene. If he could behave like that to you before marriage, think what he could have done to you after marriage. Look on this as a blessing in disguise. You are still young, and there are plenty of men out there. You will soon find one who will come forward to marry you, one who will treat you much better than that hopeless Eugene would have done."

"It is easy for you to say that, Priscilla," she said. "You are married to a very good man, and you already have four healthy children. Now, Josephine is married as well. I'm the only one of us three who is still unmarried. Look at me! I am almost thirty-one. What sort of young man will come forward to marry me now, especially since the whole town knows that I was engaged to Eugene and he ditched me? They will say that he ditched me for a good reason, and that will make it even more difficult for me to find an intended."

"You must trust in God, as your mother says. Show Eugene, Josephine, and everyone else that you are not going to allow the way you've been treated to defeat you. You can put your life together again. You have your mother, and you have your family, and good friends who love you. That is a good basis on which to build."

"What galls me most," she said, "is that it was Josephine, my own very good friend, who did this to me. Tell me Priscilla. Why is the world so bad? Why does God allow such evil people to live? How can a friend do such a thing to another friend? After all the times we spent together at Sissy Dinah's, after all the jokes and stories we shared together, how can she betray me like that and cause me such pain? Does she not have a conscience? Does she not believe in God?"

"I understand what you say," I said. "But Josephine's actions show that she was not really a friend. Maybe she was just pretending because we were all three thrown together. All these things happen for us to learn lessons. You're beginning to know that in this world there are few people that you can trust. Most people are out for their own interest. But you must take heart, learn the lessons, and go on from there. You cannot allow this to defeat you."

I visited her quite often after that, and saw that she had taken heart and was improving. I was glad. She regained some of her beauty and her figure. She also occupied herself by helping her mother with the trade. Her mother too, like Eugene's mother, started receiving goods from up country that she sold to retailers here in Freetown. Annie helped her by going to the station to receive the goods for her. She also made things like coco-nut cakes and ginger cakes that she sold outside their house. That way she was able to make a tolerable living.

Let's go back to Eugene and his mother. If Mrs. Susan Pratt had hoped that her son's marriage would enable her to hob-knob with the elite, she was sadly mistaken. Mrs. Freeman was determined that that would never happen. Soon after the marriage, Mrs. Pratt decided to pay a visit to the Freemans at their home on Circular Road. She knew that the Freemans were home because as she walked up the

street, she saw Mrs. Freeman looking through the window on to the street. However, when she got to the house and knocked on the door, she was kept standing there for a good fifteen minutes. Eventually, a servant opened the door and told her that the Freemans were not at home.

"I thought I saw your mistress looking through the window as I walked up the street," Mrs. Pratt said.

"I don't know about that, Ma." the servant replied. "All I know is that she told me to tell you that she is not at home."

"That moment I felt so small," said Mrs. Pratt, relating the incident to a friend, "that I wished the earth would open and swallow me up. I also felt like saying to the servant, 'tell your mistress that when she goes out next time she should take her head and shoulders with her.' But I refrained from doing so in the interest of family unity. However, I will have my own back. I will show her that Susan Pratt is not the kind of woman you put into a bag and walk away with. I will force her to come down from her high 'petesin' and deal with me. After all, it is my son who has married her daughter. It is my son who is her daughter's master."

However, even the snobbish Mrs. Pratt took the hint and knew that her visits would not be welcome. She never visited the Freemans after that.

And what about our newly married couple, Mr. and Mrs. Eugene Pratt? How were they getting on? They were both disappointed they could not live with the Freemans in their mansion at Circular Road. Although it was unusual for a newly married couple to live with the bride's parents, it sometimes happened, for financial and other reasons. In Josephine's case, she had hoped she would continue to live in her parents' spacious house because that would help alleviate the decline in status that her marriage to Eugene entailed; in Eugene's case, it would help confirm his rise in status, and he would be able to mingle with the people who mattered, whenever such people visited his parents-in-law.

Mrs. Freeman's opposition meant that all that was not to happen.

This was the first cause of friction between the newly married pair. Eugene discovered that his main reason for marrying the unattractive, and rather ungainly, Josephine would not materialize. Instead of living in the grand Freeman mansion at Circular Road in one of the best parts of Freetown, he had to be content with the much more lowly one-story, wooden house along Sanders Street. The area was certainly not as attractive as his parents' Percival Street neighborhood. In fact, his parents soon finished their own house along Circular Road, but though it was a concrete house in the latest style, they did not have enough money to make it a two-story building, so there was not enough room for the new couple to come and stay with them. Moreover, Eugene did not like his neighbors, and his wife liked them even less.

"They are so coarse and common, Mama," she said to her mother. "They make so much noise night and day, and some of them even sell their wares in front of their houses. It is so degrading."

"Well," said her mother, "as someone sows, so let her reap. A chicken that does not hear 'sh...sh...sh' will hear the stone. You should have thought of this before you threw yourself away on a man like Eugene. That is the sort of society he is used to. I warned you, but you would not heed my warning. Now you will have to live with it."

Another cause of friction was Josephine's expensive habits. Not having been trained for any kind of occupation but housewife, Josephine was a stay-at-home, like me, and the two of them were totally dependent on Eugene's salary. It was good enough to keep a normal couple happy and comfortable, but Josephine was not a normal young woman. She had been raised with expensive habits. It would hardly be the third week of the month, and she would say to

her husband, "Eugene, I need more money for cooking and housekeeping."

"What do you mean, you need more money for cooking and housekeeping? What have you done with all the money I gave you? It was supposed to last the whole of the month?"

"Is it my fault?" she would shout back. "Things are very expensive these days. The war is still going on, and prices are still high. They keep going up, day after day. That's just like you men. You do not go to market and shop, so you don't realize how expensive things are. You are happy and content as long as you find food on the table when you come home from work."

"But what about other wives?" Eugene would respond. "They surely manage. What about your friend, Priscilla? Her husband doesn't earn more than I do, and yet she is able to manage from month to month. And they have four children who are growing up fast. The problem is that you're too extravagant. We would be able to manage if you did not spend almost everything on splendid dresses and new hats. Do you have to buy a new pair of shoes, every month?"

"Well, don't you expect me to keep myself in the condition I was in when you married me? I have been accustomed to buying a new pair of shoes every month and going to church in nice dresses. If you marry a Freeman you should expect to keep her in the condition she has been used to. It's all very well to strut home with a well-dressed wife after church on Sunday to the admiration of all and sundry, but those dresses and shoes have to be paid for. You should have known that when you married me. I am an expensive wife. I have been used to great things. A wife like me costs money."

"Damn you, and your high and mighty family!" he'd shout and strut outside, slamming the door behind him.

"So you have started abusing my mother and father!" she would shout in return, poking her head through the window and shouting after him as he walked down Sanders

Street. "Okay, abuse my mother! Abuse my father! I only have myself to blame for marrying a good-for-nothing nobody like you. That's the reward I get for standing up to my mother and marrying you instead of one of those doctors and lawyers she'd wanted me to marry."

"Which doctor or lawyer would have married you?" he'd laugh. "They would've taken one look at you and puked. You should thank me for taking you into my house and giving you a home and my name, instead of leaving you to languish on the shelf. Just count your blessings, and be quiet."

She would then burst into tears and go inside her house.

This kind of thing happened month after month. Instead of staying home with his wife after work, Eugene started frequenting bars and staying out late. Often, he would come to our own house on Wellington Street and complain bitterly about his wife.

"This married life is not all it's made out to be," he would say. "That wife of mine is so extravagant. We are finding it difficult to live on my salary, and we quarrel very often. You are lucky, Bernard. You have managed to marry an angel. I have a real virago at home."

"Ah, ah, ah," Mr. T would say, "don't complain to me. You abandoned your beautiful and decent Annie, so that you could marry Josephine. It was your own deliberate choice. So you should not complain. Besides, I am not the one to interfere with other people's marital disputes. You have to solve your problems yourself."

"To tell you the truth, Bernard," Eugene would continue, "I am beginning to regret that I did not marry Annie. I saw her last week and she was looking as beautiful as ever. She spoke quite cordially to me, in spite of everything I did to her. She is such a nice girl. She would have made a good wife, just like your Priscilla."

"That way lies disaster," warned Mr. T. "Don't start having regrets now and wishing that you'd married the other girl.

You've made your bed and you must lie in it. Josephine will probably mellow out once the child arrives. There's nothing like a baby to cement the bond between two people."

In mentioning the child, Mr. T had inadvertently touched on a sore spot and on another major cause of friction between Eugene and Josephine. Remember, I said that one of the main reasons why Eugene married Josephine was because she was pregnant. I should have said she *claimed* to be pregnant.

About four months after the wedding, she and Eugene launched into a fight that was more vicious than usual. Apparently, Eugene's mother had told her son that his wife had treated her badly, during one of her visits.

"She didn't even bother to ask me to sit down," Mrs. Pratt said. "She told me that she was going out to meet some friends, and that I would have to leave. Does she not realize that I am her mother-in-law, and that, in our society, one has to respect their mother-in-law? If I had not carried you in my belly for nine months, gone through all the pains of childbirth, and raised you all these years, would she have been able to marry you? She does not show me the respect that a mother-in-law deserves."

When Eugene went home that evening and confronted his wife with these allegations, that spirited woman replied haughtily, "and who does she think she is that I should respect her? Does she not know how much of a laughing stock she is? The whole town laughs at her because she's so pretentious, but can't even use the English language correctly. She pretends that she went to the Annie Walsh, but she could hardly read an "O" even if it were printed as large as the moon?"

"Don't you dare insult my mother," Eugene shouted and gave his wife a stinging slap on the face.

"And how dare you strike me?" she asked, slapping him back. "How dare you, a nobody from the slums of Freetown, dare strike anyone who is a thousand times better than you? Do you think I won't fight back?"

By this time, Eugene was mightily enraged. He hit her again very hard on her face, and she fell to the floor, whimpering and shouting: "Oh God! Oh God! He is going to kill me. Neighbors, please come. He is going to kill me."

Many of the neighbors poked their heads outside their windows. "Mr. Pratt, Mr. Pratt," they shouted. "What's happening? Take surrur! Take surrur. She is a young wife! Do be careful! We beg you!"

Josephine floundered and whimpered on the floor. Then, she started vomiting, and that's when Eugene noticed that she was sitting in a pool of her own blood. He immediately relented and took her into the bedroom. She was obviously very ill, so, after a short while, he rushed her to the hospital where she was immediately attended by a doctor friend of her father's.

Josephine was kept in the hospital for a day, after which she returned to a suitably contrite Eugene. She refused to speak to Eugene for a whole day after she returned, but he, realizing that he had been at fault, took her silence as part of his punishment, and even decided to cook the meals for both of them. Shortly after that, when he was at a lodge meeting, he met the doctor who had treated Josephine.

"Young man," said the doctor, "you should have had more sense than to strike a pregnant woman."

"I am very sorry," said Eugene. "I will never do it again."

"I should hope not," the doctor replied, "particularly considering the tragedy you have caused."

"What tragedy," Eugene asked, fearing the worst. "She didn't tell me anything. She has hardly spoken to me since she came back home."

"I am not surprised," the doctor exclaimed. "She has lost the baby! Your baby!"

"Oh my God!" Eugene almost sobbed.

"Well, you should have had more sense than to strike a pregnant woman, even if she was only two months pregnant."

"Only two months pregnant?" asked Eugene, in disbelief.

"Yes," replied the doctor. Does that surprise you? After all, you have been married for just over two months."

"Yes, yes, of course," said Eugene. And he said not another word more.

As he walked home that evening, however, the implications of what the doctor had said hit him full in the face and, instead of feeling sorry for his wife, he now felt nothing but hatred for her. If she'd been no more than two months pregnant at that time, it meant that she wasn't pregnant at all when he married her. In other words, she had deliberately lied that she was pregnant in order to get him to marry her. He genuinely thought at the time of the accident that she was more than four months pregnant. Maybe he should have been able to tell the difference between a two month's pregnancy and one of four months, but Josephine was naturally stout, and it was difficult to tell how pregnant she really was. "Oh! The deceitfulness of that woman!" he said. "She is indeed a monster. I have married a monster."

He now realized he need not have married her at all; through her machinations, she had condemned him to a life of misery. As he walked home, he felt a double blow: the realization he'd married her under false pretences, and that they'd just now lost their first-born, because of the disrespect Josephine had showed to his mother. She had lied to him. How could he have been such a fool! He walked back home in a daze. He scarcely heard the shouts of traders selling their wares or the moaning of the wind heralding the tornado that was about to burst and sweep through Freetown.

"You whore," he shouted at her when he got home. "You lied to me that you were pregnant."

"I suppose that your small brain has finally worked out the fact that I have lost my baby through your beastly behavior. But is it too slow to figure that I could not have had a miscarriage without being pregnant?" She retorted.

"You were pregnant all right," he replied. "But you got pregnant only after we married. I spoke to Dr. Moses, and he told me that you were not more than two months pregnant, when you lost the baby. You lied to me. You forced me to marry you with a lie."

"I did not force you. No man is ever forced into a marriage he does not want. Wasn't it you who came chasing after me? Wasn't it you who broke off your engagement with Annie, because you wanted to marry a woman who you thought would raise your lowly status? How dare you say that I lied to you? You wanted it. And now, after you have almost killed me and caused me to miscarry, you come here accusing me of lying to you. I do not blame you," she continued. "I blame myself. I should have listened to my mother and not married a ragamuffin, a low class nobody like you. You are a beast! You behave like a beast. That is all you know." In a fit of rage, she went into her room and slammed the door. Eugene went into his own room with all kinds of strange thoughts roaming in his head.

Strangely, Josephine did not tell her parents that she'd had a miscarriage through Eugene's brutality, because she was afraid that if they confronted Eugene, he would tell them about the lie she had told him about her pregnancy. Similarly, Eugene did not tell many people about the lie, because he feared that they would find out that he had beaten her and caused her to miscarry. We only found out the full truth of these things much, much later.

So, when Mr. T said that Josephine would mellow after the arrival of the baby, he still had not learned about the

miscarriage. Eugene sighed and told him right then that there would be no baby; Josephine had miscarried. He did not tell him why she had miscarried, however, nor about the lie. Maybe he also did not want to appear a fool, for only a fool of a man would be caught in that kind of trap.

"I am so sorry," Mr. T said, with true concern. "Poor Josephine! Well, don't worry. You are both still young. You can make another baby. You can make several more babies." And he left it at that. Eugene's mother, Mrs. Pratt, was by no means so subtle. She badly wanted to have a grandson that would carry on her husband's line, so she, speaking as though the miscarriage was Josephine's fault, kept urging her daughter-in-law to try again and have a baby soon.

"Try for us," she would say. "Try for us. We need a grandson. Hurry up and give us one." And as the months went by and turned to years without a baby appearing she would say:

"What is the matter with you? Why don't you hurry up and give us a grandson? My husband needs a grandson to carry on his name and his line. Try for us."

After years had gone by, and Josephine showed no sign of conceiving again, Mrs. Pratt said to her son, "Aren't you going to find out what is wrong with your wife? I know she's had a miscarriage, but I also know of several women who had miscarriages and then went on to have several children after that. There must be something wrong with her. You should try to find out. Barrenness has never existed in our family. People will begin to talk. What good is a wife if she does not bear children for her husband?"

"What do you want me to do, mother?" asked Eugene.

"Well, I know a medicine man who can solve these problems. I'll go and see him. He'll arrange to have Josephine's stomach cleaned. That is what we must do."

"Knowing Josephine," said Eugene, "I doubt whether she will agree to that, but I will ask her."

Eugene was quite correct about Josephine. She reacted with the utmost revulsion when her husband told her that his mother had found a medicine man who would cleanse her stomach so that she could conceive.

"I knew that you and your mother belonged to the lowest possible class, but I didn't realize how primitive you actually were," she shouted. "Do you expect me, Josephine Freeman, daughter of Columbus Freeman, a college graduate and the highest African official in the Sierra Leone colonial service, to go to some stupid herbalist in some dirty street to have my stomach cleansed, as you say?"

"There you go again," shouted Eugene in return, "insulting my mother. Take care before you insult my mother. You know what happened the last time you insulted my mother. I will not have it. If we belonged to such a low class, why did you marry me? Answer me that. Why did you marry me? And moreover, do you think that I do not know that in spite of all the airs you put on, you used to consult medicine men yourself? Do you think I do not know? Do you think I do not know that you consulted a medicine man at Aykaymori to turn my head so that I will ditch Annie and marry you? Do you think I do not know? You pretend to be high and mighty and to shun superstition, but when night comes you dress in old clothes and consult the same medicine men as poor people in order to do your dirty deeds. Do you think I would have married you if you had not used medicine to turn my head? Answer me that."

"So now, it was I who turned your head with medicine so that you would marry me. Was it not you who came chasing after me? Did you not go down on your knees and beg me to marry you? Did you not swear that the managers in your company were fond of you and had promised you rapid promotion? Did you not swear that one of the managers was so fond of you that he had wanted to treat you as a woman and you would blackmail him into giving

you the promotion? Who knows whether you did not give in to him? And now you come and accuse me of turning your head. You had better be quiet, otherwise I will let the whole world know the kind of rotten person you are. You beast of no nation!"

It's not that Josephine was above superstition; she may indeed have gone to a medicine man to ensure that Eugene married her. That sort of thing had been known to happen and people of all classes were doing it. That wasn't the problem. It was simply that Josephine strongly objected to any suggestion made by Eugene's mother. It is quite possible that if the suggestion had come from her own mother she might have accepted it. Here Eugene and his mother showed that they were lacking in diplomatic skill. Perhaps they would have got their way if they had made the suggestion, in the first place, not to Josephine herself, but to Josephine's mother.

"You can say what you like," shouted Eugene as the argument continued, "but I tell you now once and for all. I want a child, and I want a son. I want a son to carry on my line. That is but natural. Every man wants to have a son to ensure that his name lives on after he dies. What do you think my friends will say of me if I never have a son? What do you think they say, already? Look at Bernard! His wife Priscilla has already borne him four strong and healthy sons. He has already proved his virility and ensured his immortality. I have to do the same. What use are you to me as a wife if you do not bear me sons to ensure my immortality and prove my virility?"

"It is just like a primitive man like you to talk such nonsense," Josephine replied. "So, I am the one to prove your virility and ensure your immortality! And that's my only use to you. How do we know that the problem does not lie with you? Answer me that. How do we know? After all, I have proved that I can conceive. I conceived a baby who would have been a beautiful toddler, by now, if you had not killed it with your primitive brutality. The fault can't lie with me. Would you be prepared to go to some medicine man and get him to wash your thing?"

"You're not making any sense. The fault does not lie with me either," Eugene replied. "I gave you that child, did I not? Do you know how many other women had children by me, before I married you? Three! Three! I have already proved that I am a man and that I can do it. It is you who seems to be a barren, dried up woman. What a mistake I made in marrying you!"

"So, you're a man? Do you tell me that you are a man because you had three children by other women before you married me? Do you support those children? Do you even know them? You call yourself a man, and you do not even know the children you claim other women had for you, let alone support them. What kind of a man are you? A real man not only begets children, but he also supports them. You are not a man! You are a petticoat man. How do I know that even if I had children by you, you would not leave us to starve while you waste your substance on foolish women outside the home? But I blame myself in throwing myself away on you when I could by now have been married to a doctor and living in luxury." And so this worthy couple's arguments went on and on and on like this, day after day, month after month.

Their relations and in-laws also played a part in the controversy. Once, after a Mothers' Union meeting, one of Mrs. Susan Pratt's friends asked her, "How are Eugene and his wife? Have they had a child yet?"

"No, my sister," Mrs. Pratt replied. "She had a miscarriage years ago, and she shows no signs of being pregnant again. If you ask me," she said, inclining her mouth to her friend's ear and whispering, "I don't think that girl is clean." She meant that Josephine must be a witch.

"Ibosio!" shouted the friend. "I am sorry for Eugene. There is nothing worse than having a wife who is not clean. She could put things in his food. You had better warn Eugene and tell him to be careful."

"I have already warned him," Susan replied. "But she will know that she has a mother-in-law that she must not play around with. I also know how to play that game. I have consulted medicine men who have confirmed my suspicions. They have confirmed that she is not clean, that she is a witch, and that she sacrificed all the children in her womb. One medicine man even told me that was the sacrifice she had to make in order to marry Eugene. She badly wanted to marry because she was so ugly that few men would look at her. So the medicine man told her that she would only marry if she was prepared not to have any children. She has tied up her womb. But I also know how this world works, and there is nothing I won't do to save my son, even if it means detaching him from that terrible woman."

"God will help you my sister," the fellow member of the Mother's Union chimed in.

However, Mrs. Pratt's rumors found their way to Josephine's ears. Freetown was, back then, a small place, and one could never be sure that anything one said would not be repeated. It soon got to Josephine's ears that her mother-in-law was spreading rumors that she was a witch who had tied up her womb or sacrificed all the children in her womb in order to get married. She was, therefore, determined to prove her wrong, to make her enemy ashamed. She would do her damnedest to bear a child and then she'd crow over her despicable mother-in-law. Her resolution was strengthened when she told her mother about Eugene's proposal to have her stomach cleaned.

"Well," said her mother, "maybe he's got a point. Sometimes, even the most despicable people can give us ideas, or say things that contain a germ of truth. I know of women who went for several years without having children and were forced to consult medicine men. They told them that someone had tied up their wombs, or that their stomachs were dirty and had to be cleansed. Within a short time after their consultation they became pregnant and went on to have several children after that."

"But mother," replied her daughter, "just think of some nasty old man rubbing my stomach with his claw-like hands! The idea is revolting."

"You're mistaken. You have got a wrong conception of the idea of cleansing. He may not have to touch your stomach at all. He may simply give you something to drink; that is all. It will be no different from taking a laxative. After all, are there not times when even Western doctors prescribe laxatives for us to cleanse our insides? This will be no different. Do you know Mrs. Tabitha Findlay?"

"Do you mean Canon Samuel Findlay's wife?" asked her daughter.

"The very same woman," the mother replied. "For six good years after they got married Tabitha had still borne no children. Then she went to a medicine man. He told her that she needed to have her stomach cleansed. Part of the problem, he said, was that some enemy, who had been a contender for her husband's hand, had tied up her womb so that she would not have children. I know this for a fact because it was her own sister who told me one day while we were cleaning the church. So, the medicine man performed some ceremonies, told her that she had to make a sacrifice, and gave her a potion to drink every night before she went to bed. Within two months she was pregnant. She went on to have eleven children after that."

"Imagine that!" said Josephine. "You mean Mrs. Findlay who always pretends that if you mention a medicine man in her presence she would spit at you?"

"The very same," said Mrs. Freeman. "You must not underestimate African science. We trust in God and go to church, but, sometimes, God fails us, and it is right for us to fall back on African science. I even know of some ministers of religion who consult medicine men after dark. If you're stubborn and won't ever do it, saying that sort of thing is only for primitive people, you put yourself at a disadvantage and give your enemies the whip handle over you. Who knows whether it is not your stupid mother-in-law who has tied up your womb? I do not trust that woman. She has never forgiven us for not admitting her into our circle. I would not put it past her to do anything to separate you from your husband.

"I believe you, Mama. I think she is quite capable of doing it. Besides, she has been spreading rumors that I am a witch, and that I have sacrificed all the children in my womb to my witch medicine. I will do whatever it takes to shame her."

Mother and daughter agreed that the best solution was to consult a medicine man. So, one Tuesday evening, when the moon wasn't out and it was so dark that you couldn't see your own hand, they meandered their way up a steep dirt road in the Aykaymori area of Central Freetown and knocked on Pa Santigie's door. They were let into Pa Santigie's inner room that was musty and reeked so strongly that Josephine almost threw up. The room was lit only with a small tin lamp, and was otherwise so dark that Josephine could hardly make out the few items of furniture: a wooden bed with a raffia mat spread on it and two grimy boxes on which the encrustations of dirt acquired over the years were visible in spite of the darkness. On a shelf above the bed, there were jars of all kinds and sizes, containing, no doubt, all kinds of ointments and lotions. Hung over the black, wooden door was a skull; Josephine could not make out in the darkness whether it was that of an animal or a human being. She gave an involuntary shudder. Pa Santigie, a thin old man whose eyes looked as though he was blind, was seated on the bed.

"Sit down my daughters, please sit down."

Josephine regarded the two grimy boxes and almost said she'd rather stand. But when she received a slight nudge from her mother and saw her sit down on one of the boxes, she also sat down on the other box.

"I know your trouble my daughter," said Pa Santigie, grabbing Josephine's plump hand with his thin shriveled claws. Josephine shuddered afresh.

"You have come to me because you seem to be barren and you want children to prove to the world that you are a good woman."

"How do you know?" Josephine gasped.

"Ha! Ha! Ha!" Pa Santigie laughed. It was a mirthless laugh that sent shivers right down Josephine's spine. "These eyes cannot see, but they can see. These hands might look old, shriveled and lifeless, but they can feel and get through to the desires of all kinds of hearts. You have never had children," he said, "but you want children badly, so that your enemies will be ashamed, those enemies that have invoked evil spirits to ensure that you do not conceive." At this, Josephine and her mother looked at each other as if to say, "I told you so."

Pa Santigie continued with his mirthless drone: "you are a tough, strong woman, but, like any woman, you would like the feel of a babe in your arms. And God willing, you will have children, provided your heart is clean and you do what I tell you to do."

"Tenke, tenke, Pa Santigie," Josephine blurted out in relief.

"God bless you, Pa," her mother exclaimed.

"But your heart must be clean," Pa Santigie continued. "You must not intend any evil toward anyone. Look!" At this he took some cowries from the pocket of his old brown, dirty gown, and rattled them for a few seconds in his right hand, while chanting some words that Josephine and her mother could not understand. He then threw the cowries onto the floor. The cowries seemed mysteriously to separate into two distinct groups. One group was smaller than the other and consisted of about four cowries, while the other had about six cowries in it. "Look," Pa Santigie continued, pointing to the smaller group of cowries, "these are the children you could have had in the past if your enemies had not put a spell on you. Now look at this other group. These are the children that you can still have, the children whose seeds are still in your womb, provided your heart is clean and you do what I tell you to do. It is all very clear."

Pa Santigie then got up from the bed and onto his shaky, old legs. He moved his hands along the shelf and selected two of the jars. He then sat down again on the bed and poured some of the contents of one of the jars into a small black bottle which he proceeded to cork up with some old pieces of paper.

He handed the bottle to Josephine and said, "you must rub your belly with this lotion each night before you go to bed. You must do so again first thing every morning before you eat anything. Make sure you do it after your husband has lain with you. And you must be lying flat on the bed. I warn you, the lotion has a very strong smell. Some people might even say it is a nasty smell, and they might not want to sit or stand or lie near you once you have rubbed it on. But don't let that bother you. A price has to be paid for success, and success in this case means having lots of children. In years to come when you are surrounded by children, you will be laughing at those people who avoid you because of the way you smell."

Pa Santigie then poured some of the contents of the other jar into an even darker bottle, corked the bottle, and said to Josephine, "you must drink some of this every morning. Make sure you do not speak to anyone before you drink it, and do not wash your mouth for at least one hour afterwards. Make sure you do not get the bottles confused and drink the lotion you are supposed to rub your belly with, or rub your belly with the one you are supposed to drink. That is very important."

"I will do my best, Pa Santigie," Josephine blurted out with immense gratitude, clutching both bottles in her right hand as if her very life depended on it. "Tenke, tenke, Pa Santigie," she said.

"God bless you," Pa Santigie, said her mother. "Kushe, kushe sir."

With that they paid Pa Santigie the fee he demanded and took their leave.

CHAPTER 8

In a sense, Josephine was relieved when she and her mother got out of Pa Santigie's den. It was not the first time she had been in a medicine man's consulting room; in spite of the haughty stance she took with her husband accusing him of being primitive, she and some of her friends had consulted medicine men in the past to find out whether they were likely to get married. Pa Santigie's den, however, was the creepiest den she had ever experienced. She would never forget that skull hanging over the door. The more she thought of it, the more she was convinced that it was a human skull. However, all this helped to convince her that Pa Santigie was a very powerful medicine man who knew what he was doing, and that if she did as he had asked her, she would soon have children. The thought of having many children that would shame her enemies brought smiles on to her rather plain face as she walked buoyantly home with her mother.

In the weeks that followed, Josephine did her best to carry out Pa Santigie's prescriptions. She assiduously rubbed her belly with one lotion, just after her husband had lain with her. She made sure to lie flat on her back as she did so. Fortunately for her, married couples did not share the same room in those days. The husband had his own room, and the wife had hers. After having relations with his wife in her room, the husband would retire to his. So, Eugene did not see Josephine rub her belly with the smelly lotion.

He noticed, however, that she had started giving off a very offensive odor, but he put it down to bad personal hygiene, and made a mental note that he would have to speak to her about her cleanliness. That kind of thing could put a man off a woman completely and intensify his aversion for her. If she did not take greater care with her personal hygiene, she would have to go. He also noticed that Josephine was hardly speaking to him in the mornings. Even if he woke up in a good humor and said a cheery "Good Morning" to her, she would only answer with a grunt. And until he left home for work, not a word passed between them. Again, he put it down to her bad temper and her growing aversion for him.

"This whole marriage is falling apart," he thought. "Now, I know I made a big mistake. Here I am, stuck with a wife who is beginning to smell, and, what's more, she can't even bring herself to speak to me." How was he to know that Josephine was merely carrying out Pa Santigie's prescriptions to smear her belly with a stinking lotion and not to speak to any soul before and after she drank the other!

And so the weeks turned into months, and still Josephine saw no sign of pregnancy. She mentioned it to her mother, and could not hold back her suspicions that, after all, Pa Santigie, like so many other supposed medicine men, might be a fraud. Her mother, however, advised her to be patient. "The patient dog eats the fat bone," she said. "If you want to see an ant's intestines," she said, "you must take your time killing it." And so she advised patience. She was sure that one day the happy event would occur.

The happy event, however, stubbornly refused to occur. Instead, Josephine discovered that several of her friends were shunning her. One day, at church, one of her friends actually moved away from her, under the pretense that she had seen some relatives of hers in another pew and would have to go and sit with them. It was New Year's Sunday, and Josephine had turned up at the church in a new, blue floral dress, a new white and blue hat, and white shoes. She was gorgeously attired, like all the other women, as was the custom on New Year's Sunday. She had taken her place in her pew with studied stateliness, and had started fanning herself. Eugene, being a society steward, was not with her, since he was one of the stewards on duty that Sunday. He was busy showing worshippers to their seats or giving out hymn-books to those who needed them.

Josephine suddenly noticed that almost everyone around her was sniffing, whispering, and looking around as if they thought that some naughty boy had fouled the air, or there was a lump of feces lurking around somewhere, or some negligent mother had brought her baby into the church and not bothered to change its nappies. It was then that this friend saw her, greeted her and decided to sit by her. Suddenly, she too started sniffing, realized the source of the odor, and made that pretended dash for her "relatives" who were sitting in another pew.

Needless to say that after that embarrassment Josephine did not rub her belly with the smelly stuff before going to church. Of course, this in itself constituted an infringement of Pa Santigie's orders. It did not take long, however, for Josephine's friends and acquaintances to realize the reason for the smell, that she was anointing herself with some foul herbal lotion.

"Why is she doing it?" asked one friend.

"She must want power," replied another. "Some women do that sort of thing you know. Maybe she wants control over her husband. Or maybe she wants power in the church. She wants to be President of all the organizations she is a member of."

"Some do it to get money," said another.

And so the rumors ran from one end of Freetown to the other. Yet, several weeks after both lotions had been completely used up, those eggs in Josephine's body stubbornly refused to be fertilized. Instead she woke up one morning with a terrible pain in her stomach. She started vomiting and literally howled in agony. She was in worse pain than on that famous occasion when she'd had the miscarriage. Her husband became thoroughly alarmed and rushed her to the hospital. It was just as well he did. The doctor who saw her gave her an enema, an antidote against poison. He said that she was lucky. Had she arrived at the hospital one hour later, she would have been a corpse. She had apparently drunk something that was a ghastly poison, something that had been poisoning her slowly, and would have achieved its gruesome culmination had he not been there when she arrived at the hospital and he could use his medical skill to save her life. She remained ill for about a month afterward, but she also remained alive and regained her health. When her mother consulted Pa Santigie again and told him what had happened, he said, "Don't blame me; my medicines never fail if taken as I direct. They have never been known to fail. Either her heart is not clean, or she drank the lotion she was supposed to rub on her stomach and rubbed her stomach with the one she was supposed to drink. The lotion that she was supposed to rub her stomach with is a deadly poison. It will kill anyone who drinks it. That was why I warned her not to confuse the two."

When Mrs. Freeman went back to her daughter and asked her to show her the bottles, it became quite clear that Josephine had been careless. She could not remember exactly which lotion was to be drunk and which she was supposed to rub her stomach with. So she must, at times, have drunk the lotion for rubbing on the belly, and rubbed her belly with the potion she was supposed to drink. That

was why she had failed to conceive; that was why she had almost killed herself.

After that terrible and nearly fatal experience with the lotions, Josephine refrained from going to any more medicine men. She still badly wanted a baby, though. She wanted to shame all her enemies, especially her now quite hostile mother-in-law who was still spreading rumors that she was some kind of witch, and that was why she could not conceive. The mother-in-law had even suggested to some of her friends that Josephine had not been a virtuous woman before she got married. Had she been virtuous, she claimed, she would have conceived very easily. She must have been running around with a number of young men before marriage. Was it not true that it was she who took the initiative and tempted and then seduced her innocent son, Eugene, into marriage, when he could have married that nice girl Annie Macauley? She must have been doing the same thing with other young men. Who knows, she might even have had any number of abortions. That sort of thing ties up a woman's womb forever and prevents her from conceiving. Besides, it could be God's punishment on the woman for killing her unborn baby.

So, according to Mrs. Pratt, God, in his anger, denied Josephine the pleasure of having a child when she wanted a child. It was a pity, Mrs. Pratt went on, that her son, Eugene, had tied himself up for life to such a bad woman. The wives of all his other friends were having children.

"Look at Priscilla," Susan Pratt would say, "the wife of Bernard Thompson! She now has five children, four boys and a girl. God has blessed her and made her a fruitful vine on the walls of her husband's house and their children are, in the words of the psalmist, like the olive branches round about their table. Theirs is such a beautiful family! Yet, this ungodly daughter-in-law of mine refuses to bless me with grandchildren to cradle in my arms. What have I done to deserve such a fate? Have I not been to church regularly? Do I not pay my dues with unfailing regularity at the end of every month? Am I not a member of several church organizations? Do I not also contribute regularly towards the "poor rate"? Why is it that I, of all my friends and relations, should be without grandchildren? But, mark my words, such goings-on never have a good end."

And so Mrs. Susan Pratt went on spreading those foul rumors about her daughter-in-law with whom she was now hardly on speaking terms. Whenever she went to the house at Sanders Street, she made sure it was at a time when her son was at home, so that she would not subject herself to humiliation at the hands of her daughter-in-law. One evening, however, she had the misfortune of visiting when Eugene had gone to a meeting of Society Stewards and only Josephine was at home. She would never forget that experience, and she was fond of relating it to her friends:

"I greeted her quite jovially as is my custom."

" 'Good evening, Mrs. Pratt,' she answered. Can you believe it? She actually referred to me as Mrs. Pratt. Me, her mother-in-law-law! She didn't say 'Ma' or 'Mama' or 'Mama Pratt,' just 'Mrs. Pratt' as if we were both equals. Me! Her mother-in-law! She called me 'Mrs. Pratt'! She spoke so coldly, and you could see the look of contempt in her face. If it had been in her power to strike me dead at that moment, she would have done it. She didn't even offer me a seat. She went on doing what she was doing as if I wasn't even there. Anyway, I asked her kindly, as is my custom, 'how di bodi?' "

" 'I am very well thank you,' she said, and continued with what she was doing. That was exactly how she said it, too. She spoke in English, as though Krio was beneath her. 'I am very well, thank you.' And she did not bother to ask me how I was. She did not even offer me water to drink. She made it quite plain that I was not welcome in her house. Just because her father used to be Colonial Secretary, she thinks she can behave as she pleases to anyone. Was her father always Colonial Secretary, hmm? I know her father's grandfather was a carpenter, and he met his death by falling off a roof. But now this Josephine behaves as though butter will not melt in her mouth and she does not know how to speak Krio. But you wait. I will teach her. I will let her know that she married my son, and that it is my son who is her master."

And so relations between mother-in-law and daughter-in-law continued to deteriorate, as did relations between husband and wife. Of course, Eugene regularly related the details of the quarrels with his wife to his mother.

"And do you know, mama," he said on one occasion, "she now regularly gives off an offensive odor and hardly speaks to me in the mornings before I go to work."

"Ibosio!" shouted the mother. "She must be using some very powerful medicine. She must be rubbing something on her body to make her smell like that. I have known of such cases. She is using some medicine to gain power over you. You will have to watch your step. Be very observant. If you are at home when she is cooking, watch her closely to see what she puts into the soup. Watch her as she dishes out your food. That kind of woman can kill her husband. You must be careful."

It was after all this that Josephine almost died through confusing the two lotions. By then, as I have told you, she had completely used up both lotions, but it was some time before the offensive odor left her body completely. She now gave up all thoughts of conceiving through using potions and things like that, and decided to trust in God's providence for the time being. If God wanted her to have a child, she would have a child.

And so the months and the years slipped by, and the war came to an end. I remember it all now. It was 1945, and with the war at an end many of our young men who had gone to fight returned home, although a few never made it. By that time, I was the proud mother of six children, four boys and two girls. Moreover, my four children who were going to school were doing very well indeed. My eldest, Junior, was always top of his class. He was now in form two at the Prince of Wales School. The next was about to take the examination to enter secondary school. So, you see, I was not only blessed with children, I was blessed in my children. They were all doing very well indeed! God be praised!

As was to be expected, young unmarried women took a tremendous fancy toward the soldiers who were now returning home from the war. They were objects of attention and subjects of conversation. They were heroes, you see, strong men who had actually fought in a war on the winning side. They had also had all kinds of experiences denied to men who stayed at home. Some of them had been in the jungles of Burma, and had all kinds of interesting stories to tell about the jungles they had fought in, the strange peoples they had seen, the strange and powerful equipment they had used, the might of the Germans and the Japanese they had helped to defeat, the strange animals such as tigers they had encountered and sometimes killed with their bare hands, and about the skill of the British and their allies who had won the war. Those who had actually been to the Western world, to places like Britain, France and Germany, were regarded with particular admiration because they had got to know the ways of the white man, whom they had seen in his own country. They had fought side by side with him and, at times, against him, and actually defeated him in battle. These Sierra Leoneans seemed to have acquired an extra veneer of sophistication. Some had even learned to speak some of the Western languages like French and German, or, at least, so they claimed.

I remember the stories that one of them, Old Pa Faux, used to tell. Mr. T and I now rented his house at Cline Town.

Our family was growing and Mr. T's fortunes were improving, so we now needed a much bigger and better house than the one we had at Wellington Street. It was a grand two-storied concrete house in the modern style, and it was painted white all over. Though the kitchen, the bathroom, and the toilet were outside, they were quite decent concrete structures. There was also a wide compound in which I planted all sorts of things like cassava and potatoes and other vegetables. There were paw paw trees and banana trees in the yard, and about four mango trees. We had this grand house almost completely to ourselves, because although Pa Faux lived on the premises, he only used one room on the bottom floor and left the rest of the house to us.

It was this Pa Faux who used to regale us with his stories about the Second World War. Surprisingly, although the British, on whose side he fought, wanted him to harbor great aversion for the Germans, he actually spoke of the Germans with a certain amount of admiration.

"The German man is a very brilliant species," he used to say. "Boy, he gave us a hard time in the war. It took all the ingenuity of Churchill to defeat him. And if Churchill had not had the support of troops from Africa, of brave soldiers like myself who fear nothing, he wouldn't have been able to defeat the Germans," he would say. "You should have seen some of the weapons that the Germans built! You should have seen the grandeur of their tanks and heard the noise they made as they rumbled through the desert. You should have heard their aeroplanes flying overhead. Some soldiers, even British soldiers, peed in their pants when the German planes came flying overhead. But not us, the Africans! No! No! We stood our ground. We let those mighty Germans know that we could take any amount of pounding they chose to give us. 'Pa-ta-ta-ta-ta,' was the noise the bullets made, as those indomitable German pilots fired them at us from their cockpits. 'Boom! Boom! Boom!' was the sound we heard as bombs exploded all around us. Some men, even British men, cursed the day they were born and ran for cover. Not us the Africans! We stood tall on our feet and hurled defiance at the Germans. 'Come on, my German man,' we shouted, 'come on! Give us all you've got. We can take it!' And we fired back."

No doubt, some of these stories were gross exaggerations, but it is in the nature of soldiers to exaggerate. Anyway, they were good stories and we believed them. Pa Faux always talked about the Germans in affectionate terms. He used to refer to "my German man." In fact, he used to call my second son, whom he had a particular fondness for, "my German man."

Well, these returning war veterans had a lot of money. They'd accumulated a lot of back pay, or they were given considerable sums of money on being discharged. If you remember, I told you that the British had lured some of the more educated ones to go and fight with the promise of lucrative jobs and eminent positions on their return. Well, now that the war was won, the British were true to their word. Some of the more educated veterans found themselves promoted to positions of responsibility in the Civil Service, particularly if they had acquired some special skills during their war service. And many of them had acquired skills. They were now promoted to senior positions in the Public Works Department, the Post and Telegraphs Department, the Railway Department, the Customs Department, the Cable and Wireless Department, and the Treasury. If they were unmarried, they were very eligible bachelors indeed, and they turned many girls' heads.

Apparently, Josephine was one of those young women who allowed their heads to be turned. She was over thirty-five at the time, and not, by any means, pretty. But, as you know, she was given to flirting, and there was no reason to believe that she loved her husband. If she ever did, the constant quarreling must have put an end to it. I think she met some of these prosperous young veterans at her father's house, because he was still Colonial Secretary, and these young men occupied important senior positions in the Civil Service. They moved in the same circles. Whatever the case, Eugene inevitably realized what was going on, and his jealousy was aroused.

There was one terrible incident that Mr. T related to me. One of these new, top Sierra Leonean civil servants had a party at his quarters at Brookfields. Eugene and his wife were invited, I suppose because Josephine was the daughter of a top official in the civil service whom this top civil servant had got to know. My own Mr. T was also invited. He, through his own honest exertions, was also making headway in the civil service. In fact, he was now Chief Clerk at the Public Works Department, a very esteemed position at the time. I could not go, of course, because I had six children to look after, so Mr. T went alone. When he returned home, rather flustered, he related the details to me.

"The party had been going very well indeed," he said. "There was a lot of good food and plenty to drink. Almost everyone seemed to be having a very good time. Those who weren't dancing in the parlor were sitting on the verandah drinking, eating or chatting. I said almost everyone was having a good time, because it was clear that Josephine looked very unhappy. Perhaps she was thinking that if she hadn't been so hasty, she would now have the chance of marrying one of these well-heeled young veterans who were making so much money and such a name for themselves in the civil service, men who, more or less, belonged to her father's circle. She might now also be occupying luxurious government quarters with lots of grounds for a garden and quarters for servants, instead of the lowly, one-story wooden building Eugene and herself were still occupying at Sanders Street."

You see, though Eugene had hoped that membership of the Masonic lodge and his friendship with the managers of his company would earn him rapid advancement, he had not really made much progress, at least not as much progress as he had hoped in his job. Besides, what with his drinking, the expenses associated with being a member of the lodge, and his wife's extravagance, he had not been able to save much money, and they had been unable to move out of that house into more comfortable accommodation. So they were still living in what Josephine undoubtedly considered a squalid environment.

Anyway, let me continue with my husband's account of that eventful evening, as he told it to me.

"Josephine was looking very glum and was hardly speaking to anyone. Then, at a certain moment, Ben Sawyerr, an up-and-coming young man at the Cable and Wireless Department, walked up to her and asked her to dance. She told him she was not in a good mood and did not feel like dancing.

" 'What can be the matter?' Ben asked. 'Look, everyone is having a very good time. It is near Christmas; it is the time for fun and enjoyment. Put on a happy face and enjoy yourself.' "

" 'I don't know,' replied Josephine. 'Maybe it is the heat. There are so many people here, and it's rather stuffy.' "

" 'In that case, let's take a walk down the drive as far as the road. The fresh air will do you good. I am sure Bernard will accompany us. Bernard, let us take her for a walk down the drive. She needs some fresh air.' "

" 'Okay, let's go,' Josephine said, and got up."

"I am absolutely sure that Ben's offer was innocent and made in very good faith. He had no designs on Josephine. He was just trying to be polite and kind. Maybe he even asked me to accompany them so that no one would misunderstand and misrepresent his motives. Had he had any ulterior designs on Josephine, I am sure he would never have asked anyone else, particularly me, to accompany them. Of course, I accepted, got up from my seat, and took my beer bottle in my hand; we went out of the house and started walking down the drive. We were chatting gaily, and it was quite obvious that Josephine's spirits had risen somewhat. We were quite loud, so that anyone in the house could have heard what we were saying and realized that we were not up to anything immoral.

"It seems, though, that some friend of Eugene who wished to worm himself into Eugene's favor, went up to him and, like a snake, whispered in his ear, 'Are you just sitting here drinking, Eugene? This very minute, your wife has gone out of the house with two men, and they are heading toward the bushes. I am sure they are up to no good.' "

"He must have said something like that, for within a few minutes we saw Eugene, who was now obviously plastered, rushing toward us from the house, shouting the most obscene oaths."

" 'Where are you going with those two men you bloody slut, you harlot?' he shouted. 'Stay where you are. Don't you move a step further or I will kill you with my bare hands tonight.' "

" He was obviously drunk and not in complete control of himself."

" 'We are not going anywhere,' Ben Sawyerr said. 'Josephine said it was too stuffy inside, and Bernard and I were just taking her for a breath of fresh air outside.' "

" 'Shut up!' Eugene shouted. 'You don't know that harlot I have for a wife. You don't know the dirty tricks she can get up to.' By now he was very close to us, and he grabbed Josephine by the hand and screamed at her, 'I was keeping my eyes on you, but the moment my back was turned you sneaked out of the house toward the bushes for your nasty and filthy purposes, you filthy whore.' "

"With that he gave Josephine a stinging slap on her cheek and kicked her on her shins."

" 'Stop that Eugene,' I said. 'It is I Bernard, your friend. What Ben has said is the truth. I swear. Do you think I'd head for the bushes with any ulterior designs on your wife, after we have known each other for so many years? Stop this nonsense. You are making a fool of yourself.' "

. "But he hardly heard what I said, and was now beside himself with rage. He was now raining thundering blows on the unfortunate Josephine and kicking her on whatever part of her body his right foot could land on, swearing and cursing all the while. By now everyone at the party had heard what was going on, and people came streaming out of the house, shouting at Eugene to stop."

" 'I'll beat you within an inch of your useless life today, you whore. I'll teach you to look at other men and sneak into the bushes with them. I will disgrace you before the whole world. I'll strip you, so the whole world can see your nasty nakedness.' "

"In his drunkenness, he seemed to have the strength of ten men, and it was all that Ben and I could do to restrain him. He had got hold of Josephine's dress and was proceeding to tear it off her body. Realizing this, Josephine, whose first reaction had been to fight back, stopped that and started pleading with him."

" 'Please, Eugene, I beg you. Don't disgrace me before all our friends. Please stop. Don't do this to me.' "

"But her pleas seemed to enrage him even more, and he probably thought that they were an admission of guilt. He proceeded to rip her dress, her petticoat, and slip right off her body, leaving only her bra and panties."

" 'So, is this what you married me for?' She asked. 'Did you marry me to disgrace me before the whole world?' She was now in tears, while some of us tried to form a ring round

146

her, so that the whole world would not see her nakedness. Others were trying to restrain the enraged Eugene."

" 'This was not what I married you for,' he said, 'but if you disgrace me by running off with other men, I will disgrace you and show the world what you really are: a harlot! A whore! Senjago!' "

"By now most people devoted their efforts not so much to restrain the madman Eugene, but to cover up the nakedness of his unfortunate wife, Josephine. Some people managed to get her clothes together, and we hurriedly wrenched her away from her mad husband's hands and into a car, so that she could be taken home. Some other people led the still protesting and cursing Eugene back into the house.

"I went into the house myself, intending to remonstrate with Eugene and to ask him whether he had so little trust in me, one of his closest friends, as to suspect me of having ulterior designs on his wife. I wanted to tell him how hurt I was, and that this display would probably put an end to our friendship forever. I found him sitting down on a chair, still mumbling imprecations and talking to the young man who, apparently, had made the infamous report to him about his wife."

" 'For what you have done for me tonight, Gustavus,' Eugene was saying, still in a drunken kind of stupor, 'I will be grateful to you forever. I am deeply in your debt.' He then put his arm around Gustavus' shoulder and rubbed his cheek with his. The latter looked around with a sheepish kind of satisfaction. I realized it was he who had made the stupid report to Eugene and thereby caused the total disruption of a party that had been going very well indeed. It seemed to me that it would be useless to say anything to Eugene in the state he was, and that I should reserve my comments for another occasion. I honestly think Eugene is going downhill. I don't think his marriage with Josephine will last much longer."

What my husband told me caused me great distress, not only because of the way in which that Gustavus, whoever he was, tried to implicate my husband in an alleged sordid affair, but also because of the implications for our friendship with Eugene and Josephine. Despite Eugene's poor treatment of Annie, Mr. T and I had somehow managed to remain on friendly terms with him and Josephine. But how could we continue our friendship with him after he, whether in a drunken rage or not, actually suspected my husband of having designs on his wife?

If there is only one thing I could say about my husband, it would be that he was never unfaithful to me in all our fifty years of marriage. He never gave me any reason to doubt him. He did not have sweethearts outside the house, and he did not lust after other men's wives. He was as faithful to me, as I was faithful to him. God rest his soul! So I had no doubts that Eugene's fears were completely unfounded. I am sure that, deep down, Eugene also knew this. He never upbraided my husband after this about this apparent and alleged liaison with his wife, though he might have felt that Josephine had her eyes on one of the up-an-coming young men in the civil service. The next time my husband met him, their conversation was quite cordial, and he even told Mr. T, in confidence, that he was beginning to have serious doubts about his wife's fidelity. You do not say that to a man you suspect of having, or wanting to have, an affair with your wife. Mr. T, in fact, seized the opportunity to try and convince him that on the evening of the party his suspicions were completely unfounded, and that seemed to mollify him somewhat. But it didn't curb his jealousy.

From that time on, our friendship began to cool somewhat, though it didn't completely come to an end. My husband and I now realized that in addition to his other unattractive qualities, Eugene exhibited a completely mindless jealousy. It was jealousy built partly on insecurity, which

was itself the result of his feeling slightly inferior to these up-and-coming young veterans in the civil service, who belonged to the same circle and class as Josephine's father, a circle from which he, in spite of his membership of the Masonic lodge, felt excluded.

The jealousy was, of course, partly justified, because Josephine had shown that she was dissatisfied with her lot, and was quite capable of flirting with these young men. Her situation was a very interesting one indeed. At about thirty six, her biological clock, as they say, was ticking away fast, and she badly needed a child, to satisfy her maternal instincts, bring a certain measure of calm into her household, and put her enemies to shame. She might even have thought in her desperation that she could try having a child by another man, perhaps by one of these smart young men in the civil service, and let her husband believe that the child was his. Maybe that was why she had begun to flirt with other men.

After her humiliation at the party, however, she must have put all such thoughts out of her head. Her adventures with medicine men like Pa Santigie had not worked, and had produced nearly fatal results. One day, she mentioned to me in confidence that she was beginning to doubt whether the problem rested exclusively with her. "Why do people always blame the woman if a couple fails to have children?" She asked. "It takes two. It could be as much a problem with the man as with the woman." After all, she had conceived a child before, although she had miscarried. That alone should prove that she was not completely barren. She told me that in conversations with her mother the latter had told her that the problem could be Eugene's. She had even suggested that the next time they visited a medicine man they should ask him to give them some medicine to help her husband who, they suspected, had now gone sterile.

The years went by, and, one by one, the older generation started to pass away. The first to go was Josephine's father, Mr. Columbus Freeman, who had had such a distinguished career in the Sierra Leone Civil Service. He was not very old, though he had been retired for some years. If I remember rightly, he was about sixty-six when he died of a stroke. Mr. Freeman was laid out in state in the hall of his Masonic Lodge, dressed in full regalia. There was a grand funeral service at St. George's Cathedral. The choir, several clergy, and hundreds of members of the Masonic lodges were in attendance. The church was absolutely packed with mourners. The procession to the Ascension Town cemetery, led by the band of the Sierra Leone Grammar School, was about a mile long. It seemed as if the whole of Freetown was there. Many people said that they could not remember a bigger funeral. Mr. Freeman's son, who was now a doctor practicing in England, had come home by ship once it became clear that his father would not survive the stroke. Apart from Josephine and this son, the Freemans had only another child, a daughter who was married to a judge in the Gold Coast.

After Mr. Freeman's death, Eugene got his wife Josephine to suggest to her mother that the couple should move and join her in the grand house at Circular Road. There was a lot of space in that big house, and Mrs. Freeman surely needed a man about the house. That stout woman, however, rejected the idea with great determination. She would not have objected to her daughter living with her in the house, but she strongly objected to Eugene, with his peasant manners, living in her stately home. To have Eugene living in her house would also mean that she would have to subject herself to the indignity of visits by the detested Susan Pratt, Eugene's mother. And she could not stand that woman. She preferred to live on in the house with the children of some relatives whom she adopted as her wards.

You can easily see that this did not help improve relations between the Pratts and Mrs. Freeman. It didn't help relations between Eugene and his wife either. They kept on living as husband and wife together, but it was merely a façade. People, especially Eugene's relatives, were still urging her to try and have a child. There is nothing like a child, they suggested, for mending the frayed relations between a husband and his wife. There is nothing like a child to bring husband and wife together once more. Husbands who previously detested their wives had been known to fawn on them with ardent love and give them all they needed once they had children, children that verified the husband's masculinity and ensured the continuity of his line.

So Josephine decided, as a last resort, to do what one of medicine man had suggested: to give her husband a potion that would stimulate his masculinity and cure any chance of sterility. It was a dark brown potion that she was supposed to put into his soup every evening, for a whole week. The potion was virtually tasteless, so Eugene wouldn't notice that there was anything added to his food. It should be very easy. The medicine man warned her, however, not to take the potion, herself. "This potion is for men, not women," he said. The potion could not therefore be put into the soup while Josephine was cooking it, as she would have to eat of that herself. She could cook a special soup for her husband, but that would arouse suspicion. No! The potion would have to be put into Eugene's dish just before or after she dished out his food.

Unfortunately for Josephine, she did not know that Eugene's mother had warned her son to keep his eyes wide open lest his wife should try to give him something in his food, in order to have power over him.

From that day after the conversation with his mother, Eugene was very suspicious of his wife, and had watched her very closely indeed. True, he wasn't always there when she dished out his food, put it on the table, and wrapped it up with a white lace cloth. But he carefully smelled every dish she prepared for him and paid great attention to the taste of the dish to ensure that nothing strange was there. On some occasions, of course, he was at home when his wife dished up his food. He would then watch her very closely, although she did not know it.

It was on one of these occasions, a Saturday afternoon, that he saw her slyly take a brownish phial out of her dress pocket, unscrew the top, and pour some of the brownish contents into the bitter leaf sauce that went with her husband's foofoo.

"What is that that you are putting into my food?" he shouted as he jumped out of his chair. Alarmed, Josephine tried to put the phial back into her pocket, but her husband was too quick for her. In a flash he had got hold, not only of her hand, but also of the tell-tale phial.

"Ibosio," he shouted. "Lord, have mercy!" Then, he ran over to the window and cried, "Neighbors, come and see the poison that my wife wants to poison me with. People of Sanders Street, come and see how my wife wants to poison me."

He rushed back into the pantry and gave Josephine three resounding slaps on her face. He continued shouting, "so now, you want to kill me so that you can marry one of those men you've been flirting with, one of those high and mighty officials in the civil service you think deserve you much more than I do! People of Sanders Street, come and see what my wife has been doing!" With that he gave her three more resounding slaps, while Josephine whimpered and dropped on to the floor in agony.

"I caught her red-handed," he went on. "I caught her red-handed, putting this nasty thing into my soup as she dished out my food." He showed the incriminating phial to the crowd that had started to gather in the yard. "If I die

tomorrow," he continued, "you will know that it is my wife who has poisoned me. Ask her if you like. Let her deny it if she dare."

Of course Josephine could not say a word in defense. She just sat there in a heap on the floor, screaming her head off and telling him to kill her, while he administered slap after slap and kick after kick.

"All right," she screamed, "kill me. Kill me for my mother. You have done all sorts of other things to me. It is not beyond you to kill me. Kill me! Kill me!"

"Yes, I will kill you," he screamed, "and I will be justified. Who will condemn me for killing a wife who's tried to poison me? People of Sanders Street, here is the evidence. God in heaven knows how long she has been putting this poison into my food. If I die tomorrow, you will know that it is my wife who has killed me. I curse the day I married this harlot who now tries to murder me so that she will marry one of her fancy men."

"Okay, it's enough," some people said, trying to restrain him. "We have seen the evidence, but don't kill her. Let her go home to her people. Let her go to her mother."

"I will kill her and then send her back to her people," he screamed. At this he administered some more blows while some members of the crowd tried to restrain him.

"It's enough! It's enough!' they said. "Take surrur! Take Surrur! Just let her go back to her people. Don't kill her. Don't put yourself on the wrong side of the law."

"All right," he said. "But if it was not for these good people, I would show you the man you are playing with, the man you are trying to kill. Come on! Get up! Go and pack your things and leave my house immediately. You will not spend one more day in my house to kill me. You will leave my house immediately. Go and pack your things and go."

With that he pushed her into the house and into her room to pack whatever she could.

"I give you only half an hour to pack your things and leave my house," he continued. "And take only your clothes and your trinkets. All the other things, I bought with my own money. I cannot let you take them. Take only your clothes and your trinkets. Don't even take my suitcases. Pack your things into any basket you can find and leave my house this minute. This minute, I said."

Josephine knew that she had no alternative but to comply. She hastily put together whatever clothes and trinkets she could find into a large basket and a small handbag, put them on her head, and ran into the street.

"Get out, and take your filthy things with you, and don't you dare come into my house again. If I catch you in my house, I will commit murder. I swear to my mother, I will. And don't you send any of your detestable relations to come and talk to me," he shouted after her, as she ran, weeping down Sanders Street, in the direction of the Cotton tree, with her basket of clothes on her head. "You will never come into this my house again. Never again! I have finished with you."

That was virtually the end of Eugene and Josephine's marriage. Mr. T and I tried to reason with Eugene and begged him to take Josephine back, but his mind was made up. Afterward, I spoke with Josephine and found out that the potion was, in fact, not meant to kill him, but to stimulate his masculinity so that they would have children. She had done it out of desperation because she wanted to give him a child that she hoped would bring them closer together once more. But there were other influences operating on Eugene. For one thing, there was his mother whose dislike of Josephine was now implacable, and who convinced her son that a wife who went to a medicine man to get a potion to put into his food, for whatever reason, was also likely to kill him. How could he trust her after this? How could he trust her to cook his food? How could he tell that every morsel of food

he put into his mouth did not contain a deadly poison? To keep such a woman in one's house was dangerous. It was best to get rid of her.

In vain, therefore, did Mr. T and I attempt to plead with Eugene. "She did it out of love for you," we said. "She did it because she was desperate to give you a child. She did not mean any harm. In any case, we will talk to her and warn her very strongly to mend her flirtatious ways. You have sworn on God's holy altar to stick to her for better or worse, for richer or poorer, till death parts you, and you must keep your vow."

"God will forgive me," he said, "for not keeping a vow I made with such a wicked woman. I am doing this in the interest of my own self-preservation. I must look after my own life. She and I are finished."

"But what do you expect her to do now?" Mr. T asked. "She doesn't work and has no money of her own. She will be entirely dependent on her mother, who is herself a widow. What do you expect her to do?"

"They will manage," Eugene replied. "I am sure her father left a good sum of money, and in any case there is her brother who lives in England. He will send money for them. They'll manage. At least, she will have a roof over her head. But I will not, under any circumstances, take her back into my house. What have I gained from that woman since I married her? See the squalid state in which I am forced to live, because of her extravagance? And her parents have not helped me one bit in my career. Plus, she hasn't given me any children, and on top of all that, she tried to kill me."

"She didn't try to kill you," Mr. T said. "What she did, she did for both of your sakes. It was ill advised, perhaps, but she did it only to make sure that you could have children to gladden your heart."

"How can I be sure that on another occasion she will not try to poison me so that she could marry one of her fancy men? Let's face it. We were not even living like husband and wife together. Our marriage was falling apart. It is best for us to separate now. It is best for her to go and live with her mother."

And so our efforts proved fruitless, as did the efforts of many other people from both sides who tried to talk to Eugene. His mind was made up. I could not help reflecting on the unfairness of it all. After more than eight years of marriage, after her youth had gone and the woman had given her all to her husband, she was thrown out into the streets like some dirty old clothes without a penny to her name. After cleaning for her husband, cooking for him, and providing comfort for his bed, she was thrown out of the house without a penny, without even some of the furniture that they had bought together. The husband claimed that it was all bought with his own money and that none of it belonged to her. It would not have been too bad if the wife had some form of employment; but she had been a full-time housewife and had not done a day's work outside the home. She had not saved a penny of her own. Now she was cast adrift when she was approaching the age of forty to depend on the good will of her relations.

Of course, Mrs. Freeman took back her daughter. She could not blame her for what she had done because they had, more or less, planned it together. Her daughter was her daughter, and she would always find a home under her roof. There was lots of space in the house. She would never have that detestable Eugene living in her house under any circumstances, but she had no objections to her daughter living with her once more. Mrs. Freeman was now entirely dependent on the interest from her husband's savings and what her son in England sent for her, but it would support both her and her daughter. Somehow, they'd manage.

Josephine sent some friends and relatives to collect the things that she hadn't managed to pack into the basket, and

resigned herself to life with her mother once more in the grand mansion at Circular Road.

The couple didn't actually go through the process of a divorce. Mrs. Freeman was reluctant to persuade her daughter to initiate divorce proceedings. She knew that a lot of unsavory things would come out in court; even she herself had not been guiltless in that. She wanted to spare the feelings of the family.

Eugene didn't start divorce proceedings either. I remember Mr. T saying to him on one occasion, "If you are determined not to have her back in your life, it would be better to get a divorce so that the two of you can start your lives all over again."

Eugene replied, "a divorce would be costly and messy. Moreover, some of my friends who have gone through the process say that the wife and her family almost cleaned them out." He went on to say that they might have to share the few things that they had possessed in common. Mr. T warned him, "if you do not divorce her, she would still be your lawful wife, and if you were to die tomorrow, which God forbid, she would have the right to claim all your belongings and your gratuity, and even the right to determine how you should be buried."

"From what I know of her and her family," he replied, "I don't think they would want to come anywhere near me when I die. In any case, I will make sure that I leave a will that will clearly spell out how my few possessions should be distributed."

And there the matter ended. I suppose also that Eugene refused to have a divorce because he now enjoyed all the privileges of a divorced man without going through the messy and expensive legal process.

CHAPTER 9

Oh friendship! It is a wonderful thing. Friends can be very helpful, and moments with our friends can be among our most memorable and fulfilling experiences. But friendships can also lead to betrayal and complications. It is amazing to think that Annie, Josephine and I all started out as great friends. But see what happened! Mr. T and Eugene were also the best of friends, and they became involved with the three of us: Annie, Josephine and me. But see what complications came out of that! Now, Mr. T and I found ourselves in a very difficult and somewhat embarrassing position. We were great friends with both Josephine and Eugene. Now, those two had gone their separate ways, but we still had to continue being friends with both of them. After all, one was godfather to one of my children and the other was godmother to another. We saw their faults and the problems that they may have created for themselves, but it was difficult for us to take sides. We gave advice when we felt it could help, but our advice was not always taken, and we could not put an end to the friendship because of that, or because those two people had now gone their separate ways. We still kept hoping that in course of time, after some of the wounds had healed, we might still be able to effect a reconciliation, though we realized it would be an uphill task because the wounds were still very raw.

So, we still remained on good terms with both Josephine and Eugene. We continued to visit them separately, and they, individually, came to visit us.

I remember one occasion when I visited Josephine, just after the separation. She was still badly shaken, but was, nevertheless, defiant.

"Did you see how that beast of a man humiliated me, Priscilla?" she asked. "After I'd given him the best years of my life, he humiliated me before the whole world."

"I know," I said, "but we must be patient. Perhaps things will change."

"It was the second time he humiliated me in public. The first was at Ben Sawyerr's party at Brookfields, when he stripped me naked. Can you imagine that Priscilla? That man doesn't fear God. He beat me and stripped me naked in front of all our friends and called me harlot and senjago, all for no reason at all."

"I know," I said. "Mr. T told me about it. It was very disgraceful conduct indeed."

"Can you believe it? I had done nothing, absolutely nothing at all. He was dead drunk, and he kicked me and slapped me, gave me a good beating and disgraced me in front of all and sundry. I wanted the earth to open up and swallow me. He did that to me, me, Josephine Freeman, the daughter of Columbus Freeman! He stripped me naked, beat me like a dog, and called me senjago. Hey, Priscilla, up till now I cannot find the mouth to talk of my disgrace, that night. I did not go out of my house for a whole month after that, because the word was all over town. Some people even said that Eugene Pratt found his wife naked in the bushes with another man. And he almost killed her. You know Freetown; that was what they said."

"Take surrur, take surrur," I said. We know that Freetown is given to gossip and to exaggeration. We know what happened. He was virtually accusing my Mr. T of wanting to have an affair with you."

"Yes he was, because your Mr. T and Ben Sawyerr were the ones who were with me on the walk down the drive. How on earth could he seriously think that your Mr. T, who is a model of propriety and probity, would do such a thing? Eugene is an irrational beast. Believe me! I was seriously ill for a whole month after that."

"Well," I said, "at least give thanks to God that you regained your health after such a savage beating, and that you are still here."

"But God will punish him for me," she continued. "God will take my part, because he knows that I am innocent. I go down on my knees every morning and night and pray that God will make him die like a dog, like the dog he is. I take cold water and go into the yard and call on God every morning to give him his just deserts. I am sure God will hear my prayers."

"Don't speak like that, Josephine," I said in alarm. "The mouth that eats salt and pepper should not speak like that. Instead, we should pray for God to soften his heart and change him, so that in time there may be a reconciliation."

"Do you think I want to go back to the house of that beast, that heathen? Not on your life," she said. "He will only humiliate me again, if he doesn't kill me. He has threatened to kill me, and on the first occasion, when I had that miscarriage, he almost killed me. No, I will not go to his house again. I will only be asking for my death. I will be a fool to go back to him. I was a fool to marry him in the first place. Just think of it! He, the son of a shoemaker, to humiliate me like that, to shout out to the whole of Sanders Street, to the whole world, that I wanted to kill him, to beat me and kick me out of his house with only a few clothes in a basket! Without a cent to my name! Can there be greater humiliation than that? But you wait. I will have my revenge. Every

minute of every living day, as I sit down, or before I go to sleep at night, I think of how to have my revenge on him. And God will show me how. God will give me my revenge. You just wait."

"Please don't talk about revenge, Josephine. Do, I beg you. Revenge is not very Christian. Leave everything to God. Place your problem in his hands, and he will surely give you justice, if you need justice."

"Oh, I need justice alright," she said, "but I also need revenge. And if God does not give me revenge, I will seize it with my own hands. I will make him pay for the harm he has done to me, my family, and my good name. Oh death, you are great indeed! Do you think if the mighty Columbus Freeman were still alive, Eugene would dare to do what he has done to his daughter? But he has underestimated me. I will show him whose daughter I am. I will seize my revenge with both hands. I will make him curse the day his miserable mother gave birth to him."

I must confess that I was thoroughly alarmed at what Josephine was saying. She had been badly hurt and humiliated, I know. But I began to shudder when I thought of what she might be planning to do. I would have to do my best to pacify her. She was certainly working herself up to a terrible passion, and I began to fear what the aftermath might be. After all, Eugene was still a friend. I would have to talk to Mr. T and we would both have to talk to Eugene and see what could be done.

"And I will never give him the satisfaction of knowing that I suffered," Josephine raged on. "Perhaps he thinks that by throwing me out of his house he will make me beg for my bread. But I will show him that I am a woman. I will show that dog what a proper Krio woman can do. I will rise again. I may be down now, but I will surely rise again. If he thinks he will have the satisfaction of laughing at my discomfiture, he is very much mistaken. I will show him that I am a woman with steel, with backbone. I will rise again. He will see."

"That's the spirit," I said. "Don't let this get you down, Josephine. Take it as a challenge, or an obstacle that you must and will overcome on the way to higher things. I know that it's a man's world, but there is no law that says that we women cannot succeed on our own if we try. Show him that you don't have to depend on him."

With those words, I took my leave of Josephine. I must confess that, though I was alarmed by some of the things she had said, I did greatly admire her spirit of defiance and determination. She didn't tell me what precisely she planned to do, and maybe there wasn't much that she could do; but it was enough that she was not prepared to let her husband's treatment break her spirit. That would have been defeat indeed.

I told Mr. T about this conversation, and about some of the things Josephine had said and her apparently unshakeable determination for revenge. He too shared my misgivings, and he thought it would be best to go and talk again to Eugene.

"But we will also have to talk to Josephine," said Mr. T. "Some people would say that any woman who puts something in her husband's food, whatever the reason for that may be, is a dangerous woman, and the man should not continue to live with her. We will have to tell her to stop her superstitious ways. One of the worst things that can happen to a man is to have a superstitious wife who is constantly consulting medicine men. She will have to stop that."

"I agree," I said.

So, one Tuesday evening, after Mr. T had come home from work and had his dinner, he and I made our way to Eugene's house at Sanders Street. Our children were growing up fast and they could be left by themselves, the

older ones looking after the younger ones. We arrived at Eugene's house and knocked at the door.

"Who is it," answered a female voice. Mr. T and I looked askance at each other. We had expected Eugene to answer the door. He had not told us that there was a female in the house.

"Friends," we said.

We heard light, slippered footsteps walking to the door and in a few seconds, the door opened. Who do you think we saw standing there, right in front of us? It was Annie, Macauley.

"Annie," exclaimed Mr. T in great surprise, "what are you doing here? Where is Eugene?"

"Oh please come in and sit down," she said. "Eugene has gone to an emergency meeting of his Stewards Society, but he'll probably be back soon."

"But what are you doing here?" I asked. "You are the very last person we expected to find here."

"It's a long story, my sister," she said.

As you might expect, Mr. T and I were dying to hear the story.

"After his violent quarrel with Josephine" Annie said, "Eugene and I met at a funeral. I think it was at Christ Church. As he entered the church, he caught sight of me sitting in a pew and he came and joined me. He greeted me affably and started to chat me up. What could I do? I couldn't ask him to move to another pew. And it would've been just as rude for me to move and leave him sitting by himself. One doesn't do that kind of thing in God's house. Besides, in spite of what he'd done to me, I'd never hated him, and I must confess I've always had feelings for him. You know how he won my heart. No, I did not have the heart to ask him to move.

Well, he started conversing about this and that, and during the entire service he wouldn't stop talking to me.

When the service was finally over, we walked in the procession to the cemetery together, singing all the way with the other mourners. I couldn't detach myself from him. In fact, as we walked together in that crowd of mourners, the old feelings started to return, and I almost forgot how badly he'd treated me, and how badly he'd treated his wife. You know how charming Eugene can be when he has the mind to be. Anyone who saw us in that procession would probably have thought we were husband and wife walking together.

After the funeral was over, we walked back together out of Kingtom cemetery. He started talking to me about his troubles with his wife Josephine, and he swore that he had now realized how bad a mistake it was to have married her and not me. They'd never been happy together, he said. There had been nothing but quarrels throughout the marriage, and in the end he could have sworn that she wanted to kill him in order to marry someone else. That was why he kicked her out of doors, and he would never allow her to enter his house again. The long and the short of it all was, he also swore that he'd made a big mistake in not marrying me, and he now wanted to rectify that mistake."

"Did he say that he would marry you?" asked Mr. T.

"Well, he did not say that exactly, but he did say that his goal was to divorce Josephine. However, that would take a long time, and he was not sure that Josephine would agree to a divorce. That shouldn't stop us from living together, he said, since we knew each other very well and had been engaged to each other. Then, he swore to treat me kindly, to give me everything I want, and to marry me as soon as he was able to get a divorce from his wife."

"And you believed him and agreed?" asked Mr. T.

"I did not agree immediately," she said. "I told him that I'd consider it. He walked with me right up to our house on Circular Road, before he turned back to go home. I told my mother what he had proposed, and she said that it was my

decision, though after what he'd done to me, she felt I'd be taking a risk."

"A week later he came to the house, bringing presents for all of us. He was so charming and spoke so nicely to my mother. You remember my mother had really liked him before he ditched me. Also, my mother is ailing, as you know. She's not very strong now, and I don't think she will remain in this world for long. She must have felt that it would be good to have a man beside me if she were to die. So she didn't raise any objections.

To make a long story short, I agreed to what Eugene proposed. I agreed to move in with him and keep house for him. We are now living as husband and wife together, and he has been very kind to my mother, and has given us everything we want."

"But don't you realize you are taking a grave risk?" Mr. T asked. "What will people say? After all, Josephine used to be your friend. All right, I know that she was the reason Eugene didn't marry you in the first place, but you don't have to pay her back in her own coin. You will just be creating more enemies for yourself. Besides, how can you be sure that he will marry you, even if he were to get a divorce from his wife? Are you not spoiling your chances of ever getting married to a good man who will take good care of you?"

"Look at me, Bernard," she said. "I am almost forty and certainly not as beautiful as I used to be. The years and my problems have taken their toll. Who will marry me? If it were possible for me to find a husband, don't you think I'd have got married by now? I'm not even sure that I can have children any more, and men of today are looking for young wives who will bear children for them. I have not been trained in any job. Yes, I manage to get by, by selling this and that, but it's barely enough to keep soul and body together. My mother is ill and may die at any time. That sort of thing costs money. I need a man who will help me. Do not our people say that a man with a broken foot is better than an empty house?"

"But what worries me, Annie," I chipped in, "is that Eugene may never be able to get a divorce from Josephine. Even if it's possible for him to get a divorce, he might not bother to get a divorce. What incentive would he have to get a divorce and marry you when he has all the privileges of a husband—someone to keep his house and cook his food and provide him with other comforts—without the inconvenience and expense and legal commitments of a divorce and second marriage?"

"I have thought of that, Priscilla," she said. "But what choice do I have at my time of life?"

I could hardly mention the fact that I thought there might be personal danger to her from Josephine's quarter, knowing how superstitious that friend of ours was. I kept quiet on that score and merely said, "I hope you know what you are doing, Annie."

"Yes," she said. "I am prepared to take the risk. I am boxed into a corner, and I can see no other alternative. Besides, you know how much I've always loved Eugene. He was the first man I ever knew. In a sense, I consider myself his wife, even if he doesn't marry me. I find it difficult to get him out of my system."

Soon after, Mr. T and I left the house. We now realized that any hopes we might have had of effecting a reconciliation between Eugene and Josephine were dashed. We'd also have to walk a very fine tightrope indeed, if we were to maintain our friendship with Josephine on the one hand, and with Eugene and Annie on the other. It was an unenviable position.

How like Eugene, I thought, as I lay in my bed that night. He was truly getting the best of all worlds. He'd got rid of a wife he'd come to detest, and now he had a woman who'd always been the love of his life, living with him and performing all the duties of a wife, without any of the legal obligations, on his part. Who knows? Maybe he even hoped that Annie, despite her middle age, would be able to give him the son he so badly wanted. After all, some women have been known to conceive at the age of forty-two or even forty-three. Why should not the same thing happen to Annie?

CHAPTER 10

Now, I'll have to skip a few years to about the mid-50s. A lot of changes had taken place: not only in our personal circumstances, but also in the country as a whole. Politically, there were great advances. The country was moving gradually toward self-government and independence. We would soon have our first elections with universal adult suffrage and our own Chief Minister. Change was in the air. The British administration was looking for competent Sierra Leoneans who would move into the shoes of British officials both before and after independence, in order to take over the reins of government and administration. This was very important for the civil service. Fortunately for us, my husband, Mr. T, was one of those Sierra Leoneans selected to move into these positions. He had risen steadily in the civil service over the years, and had proved his competence, efficiency and reliability. He was one of the first Sierra Leoneans chosen to move into what was then called the Senior Civil Service. This meant that his stature was considerably enhanced. He was entitled to a loan for a car and for a refrigerator, as well as to a substantial loan to start constructing his house. Mr. T was therefore one of the first Sierra Leoneans in the civil service to own a car.

I remember the day he brought the car home. All the neighbors were green with envy, but some of them also rejoiced with us for our good fortune. My head swelled with pride as all the neighbors came out to admire that beautiful Triumph Herald. Every Sunday, we'd wave as we drove by, on our way to church. The children proudly mounted into it on weekdays to be taken to school, and came out of it with their heads held high when they arrived at their schools, to the great admiration of their friends. My husband had truly made it. "Seest thou a man diligent in his business," as the good book says, "he shall stand before kings, and not before mean men." My husband had indeed been diligent in his business, and he was getting ready to stand before kings. Mr. T also bought this beautiful piece of land here at Murray Town, overlooking the ocean, and started constructing this magnificent house. It would take him years to complete, because he was doing it honestly on his salary, but he had started saving toward it, and he would partly pay for it with the monthly housing allowance that he was entitled to as a member of the Senior Service, as we called it. This shows you what honesty, diligence, hard work, and devotion to duty, as well as loyalty to family can achieve.

We had indeed prospered as a family. Our eldest son, Junior, had done extremely well at school and had proceeded to the United Kingdom on scholarship to train as a doctor at Manchester University. The second was also about to proceed to London University to begin his own studies as an engineer. The others were also doing extremely well at school. They had done well because their father, though a kind father, was also a very strict disciplinarian who ensured that they paid attention to their studies. He taught them the proper values: honesty, thrift, industry, integrity, and efficiency. I also gave him as much support as was necessary, both in bringing up the children and in his work. Although I say it myself, we were a model family, and I have nothing to complain about. There were times when I thought that Mr. T was rather stingy about spending money on accessories and decorations for the home, but I realized that was because he was saving toward the construction of the house. And that was the most important thing. So I suppose we were what you would call a highly successful family: united by love, possessing a car and quite a few modern conveniences, having enough money to live on, and soon to have our own house. When I think of other families and see how they turned out, I thank God that we were so blessed.

The next great change that happened was the passing away of the older generation by the course of nature. Annie's mother, Mrs. Macauley, died. As I've said, she'd been ailing for some time, and she still lived in the small rented house at the lower end of Circular Road. Her circumstances hadn't been very good, poor woman. Her children hadn't been very successful, and her husband was dead. She'd hoped that Eugene would be the new man in the family and give them substantial help as the husband of her daughter. But in this, as we have seen, she was gravely disappointed. However, after Annie moved in with Eugene Mrs. Macauley was able to get some assistance from him. Furthermore, he took almost complete responsibility for the funeral expenses and thus enabled Mrs. Macauley to have a very decent funeral.

My mother-in-law, Mrs. Thompson, was the next to go. After all our trouble with her during those early years, she had mellowed out considerably and had become very fond of her grandchildren. I think she even became very fond of me because I had given her several grandchildren including many boys who would carry on her husband's name and line. She still remained a formidable woman up to the very end. She was in her mid- seventies, and still played a major role in the Mothers' Union at Holy Trinity Church and in the diocese in general. She was also a leading member of the Dorcas Association and the United Churchwomen. She therefore had a splendid funeral. The church was packed, and the choir was in attendance, since she had been a sideswoman in her day. Of course, the Mothers' Union from the

entire diocese, as well as the United Churchwomen and the Dorcas Association were also there in force. She was buried in the same vault as her late husband at Kissy Road cemetery.

Josephine's mother, Mrs. Letitia Freeman, also went, as did Eugene's parents, Mr. Thomas Pratt and Mrs. Susan Pratt.

After very humble beginnings as a shoemaker, Mr. Pratt, as we have seen, made some money as a trader, and he and his wife moved into their new one-story concrete house along Circular Road. Mr. Pratt was the first to go, but a calamity overwhelmed the family about six months after his death. A careless child in the wooden house next door had inadvertently started a fire. It spread down the street and burned the Pratt house completely down. In her old age, therefore, Mrs. Pratt was left without a home. She never recovered from that calamity. She moved to join her son and Annie in the house at Sanders Street, and they did their best to lift her spirits up, but she passed away about a year after her husband's death.

Of the entire older generation, therefore, only my mother survived. She lived up to the great age of one hundred and one, before she passed away.

A most significant development during this period was the complete transformation of Josephine. Remember I told you that after Eugene kicked her out of his house, she'd vowed vengeance and was determined to rise again. She was true to her word. Even before her mother passed away, she'd become a very active, successful businesswoman. With incredible purposefulness, she converted part of the lower floor of her mother's house at Circular Road and stocked it with ladies hats, shoes, dresses and other accessories. Her brother in England and his wife were her market contacts and ensured that goods were regularly shipped to Josephine in Freetown to stock her store.

I remember calling at the store one Wednesday morning. I just stood there, marveling at its elegance.

"How did you do it, Josephine?" I asked.

"Well," she replied, "my father left me a bit of money, and I used that as capital to convert the bottom floor and buy stock. Some people told me that my business wouldn't succeed because the store was not in the center of town. As if every business needs to be in the center of town to be successful! The way I look at it, you just need to locate your business where there's demand for your goods. And there are lots of women in this area and, indeed, in the whole of Freetown, who need the goods that I am selling. I merely have to make sure that the prices are right and that I keep up with the latest and most desirable fashions. That way I am able to compete with the bigger stores in the center of town. My sister-in-law in London helps me to keep abreast of the latest developments in the fashion world by observing what is happening in England and sending me catalogues. She regularly goes to sales and places like Petticoat Lane in London where she can buy things cheaply, and ships the goods to me. So I keep my store well stocked, as you can see, with the latest in Ladies' accessories; and I can sell them at much more reasonable prices than the bigger stores in town. Moreover, I can order things that are not available in the store by showing women the catalogues and getting them to select the things they want. That way I can even order things like crockery and cutlery for people. My business is flourishing and I am making a lot of money. Besides, I have found an excellent way of keeping myself occupied."

"Come round this way and let me show you something," she said.

She took me to the back of the store and showed me a most elegant blue silk dress mounted on a dummy. "It's exactly your size. Try it on."

"Josephine," I said, "I didn't come intending to buy a new dress. I don't want to be extravagant. Mr. T and I are trying to save as much money as we can for the house."

"Just try it on," she said sweetly.

I went to a small fitting room at the back of the store and put on the dress. Believe me, it fitted me perfectly. When I looked in the mirror, I could not believe how elegant I was.

"It is you to a 'T,' " Josephine said. "It will be absolutely suitable for New Year's Sunday, Easter Sunday, or a wedding. You could stand in the store and model that dress for me. It was made for you."

"How much is it?" I asked. I was sorely tempted.

"It is only five pounds," she replied, "but I'll make it four pounds for a friend. You don't need to pay me now, if you don't have that much on you; you're a friend. You could bring the money later."

I ended up buying the dress, and Mr. T, as well as everyone else, was full of admiration when I wore it for the first time the next New Year's Sunday.

That shows you what an excellent businesswoman Josephine turned out to be. She soon revealed a kind of latent charm that few people, including herself, would have guessed she possessed, and she could charm anyone who entered her store to buy something before they left. She became known throughout Freetown as "hat-hat" Pratt, and she was able to compete quite favorably with any of the leading stores in the center of town.

She once said to me, "Do you know, Priscilla, I think Eugene's kicking me out of his house was a blessing in disguise. It's made me discover my true potential. It's made me realize that I can be successful and happy, without the help of a man. I have done it all without the help of any man. I have become successful, not through a man, but in spite of a man. Even if Eugene were now to go down on his bended knees and ask me to go back to his house, I would not go. And I do not care whether he divorces me or not, because I do not want to marry again. What use do I have for a man? I have my freedom, I am successful, and I have status in the community. I even have men friends now and then, just as he has Annie in his house. If a man can do it, why can't a woman? Men have their uses in that way. But I can choose whom I go with and dump them when I want. Their friendship is not essential to my existence or my success."

I always knew that my friend Josephine was a woman of spirit, but, I must say, I was lost in admiration of her boldness and her achievement. You had to give it to her. While Annie had hardly been able to do anything without a man, Josephine had defied the odds and become successful. Maybe she was helped by the little sum of money her father left her and by her contacts in England, but still I had to admit that she would not have got anywhere without her strong will.

The ladies' accessories business was not the only one that Josephine went into. She soon discovered that drink bottling companies were anxious to buy back the empty bottles after people had drunk the beverages they contained. So, she started buying back empty bottles from the public and selling them to the companies. She built a special shed at the back of the house where she stacked the boxes and cartons of bottles until the beverage companies came to collect them. She soon became known throughout Freetown not only as "hat-hat" Pratt, but as "Mammy Bottle." The bottle business, like the ladies' accessories business, turned out to be extremely lucrative.

Josephine thus became one of the best-known women in all of Freetown. She'd become a leading member of the Annie Walsh Old Girls' Association. She was also a leading member of the Young Women's Christian Association. She was very much in demand as a Grand Chief Patron or Grand Chief Receiver whenever women's organizations had their thanksgiving services and wanted women of substance to perform those roles. Although her own marriage had turned out disastrously, she was often asked to be godmother for weddings, and on these occasions she would throw lavish parties at her house. It almost seemed as though she needed to be free of Eugene in order to blossom.

One regret Josephine had, however, was that she was never able to have a child. It seems as if she even tried to conceive a child after the separation from Eugene. But apparently that dreadful miscarriage after that terrible fight with Eugene had taken its toll; she would never be able to have children.

"That is my only regret," she once said to me. "You might think me a hard woman, Priscilla, but I am a woman nevertheless. I would've loved to have children, not in order to ensure my immortality or carry on any line, the sort of thing men rave about, but for the simple pleasure of cradling a baby in these arms. You are so lucky, Priscilla. You and your Mr. T have seven superb children to leave your property to when you pass away. I am accumulating all this wealth and property. Whom do I have to leave it all to when I die? It will have to go to relations. That is my one regret."

And what about Eugene and Annie? Sad to say, Eugene didn't make much progress. The United Africa Company, in which he had hoped to excel, was on its way out, so they weren't looking for competent Sierra Leoneans to promote to positions of great responsibility, as was the case with the Civil Service. Even if they were, it's doubtful whether Eugene would have been promoted. He had hoped to rise by making use of his contacts and his charm, not by efficiency, ability, and integrity. The European bosses who'd been fond of him were long gone, and the new ones didn't seem to have the same fondness for him. Besides, they too were about to take their exit.

His lifestyle had not enabled him to save for a house of his own, and, to crown it, his parents' house that he might have hoped to inherit, had burned down in that disastrous fire. It hadn't been insured, so there was no money to be got from any insurance company. All that was left to Eugene was the small piece of land on which the house stood.

One day I visited Eugene and Annie at the house on Sanders street. I found them both in the kitchen at the back of the house. Annie was frying plantains and putting them on a plate near her. But as soon as she finished frying a piece of plantain and put it on the plate, either she or Eugene would devour it at once. So when she finished frying the plantains there was nothing on the plate. They both giggled and we all three moved into the house. I wondered at the shabbiness of their lifestyle. Josephine, for all her faults, had managed to maintain Eugene's home in a state of comparative elegance. Annie, for all her sweetness of temper, apparently lacked the energy, and possibly ambition, to keep the home in a similar state of comfort. The linoleum carpet on the floor should have been changed at least a year ago; the table covers, window curtains, cushion covers, and door curtains, though not dirty, were of a rather cheap kind; there were no flowers on the tables, and the pictures and photographs could have done with some dusting. It was almost as though both Eugene and Annie had given up on life and had let their disappointments get the better of them. However, they seemed to be happy together. And from time to time, when Annie burst out into that infectious laughter of hers, the dimples in her cheeks would be enhanced, and one was able to recognize the beauty that had once made her such an object of admiration.

If Eugene hoped that he'd be able to have children with Annie, he too was disappointed. As in Josephine's case, maybe it was Annie's abortion that had taken its toll. So Eugene's mother, Susan Pratt, unfortunately went to her grave without the grandchildren that she had so looked forward to, at least grandchildren that her son acknowledged and that she knew. Nonetheless, as I have said, if Eugene and Annie were disappointed, they at least did not

176

let their disappointment show, and they seemed reasonably happy and contented with each other.

Eugene still had difficulty controlling his violent temper, particularly when he'd had too much to drink. Surprisingly, this never affected his relations with Annie, but it affected his relations with members of his church. He quarreled with the minister in charge of College Chapel, where he had been a society steward. As a result, he transferred to Buxton Methodist Church. In any case, as he said, Buxton Church was closer to Sanders Street and was more convenient for him. But he could not get along with the officers there, either.

One Sunday, when one of the organizations was having a Thanksgiving service, a visitor calmly walked up to Eugene and asked him for a hymnbook. But instead of giving him the book as he was supposed to do, Eugene took one look at the man, decided that he was a man of no importance, hissed, and walked away. Unfortunately for him, the man was a very senior teacher at one of the leading secondary schools and an important member of his own church. He remained quiet during the service, but at the end he went up to the Minister-in-charge, the Senior Society Steward, and the Superintendent, and in a rage told them of Eugene's despicable behavior toward him.

"What are those hymnbooks for if they are not supposed to be given to visitors on occasions such as this?" the man fumed. "I was invited to your church. I'm an Anglican and I don't have the Methodist hymnbook. Had I been a Methodist, I would have brought along my own Methodist hymnbook. But I am a visitor to your church and the books were intended for visitors. I politely asked your man if I could have a book, but instead of giving me one, he looked at me as if I were a piece of shit, hissed, and walked away. This is the very last time I come to your church. Even if a close relation of mine is getting married here I will tell him or her that I will meet them at the reception, but I will not come to the ceremony in this church. If a funeral service is being held for a relative of mine in this church, I will wait for the corpse outside or wait at the cemetery, but I will never set foot inside this church again."

The Minister-in-charge and the Superintendent were good friends of the offended man. They tried to mollify him, but he refused to calm down. A woman who had been standing near the man in the church bore witness to the truth of his complaint. The Superintendent called Eugene up and started to admonish him. Eugene said he was not aware that the offended man was a person of such importance.

"Does a visitor have to be important in order to be given a hymnbook? That is a most unchristian attitude. Mr. Pratt, you are suspended from your position as society steward until further notice."

Eugene was flabbergasted. From what you know of him, you'd have realized that he attached great importance to position and status. Had he known that the man in question was a person of such importance, he'd probably have behaved toward him with servility, rather than contempt. Now, he was shamed in front of the whole world, and everyone was upbraiding him. In addition, he was about to lose his own important position as society steward. Had he been wise he would have remained quiet and allowed the whole thing to blow over, and he would probably have been reinstated after a suitable interval. But his reaction at being thus humiliated and chastised was to fly into a tantrum and insult the offended man, the minister and the superintendent, and mouth obscenities.

"Damn you," he shouted at the Superintendent. "Who the bloody hell do you think you are? Do you think that because they made you Superintendent you have the right to chastise me in public? Damn you and your church. You can take your society stewardship and stuff it you know where."

With that, he stormed out of the church compound, still mouthing obscenities too fearful to repeat. That put an end to his association with Buxton Church, indeed to his association with any church at all. He stopped going to church, and he stopped paying his church dues. He swore that if they thought he would be a slave to anyone wearing a dog collar, they had another thought coming.

CHAPTER 11

Just before Sierra Leone became independent, Mr. T finished building this magnificent house, and we moved into it. I daresay you have seen what a beautiful house it is. Though I can no longer see, I know that even after so many years it has not lost its charm and beauty. Many modern houses have been built in this area since then, but at the time, this was one of only two modern houses in the vicinity. It was extremely well built and we had chosen the interior and exterior colors very, very carefully. Do you know it has six bedrooms and two bathrooms with all the modern conveniences, a large parlor with a large dining area, a large modern kitchen, a pantry, a store and a garage? It also has verandahs upstairs and downstairs from which you can get a very good view of the estuary of the Sierra Leone River, and even of the Atlantic Ocean. It also has a large patio upstairs above the garage.

We built this with our large family in mind, so that if those of our children who were studying in the United kingdom wanted to come and stay with us on their return, there would be room enough for everyone. It was built on ten lots, so there is a very large compound with all kinds of fruits trees. We have mangoes, paw-paws, guavas, apples, coco-nuts, palm trees, pineapples, coffee, chocolate, plums, and the list goes on. Did you notice the beautiful garden in

front with all kinds of flowers and palms? There is God's plenty here. It is a kind of Paradise.

We also have a well at the back of the house, so that if at any time there is water shortage in Freetown, we have our own supply. It is in a pleasant suburb of the city where there is not too much noise, and there is always a wonderful breeze blowing from the sea.

And you know, Mr. T completed the construction without owing anyone a single cent. He had used his savings and the monthly housing allowance he received as a senior civil servant. So he could truly say, "this house is mine."

I will never forget the day we moved into it. You should have heard the expressions of admiration and praise from friends and relations alike.

"Congratulations, Bernard," said one of Mr. T's first cousins. "You're truly a man-child. You have performed God's wonder."

"I'd never dreamt," said another cousin, "that any relative of mine would build and live in such a magnificent house."

"The little chick that will grow into a big cock," said Mr. T's very old aunt, "can be spotted from the very first day it's hatched. You can always tell that a wedding will be sweet from the bachelor's eve. I knew from the time that Bernard was little more than a toddler, when I used to hold him in my arms, that he was destined for great things. And I have not been disappointed."

"Thank you, thank you, thank you," said Mr. T, beaming with pride, "but don't forget my wife, Priscilla. A man can never complete a big project like this without a good woman beside him."

"That is word," said another relative. "A good wife is the greatest blessing that a man can have. Priscilla, we thank you for the support you have given to our brother here. You've been a tower of strength for him. God bless you!"

Needless to say that my head also swelled with pride.

Soon after we moved into our new house, about a year before independence, a singular honor was conferred on Mr. T that was another source of great pride and a vindication of the years of devoted service he had given to this country, especially in the Ministry of Works. He was named in the New Year's honors list which, since Sierra Leone was still a member of the British Empire, actually came from Buckingham Palace. He was to become a Member of the Most Excellent Order of the British Empire, M.B.E.

The award was completely unexpected, and you can just imagine our joy when Mr. T's name was read over the Sierra Leone Broadcasting service, and the citation stated that the award was in recognition of his distinguished and devoted service as a civil servant. I know that today, in these days of independence, some people tend to scoff at these awards, suggesting that they indicated that we Sierra Leoneans, particularly those from the Western area, were sycophantic members of the British Empire and lacked that consciousness of African nationalism that was to lead so many African countries to independence from the British. Some people scornfully refer to the O.B.E, Officer of the Order of the British Empire, as "Obedient Boy of the Empire." Well, let them scoff.

I only know that the award of the M.B.E. to my Mr. T was more than deserved. He had truly been a tireless, devoted, efficient, and honest employee of the government. I only wish that we had the same integrity, efficiency, and devotion in the government service today. Sierra Leone would be a much better place.

The award was actually made at Government House, now State House, at a formal and very imposing ceremony in April. I accompanied my Mr. T, who was dressed in his best dark suit. I wore the blue floral dress that I had bought from Josephine's store, with matching hat and shoes. I was very elegant beside my husband. Of course, in those days, we had to wear gloves when we went to formal occasions at Government House, so I bought some white gloves for the occasion from Josephine. You can imagine my pride when Mr. T's name was called, the citation was read, and he matched up to the dais to receive his decoration from the Governor himself! Truly, he had been diligent in his business, and he stood before kings, or the representative of the Queen. This was the culmination of all his years of honest hard work.

After the presentation of the awards, there was a kind of garden party in the grounds of State House, during which the guests mingled with each other and the recipients of awards. Everyone who was anybody in Sierra Leone was there. I knew then that my Mr. T had truly arrived. It was not the only time we went to a garden party at State House; since Mr. T was in the Senior Civil Service, we were invited on two other occasions, one just before he retired from the service.

About this time, our two eldest sons returned from their studies in the United Kingdom. Junior qualified as a Doctor of Medicine at Manchester University and returned home in 1959 to join the government medical service. Our second eldest got a Ph.D. in Civil Engineering from London University, and he returned in 1960 to join the faculty of Fourah Bay College as a lecturer in Engineering. Their father and I were swelling with pride, as we boarded the Elder Dempster Lines ships that were still running in those days to welcome them home. The joyful celebrations went on in our home for the rest of the day. My third son was, by then, a student in the United States of America, the fourth was in the sixth form at the Sierra Leone Grammar School, and the fifth would do his GCE "O" level examination, the following year. All my five sons went to university and did very well indeed. The two girls also did very well in their own way and eventually held very responsible positions.

One became a banker and the other a confidential Secretary in a major corporation. Mr. T and I were indeed blessed in our children. Children are indeed a gift from God. As the good book says, "Happy is the man that hath his quiver full of them."

As you know, independence came in 1961, and we all welcomed it with joy. The country was then quite different from what it has since become. There was not so much tribal animosity, and Freetown was, by no means, as congested as it is now. The cost of living was very low. It was two Leones to the pound, back then. Can you believe it? We didn't know anything about foreign exchange. In those days, you could take Leones to England and change them for pounds at Thomas Cook's. In fact, many people went to England on holiday, and we didn't know anything about visas and things like that. As a senior civil servant, Mr. T had the opportunity of going to England every two years on paid leave, with his passage being paid by the government. Many senior civil servants made use of the opportunity. My Mr. T, however, refused to go because, as he said, living in England for three months every two years would involve considerable expense, and he wanted to save as much money as possible toward the construction of his house. I supported this decision, of course. I know a number of senior civil servants who went to England on paid leave and never had shelters above their heads that they could call their own homes when they retired, whereas we were able to create this paradise.

My husband retired from the government service, the year after independence. He received a handsome gratuity and was entitled to a decent monthly pension from the government, on which we were able to live quite comfortably. A very pleasant retirement party was also held in his honor, and he received several nice gifts from his colleagues. He was thus able to retire to his comfortable home and enjoy the well-deserved fruits of his labor. From then on, he decided to devote his attention to gardening, to his great hobbies of fishing and hunting, and to the affairs of his church and choir. It was indeed a very comfortable and pleasant existence.

At this time, however, tragedy arose among our little circle of friends. We had kept up our relations with Eugene and Annie, and were on very good terms with Josephine. But Josephine adamantly refused to visit Eugene and Annie, and they never went to visit her. Their estrangement, however, did not prevent us being on good terms with all three of them. We knew that they all had their faults, and each of them, in some degree, shared responsibility for the estrangement. We tried to reason with them as often as we could, but we weren't judgmental. "We are Christian people," Mr. T said, "and the Christian duty is to be a peacemaker. "Blessed are the peacemakers," said Mr. T, quoting the Sermon on the Mount, "for they shall be called the children of God." So we did our best to reconcile their differences. When that failed, we still kept up our association with them.

One Sunday afternoon, Mr. T and I were sitting in our verandah, after lunch, when we saw Annie hastily walking up the street, toward our house. From the way she hurried, we recognized immediately that she was not merely coming to pay a routine visit.

"I hope there hasn't been a quarrel between her and Eugene," said Mr. T. "I don't know that I'm in the mood to settle a dispute on this God's Sunday."

"Well," said I, "we'll soon know what it is. But I hope to God it's not anything that will bring great distress to Annie. Heaven knows, she's suffered enough already. Of the three of us who started as great friends at Sissy Dinah's, she's the only one who doesn't seem to have made much progress. She's the only one who never married, and up to this very moment does not seem to have much security for the future."

We soon let Annie into the house.

"Bernard," she said, reluctantly taking the chair we offered her, "you must come and help. I don't know whom to turn to. I think Eugene is seriously ill, and he will not take my advice," she said.

"I'm very sorry to hear that," said Mr. T. "Of course, I'll do whatever I can. What is it?"

"For the past two months," she said, "he has not been able to pass water properly. At first he kept it to himself, until I noticed that whenever he came out of the toilet he was squinting very badly. I also noticed that he was getting up very frequently to go and pass water. At times he would do so several times during the night. But you know how proud he is. He wouldn't confide in me until I asked him about it. When I finally got it out of him, I told him that he should see a doctor, but he said that it was probably some small infection and that it would pass. I noticed he was taking some patent medicine that someone had obviously recommended, and about a week ago, I noticed he was drinking something out of a small brown bottle, which was probably something that some local herbalist had given him.

"But the condition seemed to persist. Of course, he refused to discuss all the details with me; he probably thought it's one of those men's ailments that he couldn't discuss in detail with a woman. This morning, I noticed he was in great anguish. When I asked him what was the matter, he didn't reply at all. He just rushed out of the bedroom and into the bathroom.

"I followed secretly, and heard his groaning through the door. When he came out, his face was badly contorted, and I noticed that his feet were swollen, and the odor that came from his mouth smelled like urine. I've been so worried. That's why I decided to lose no more time but to come ask you to go to him and give him advice. You know how stubborn he is, but he will listen to you."

"I am glad you came to me," said Mr. T. "I think I have an inkling about what might be the matter. If it's what I think, there is no time to lose. He will have to see a doctor. "

Mr. T immediately got dressed, and he and Annie got into his car and made their way toward town.

Mr. T later gave me the details of the condition he found Eugene in. He was really grunting in pain, so Mr. T decided that he should be taken to the hospital immediately. He had to brush aside Eugene's remonstrations. For some odd reason, Eugene thought it was shameful for him to go to the hospital with such a condition: that his manliness was at stake.

"I suspect, as I think you also suspect," Mr. T told him, "there's something the matter, not just with your bladder, but with your prostate. If that is the case, you need immediate attention. It's nothing to be ashamed of. That kind of thing affects many middle-aged men, and you are now past your mid fifties. But it is not something to be taken lightly."

Eventually, Eugene was persuaded to go to Connaught hospital. The Connaught hospital then, in the early sixties, was quite different from what it is now. It had not deteriorated so badly. There were still some good doctors and surgeons, some from India and some, in those early days of independence, even from the United Kingdom. Our own eldest son, Junior, was working there as a doctor, and Mr. T went straight to him. As soon as he heard Eugene describe his symptoms, he said without hesitation, "I have no doubt, Mr. Pratt, that you have prostate problems. We'll give you some medicine to relieve the pain and discomfort somewhat, but we'll also have to carry out some tests in order to find out the full extent of the problem. In any case, I think you'll eventually have to undergo a surgical operation."

In those days, people were mortally scared of going under a surgical operation. It was not that the surgeons weren't good. They were still very good in those days. But people were very scared of anything that seemed invasive, and in any case they couldn't be absolutely sure that the after-care would be up to standard. At times, everything depended on the after-care.

"Can't we avoid a surgical operation?" Eugene asked Junior.

"We try to avoid surgery ourselves, if possible, Mr. Pratt. We operate only if it is absolutely necessary. At the moment, our knowledge and the techniques available to us are such that with a condition like this, an operation is the only possibility. Your prostate gland is probably enlarged. That's why you're finding it difficult to pass water. Quite soon, we think, we'll be able to cure the condition with drugs that will shrink the prostate, so that a surgical operation won't be necessary. But those drugs are still being perfected and tested. Even in more advanced countries, the standard treatment for this condition is a surgical operation. Of course, that carries risks and has some consequences, but when it's all over, you'll be able to pass water again normally, and you won't be in any more pain."

Privately, however, Junior took Mr. T aside and said to him confidentially, "there are always two possibilities in cases like this. If it's only a matter of the enlarged prostate, we can operate and remove the prostate gland, and eventually the patient's condition will return to normal, that is, he will be able to pass water normally. However, I will have to warn him later that he will no longer be able to have children. He will still be able to function sexually, but since the prostate gland is responsible for the dissemination of the seeds that lead to the production of children, its removal will mean that he will not be able to have children any more, though at his age I don't suppose he wants to have any. For a few weeks after the operation he won't be able to pass water in the normal way; we'll have to fit him with a catheter, and

that can lead to discomfort and can be somewhat embarrassing. But it cannot be avoided."

"I don't know how he will take it," said Mr. T. "Eugene has always prided himself on his masculinity. He's had children, but he never acknowledged them and he had no children by his legal wife. I think that in his own warped way he was still hoping that somehow or other he'd still have a child that he can acknowledge and that would confirm his masculinity. Hmm! I don't know how he'll take it."

"Well," said Junior, "those are the consequences I was talking about. If we have to take out his prostate gland, having children will be impossible. But that's not the most serious possibility. We'll have to wait for the test results. It may be that what he's suffering from is not just an enlarged prostate gland, but cancer of the prostate. That is a much more serious condition, as is any cancerous condition. If it is cancer of the prostate gland, we'll certainly have to remove the prostate gland. But there's also the risk that the cancer might have spread to other organs. He should not have delayed coming to see us."

"Of course," Junior continued, "I haven't told him about this possibility yet, because I don't want to cause unnecessary anxiety."

The preliminary tests were carried out, and Eugene had to resign himself to a surgical operation, though he complained bitterly about the diminution of his masculinity. My friend Annie was beside herself with worry and anxiety. Though Eugene hadn't always treated her well, he had been her first love. And though he'd never married her, she felt herself, in a sense, married to him. Besides, she was now entirely dependent on him for sustenance. Their last few years together had been tolerably happy. What on Earth would she do if anything happened to him?

I tried to comfort her: "Put everything in the hands of God," I said to her. "We'll all keep praying for you and Eugene every day. God will see you through this. Sometimes God gives us these trials to test us. As human beings, we can't expect to avoid our share of troubles, but God never gives us burdens that are too heavy for us to bear."

Eugene was admitted to the surgical ward, and the date for the operation was set. Junior used his good offices and arranged for an excellent surgeon to carry out the operation.

Things really were much better in those days. We didn't have to take our own bed linen to the hospital, as we do now, and we didn't have to bribe nurses and attendants and even pay surgeons in advance, before they'd touch a patient. Drugs were also much cheaper. The hospital itself was much, much cleaner. There were still standards in those early days of independence. Hospitals looked like hospitals, not like prisons or cesspools. Doctors and nurses did not shout at patients or refuse to have anything to do with them unless they were given large sums of money in advance. I remember all of us going to Eugene's ward, the morning of the operation. Although he hadn't been going to church for some time after the quarrel with the authorities at Buxton Church, Eugene asked Mr. T to say some prayers for him, and Mr. T did so eloquently. After that, we saw him wheeled into the operating theater, and we waited anxiously for the outcome.

After the operation was done and he had regained consciousness, we visited Eugene in the Intensive Care Unit. He looked drowsy and hardly recognized us. The nurses assured us that this was normal after an operation. But what scared the life out of me, and almost sent Annie into tears, was a tube leading to a plastic bag attached to his side. The nurse informed us that this was the catheter and its bag. Considering the nature of the operation, she said, Eugene would not be able to pass water in the normal way for about three weeks. His urine would collect in the catheter bag, and that would have to be emptied every so often. This was normal in this kind of operation. What was even more important was the after-care. They were trying to ensure that the nurses and attendants observed scrupulous standards of cleanliness, so that no infection would set in. Quite often after an operation, she said, complications arose, not because the surgeons had not done their job properly, but because of inadequate and insanitary after care.

Eugene remained in the intensive care unit for about a week and was then moved back to the surgical ward. He seemed to be making great progress. He was already conversing quite spiritedly with visitors, and he gave the impression of someone who had been to the gates of hell and back. He was, in fact, quite jovial. Annie's spirits had also lifted considerably. She was beginning to look forward to having her man back in the house in another couple of weeks.

"God is great," she said. "Those who shouldn't die, will not die. God answers prayers."

"I told you to leave everything in His mighty hands," I said. "He will make everything work together for good. Now, you must get ready to nourish Eugene back to health with tasty soups and succulent dishes. I am sure you are up to that."

"Don't you worry, my sister," she said. "I did not go to Sissy Dinah's sewing school for nothing. Leave that to me."

Eugene's catheter was removed about two weeks after the operation. He was now passing water normally and was discharged and allowed to go home. He was, however, still groggy on his legs and had lost a good deal of weight. Annie swore to us that she'd take good care of that with her excellent cooking.

The day after Eugene was discharged, Junior visited us and said privately to Mr. T, "Dad, it would have been unwise to trouble Mr. Pratt with this information, but the operation revealed that he had prostate cancer."

"Angels in heaven!" said Mr. T. "Then he is under a death sentence. Poor Eugene!"

"I wouldn't put it like that exactly," said Junior. "The operation has taken care of the cancerous prostate gland. It all depends on whether the cancer has spread to other organs. If that is the case, then his chances are not very good. It was not possible to ascertain that during the operation. We have told him to report for follow-up tests, to make sure everything is going well, because we did not want to scare him and tell him of the possibility of cancer."

Two weeks after being discharged from the hospital, Eugene was once more in the most excruciating pain. Mr. T was called once more to rush him to the hospital in his car, and after some examinations, it was confirmed that the cancer had spread to other organs. In those days, doctors in Sierra Leone did not tell terminal patients their true situation. They gave Eugene the impression that this was just the aftermath of the operation to remove the prostate gland and that maybe some infection had set in, but they were doing their best to take care of it. Privately, however, Junior confided to Mr. T that the cancer had spread to other organs and that there was no hope. They would merely try to keep Eugene as comfortable as possible until the end.

I burst into tears when Mr. T came and told me the news. I suppose I was crying, not so much for Eugene, as for Annie. What would she do now? She had no children and very few relatives. Those relatives were hardly able to take care of themselves, let alone someone else. Also, I didn't think that Eugene was in a position to leave her much. The house they lived in was not their own. Annie would almost certainly not be able to keep up the payment of the rent, and she would have to move out. Even her mother's house had been rented. She would literally have nowhere to go. Whatever would she do?

Eugene died in great agony in the hospital, three weeks later. Annie was at his bedside as he died. She then left the hospital after the corpse had been taken to the mortuary, and made her way on foot to the house on Sanders Street, shouting and wailing all the way. As she reached the junction of Sanders Street and Krootown Road, she shouted out even louder: "Fire oh, fire! Neighbors of Sanders Street, come to my rescue. Fire has consumed our house. Eugene Pratt is dead. Fire has consumed our house. Fire, oh, fire!"

Mr. T and I heard of Eugene's death soon after it happened, and we made our solemn way to Annie's house to condole with her and give whatever help we could toward the funeral arrangements. We knew Annie had virtually nothing. Even if Eugene had savings that could be used toward the funeral expenses, we were sure he'd told Annie nothing of them. Eugene had no children who would now take charge of his funeral. He had some relatives, cousins with whom he had kept on fairly good terms, but they weren't very well off, and some of them, as Mr. T used to say, didn't even have their heads screwed on right, and would be in no condition to make adequate funeral arrangements.

It was quite clear that the burden of making the arrangements would fall on Mr. T, after consultation with Annie and, perhaps, some of the relatives. Fortunately, Eugene had died while still in the employment of the United Africa Company, and though that company was much diminished, they were bound to make some substantial contribution toward his funeral. In any case, they'd owe Eugene some kind of gratuity or severance pay, so some of that could go toward the funeral expenses.

Mr. T was discussing all this with two or three of the relatives when a storm was heard outside. There was obviously some commotion. By then, the house was full of people, and there were also quite a few outside.

"It is his wife," we heard some people say. "She has arrived." And then the thunder broke.

"So my one, true and legal husband died, and no one thought it fit to go and inform me. All during his illness, nobody thought it fit to go and inform me. Well, I have arrived. I am his wife. His true and legal wife! And I am going to take charge."

Yes, it was Josephine who had arrived. I had thought that after their years of estrangement, she would not even bother to appear at the funeral and would allow him to be buried by others. She would want to play no part in his final rites. I was very much deceived. She now stormed into the house like one of the furies.

She had put on quite a bit of weight since her business had started to prosper, and she now looked even tall and majestic. As she strode into the parlor, pushing her voluminous bosom in front of her like the Venus De Milo, she was a veritable virago who defied anyone in heaven or on earth to challenge her right.

"Well I am his true and legal wife," she re-emphasized. "I am now the only one who has any right in this house. I am going to take charge of everything, and I dare anyone to challenge me. They will have to answer for it in court. I know the law in these matters as well as anyone else, and I dare anyone to challenge my right. I have come to bury my husband, as his one and only and true and legal wife, and I have the right to ask anyone who says 'no' to me to get out."

"No one will challenge your right," said Mr. T in a calm voice. He intended to mollify her. "In fact, we were just wondering how to proceed with the funeral arrangements. Now that you have arrived, you can most certainly take charge, and we will be only too happy to do what we can to help you."

"I am glad to hear that, Bernard," she said. "I was sure that you, as a man of the world, would see reason."

"In fact," said Mr. T, "we're delighted that you have arrived, because there are financial implications. A funeral, as you are aware, is a costly business, and Annie has no money. Eugene doesn't seem to have had any savings; we were on the brink of going to ask the United Africa Company to help, but you are certainly in a position to give him a decent funeral."

Mr. T, in his innocence, thought that Josephine Pratt had deliberately come to ensure that her husband had a decent funeral. We knew of several such occurrences in the past when, after years of estrangement, the wife turned up as the dear grieving wife, dressed in black, at the somber and grand funeral of her husband. Perhaps that was how Josephine intended to behave. We were in for a rude shock.

"I shall bury him in the way I see fit," she said, "and no one will question my right."

Josephine then sat down in the best chair in the parlor. Annie went and sat close to her and said, "As you know, I don't have much experience with these things. I leave these matters to men. Bernard says that he will give all the help he can. There is so much to be done."

Josephine's reaction exploded like a thunderbolt. She put both her hands on to the two edges of the chair, raised her massive shoulders, pushed her great bosom forward, looked at Annie as though she were the vilest creature in the whole of creation, and said to Mr. T in a voice full of contempt, "and who is this person who dares to come and talk to me about my husband's funeral?"

"What do you mean?" asked Mr. T. "This is your friend Annie who has been living with Eugene, all this while. We will need details such as where Eugene's suits and other clothes are, in order to make proper preparations, and Annie can give us that information."

"Did you say friend?" Josephine bawled out. "No, you must mean the harlot who's been living with Eugene, pretending to be his wife and depriving me of my rightful position in this house. No friend would do that to another woman. What friend contrives to get a man to drive out his true and lawful wife, to disgrace and humiliate her in public, so that she could come and install herself in the wife's rightful position? No, this is no friend. This is just a kept harlot."

"Come on, Josephine," I said. "You know that it wasn't Annie's fault that Eugene drove you out of the house. You know that it was well after he'd asked you to leave the house that Annie came and stayed with him. Let's not go over all that again. It will only bring back painful memories. The thing to do now is to make arrangements for Eugene's funeral."

By this time poor Annie, weak creature that she was, had burst into tears.

"Don't you try to put in a word for her, Priscilla," said Josephine. "You don't know what a Jezebel, what a snake in the grass this woman is. All the while, she was pretending to be my friend, but she was secretly plotting to get Eugene to throw me out of the house, so that she could get what she thought was her rightful position as the woman in Eugene's house. She never forgave me for being the one that Eugene married. As if I was the one who forced Eugene to lead me up to the altar! She was always plotting my downfall. Well, now the shoe is on the other foot. I am the one who now has the upper hand. I am the true and lawful wife, and I am asking this harlot to get out of my house this instant."

At this Josephine stood up to her full height, and, for a moment, I thought she was going to lay a heavy hand on Annie. "Come on, get out of this house this instant. You have no place here. Eugene did not marry you. You were nothing but a harlot here. You have no more right here than any of the sympathizers who are sitting outside. I will not allow you to remain inside this house one minute longer. Get out and sit in the compound like any ordinary sympathizer, for that is all you are."

As you can imagine we were all shocked by Josephine's venomous words, and the drastic measures she planned to adopt. Mr. T tried to reason with her; he thought that, at least, she would listen to him because he was a man of some importance in the community, not to mention a true friend.

"Please Josephine," he said, "it's not a good thing to cause dissension in a house of mourning. The news will soon spread all over town and we will all be disgraced. It will not show any respect for the dead. At least, for Eugene's sake, let us maintain peace and tranquility until the funeral, and then we can sort all these problems out."

"I do not care two hoots for respect of the dead," she shouted. "Did he show any respect for me? Why should I show any respect for him? Why should I revere his memory? Anyway, all this is his fault. If he had continued to live with me, he wouldn't have died like a dog. But he kicked me out of his house, disgraced me in public like a prostitute, and called me senjago. This is the result of it all. As a man sows, so let him reap. It is his works that are following him. Now, I am the one who will have to come and bury him, and I will bury him, but this woman will not remain in this house one minute more. Let her get out of this house this instant. I cannot stand the sight of her. Get her out of my sight, or I will get the police to come and remove her. Let her go into the compound like any other sympathizer."

It was obvious that Josephine was determined and was not to be deflected from her purpose. Some of Eugene's relatives tried to intervene, but they were not very important people, and they saw that they carried no weight. If Mr. T was unsuccessful in persuading Josephine to change her mind, how could they succeed?

In any case, no one disputed that Josephine had right on her side. She was still the legal wife. There weren't any children, and only she had any right in that house. So, Annie, not wanting to create any further difficulties or cause further uproar, got up herself, and went outside, in a flood of tears.

People who came to the house of mourning to sympathize with Annie for the death of her man were surprised to find her sitting outside. The more people who came, and they were many, the more her tears flowed. She could not have felt more humiliated. If she had thought, at any time during the relationship with Eugene, that she had no real rights, it was now forcefully and painfully brought home to her. She even had to ask some people to ask Josephine's permission, on her behalf, to go into the house, and into what had been her bedroom, to select a dress to wear to the funeral.

I went outside the house and sat close to Annie to comfort her.

"My sister," I said, "I m so sorry for the way things have turned out. I thought, all this time, that Josephine was our friend. Heaven knows the three of us go back a very long way. Why, I was going to ask both of you to be my chief bridesmaids. How can she treat you like this? But take surrur; God is above. He will decide everything."

"I knew that Josephine didn't like me very much," Annie replied. "Throughout our relationship, she has done everything in her power to hurt me and make me feel inferior. First she took my man away from me. If that wasn't enough, she has now humiliated me like this. This is what it means to be poor. But God is in his heaven. He is his own interpreter and he will make it plain."

I remember now that, on one occasion, years before this, Mr. T had said, "I've tried to reason with Eugene to make up his mind about Josephine. 'If you no longer wish to be reconciled with her,' I said, 'then divorce her. You can then properly marry Annie and make her your wife. If you don't divorce Josephine, she will remain your legal wife and if, God forbid, anything were to happen to you, all the right will be on her side, and she will come and bury you as she wishes. If she decides to put your corpse naked into the earth without clothes and without a coffin, to bury you like a dog, in fact, she will be well within her rights, and no one can stop her. Make up your mind what you want to do with her.' But he didn't listen to me. No doubt, he thought that if he divorced Josephine, there would be pressure on him to marry Annie, and why should he marry Annie, when, as they were, he had all the privileges of a married man without the legal obligations?"

Now it seemed that everything Mr. T foresaw was about to come to pass.

Mr. T asked Josephine what arrangements he should make for a coffin. Josephine said that she'd already asked an undertaker to go to the mortuary and measure Eugene's body in order to make a suitable coffin. So, that was already in hand. Mr. T mentioned the need to make an announcement over the Broadcasting Service. Josephine said there would be just one announcement, the day before the funeral. She would take care of that.

"But if there is only one announcement," Mr. T said, "a lot of people will not know. Eugene knew a lot of people, and they'll all want to attend his funeral. Besides, the members of his Masonic lodge will want to officiate before, during, and after the funeral service. They would have to know."

"Do you think it's my intention to give him a grand funeral?" Josephine asked. "I don't care if none of his fellow lodge members attend. That is their affair. I have told you: I will bury him as I think fit."

"What about the church?" Mr. T asked. "He hasn't been in touch with his church for some time and I am sure he is behind with his class dues. The church will want his arrears to be paid before they will agree to give him a fitting funeral service. Leave it to me. I know the minister-in-charge. I will go and ask him how much Eugene owes, settle the arrears, and then fix a suitable date for the funeral."

"You will do nothing of the kind," Josephine replied. "He has spent nothing on me for the last several years. Do you think I'm prepared to waste precious money settling his church arrears, so that he can have a grand funeral service in Buxton Church? Not on your life! We will drive with him straight from the house to the cemetery. If any minister feels like going to the graveside to say prayers, he may. But there will be no funeral service."

It was quite clear that almost everything that Mr. T had feared was coming true. Josephine was now in charge, and she was determined to give Eugene the plainest of funerals.

What the writer says is true: "Hell hath no fury like a woman scorned." Josephine had vowed deadly revenge, when Eugene threw her out of his house and humiliated her. I thought she'd forgotten about everything, after all these years. It wasn't enough that she had prospered in the meantime, and Eugene had hardly made any progress. It was clear that she now intended to have her full revenge. She would bury Eugene like a dog.

Normally there would have been three obituary announcements a day until the day of the funeral. Once the arrangements had been finalized, the announcements on the last few days before the funeral would include all the information: a long list of relatives and friends of the deceased, the time of the vigil, the time of the laying-out in state, the time of the funeral, the church where the service was to be held, and the cemetery where interment was to take place. Where relevant, there would also be a long list of organizations that were expected to take part.

Eugene, for all his faults, had been a very sociable person and had a very wide circle of friends and acquaintances. Normally, hundreds of people would have been expected to attend his funeral, and Buxton Church would have been packed to capacity. There would have been some people standing outside. Though Eugene had quarreled with the minister-in-charge, the quarrel would easily have been forgiven if Mr. T had approached the minister and had settled the arrears of his church dues.

Since Eugene had been a society steward, the association of society stewards would have been in attendance, and the choir and several ministers would have officiated. As a member of one of the Masonic lodges, his body would have been laid in state in the temple of the lodge, dressed in his Masonic robes, and the lodge would have been in attendance both at the church and at the graveside. Several other lodges would also have attended. It ought to have been a very grand funeral.

Josephine, however, was determined that this should by no means be the case. There was only one announcement the night before the burial, and it was a very short one. It did not mention any relatives or friends. It simply mentioned the wife and the fact that interment would take place the following day at the King Tom cemetery. It did not even mention the time of the interment. Josephine clearly didn't want to have many people at the graveside, not even members of the Masonic lodge who would normally have to perform some final rites. The announcement did not mention a vigil, because there would be no vigil. It didn't mention a laying-out, because there would be no laying-out. It didn't mention the time and place of the funeral service, because there would be no funeral service. There would be no procession from the Masonic lodge to the church, and from the church to the cemetery, with a great crowd of mourners singing lustily behind the hearse. In fact, the announcement was itself meant to be a tremendous source of humiliation. Everyone listening would know that the corpse would be taken direct to the cemetery at some point during the day.

It was almost as if some pauper were being buried. Josephine's intention was that at a time of her own choosing the corpse would be put into the coffin, put into a lorry, driven to the cemetery, and buried like a dog. In vain, Mr. T and I, not to mention members of Eugene's family, tried to plead with her and remind her that Eugene had suffered enough during his illness, that he had also suffered because he had made little progress after their separation while she had gone from prosperity to prosperity, that it was undignified to punish a corpse, that a Christian should also have a spirit of forgiveness, that none of us knew how we were going to die and how we were going to be buried, that she should try to remember the past and those early days of marriage when they were happy together, that Eugene was a useful member of the United Africa Company and his colleagues at least would like to see their friend have a decent funeral, that she should at least have the fear of God in her heart, and that she would probably regret it after it was all over and she would be unable to undo what she had done. She remained inflexible. It was like talking to a brick wall. Her mind was made up. She would have her revenge, and for her revenge would be sweet.

Some of us gathered at the house at Sanders Street on the day of the funeral because we at least knew that the funeral would be that day, even if we didn't know when exactly it would be.

Suddenly, at about half past two, we saw a Ministry of Health lorry draw up outside the house, followed by a truck. Some men came out of the lorry and proceeded to take out a long object, wrapped in a red hospital blanket.

We quickly realized that it was Eugene's corpse. Annie let out a tremendous wail and could hardly be restrained. She gave true vent to her feelings, feelings that were exacerbated by the horribly shameful way in which Josephine intended to bury her man, a man with whom she had spent so many years together. I couldn't help crying myself. I was crying, not just for Eugene and Annie, though. I was also crying for Josephine, for the way in which she had exposed the uglier aspects of her character. And I cried for those moments we three had shared together at Sissy Dinah's establishment, those moments that were no more.

The men brought the body into the house and were instructed to take it into Eugene's bedroom, where it would be washed and made ready for burial. Josephine had hired two men for that purpose, and they went in after the corpse and started the business of preparing the body.

About an hour later, the men came out of the bedroom and said they were done. Josephine then instructed two men to take the coffin out of the truck and bring it into the house. Two upright chairs were arranged facing each other in the parlor; this was where the coffin was to be placed. I soon heard shouts of "Lord, have mercy!" coming from outside, and I realized why when the coffin was brought into the parlor and laid on those two chairs. It was the plainest and roughest coffin you can imagine. It was made of the cheapest wood. The wood had been hardly planed, let alone varnished. There was no name on the lid, and no brass handles on the sides. When the lid was removed, I noticed that the cheapest, white, shirteen material lined it.

But if we were horrified and surprised when we saw the coffin, we were in for greater horror when Eugene's corpse was brought out of the room to be put into the coffin. It was not dressed in a suit with a tie and gloves, as one would have expected; it was merely wrapped in an old, gray and white rough "country cloth," with only the face showing. Gasps of horror went round the room.

"But Josephine, this is an outrage," said Mr. T. "You cannot bury Eugene like this. He has several lovely dark suits, any one of which would be appropriate. This is not how we Creoles bury our dead."

"I have said that I will bury him precisely as I want to bury him," the virago replied. "And no one can stop me. I will not waste any suits on him; I would rather give the suits to charity. Close the coffin."

I suppose we were all too shocked to realize that no hymn had been sung and no prayers were said before the coffin was closed. Within a few minutes, Eugene's coffin was borne out of the house for the last time. Josephine went into a taxi she'd hired for the purpose, and Mr. T and I took Annie and two other relatives with us in our car. Those who could manage it, squeezed into the truck in which the corpse was placed, and we sped to King Tom Cemetery.

When we got there, we discovered that a few members of Eugene's Masonic lodge had somehow found out the time of the funeral and had turned up, though they were not in their regalia. They were standing by the graveside, and they asked to say a few prayers in private. We left them for a while to carry out their rites. Those were the only rites that were performed over Eugene's corpse. There was no minister of religion there. There were scarcely twenty people altogether by the graveside.

After the members of the lodge had finished we went back to the graveside. Would you believe it? Josephine actually took up a spade and threw some dirt in the traditional way on the coffin in the grave. Then she burst into tears:

"You threw me out of your house like a dog and kept me out for so many years. You forced me to do this. You are responsible, not me. You have done this to yourself."

So, Eugene was buried like a dog. I would not be surprised if, even to this day, there is no headstone marking the spot where he was buried.

After it was all over, I could not but wonder at the vindictiveness of the human heart. Yes, Eugene had his faults; yes, he had humiliated Josephine and driven her out of his house in the most terrible circumstances. But how could

Josephine have harbored so much hatred in her heart after so many years? Did she take satisfaction in her revenge? I wonder what was going on in her mind when she went back to her bed that night. Did she regret what she had done? Or did she say revenge is sweet? It also occurred to me that maybe after all these years we had not fully known Josephine. We knew she was a strong-minded woman, but we did not know she would descend to such depths. There was more to come.

After the burial and we all went back to the house at Sanders Street, she shouted out at Annie:

"Now collect all your things and move out of this house immediately. You will not spend one more night in this house. You have no business here."

"Where do you expect her to go?" asked Mr. T. "At least, allow her a few days to settle her affairs and make some arrangements."

"No," said Josephine. "She will not spend one more night in this house. She will leave immediately with her clothes. She must take only her clothes and any trinkets she has. She must not take any item of furniture, or any pots and pans, because I am sure they were bought by Eugene, and they now belong to me. I give her just one hour to get her things together and move out of this house."

After what we'd seen during those last few days, we knew it was pointless to argue. Annie packed her things and moved out of the house. I believe she went and stayed with some relatives. Soon after that, Josephine sold all the furniture, and gave the keys of the house to the landlord. Then, she then went back to her own very spacious house at Circular Road.

"It's wicked, very wicked," said Mr. T. "I did not know that Josephine had such a capacity for evil, because there's no other word for it; it's evil. Even if she was mad at Eugene, whom she succeeded in burying like a dog, why extend her revenge to Annie? After all, she was the one who first offended Annie by grabbing her fiancé. She should have thought of that. Suppose Annie had had the same kind of revengeful spirit and had contrived to have her killed, as some women would almost certainly have done, what would she have said? She at least owed it to Annie to be kind to her."

"I cannot believe it myself," I said. "It all seems like a kind of dream to me. I can't believe that Josephine, the godmother of one of my children, could behave like that. It is incomprehensible."

"You must realize," said Mr. T, "that this will be the end of any meaningful relations between us. During all these years we have been careful to maintain some kind of friendship with her. But after the way she's behaved, she cannot expect us to be close to her."

CHAPTER 12

After all these painful events, I did not see any of these my friends for some time. Murray Town, where we lived, was quite some distance from Central Freetown anyway, and it was not very likely that our paths would cross often. Mr. T and I concentrated on our watching the careers of our seven children, and trying to enjoy our retirement. I believe Annie went to stay with some relatives along Krootown Road.

We visited her once or twice during the weeks following Eugene's burial, and we noticed she was living in indescribable squalor. The house was much worse than the one at Sanders Street where she and Eugene had lived. It was an old, gray one-story wooden house with wooden windows, and the curtains, where there were curtains, looked as though they'd been rubbed on the dirt by a mischievous child and smothered all over with palm oil. There were holes in the wooden floor, and the boards creaked loudly as you walked on them. I looked up and saw that instead of a proper ceiling, there were mats overhead, but there weren't enough of them to cover the rafters and the rusty corrugated iron sheets that formed the roof. There must have been about twenty people living in that house, although I noticed only three bedrooms. There were obviously people living in the outhouses, outside.

There was no kitchen. Apparently, those who wanted to cook had to place their three firestones wherever in the yard they could find a space. I wondered what they did when it was raining. I dared not imagine what the toilet looked like. Far from having a room to herself, Annie had to share one with about three other people, some of whom were children. The house and the compound resounded with noise. At least three separate quarrels broke out among the children while we were there.

"Oh Annie," I said, "what's happened to you?"

"Ah! This is how you find me my sister," she replied. "I had nowhere to go when Josephine asked me to leave, so I had to come and manage here with my cousin. I'm trying to make arrangements to go and stay with my younger brother, but he lives with his woman and five children out in Waterloo. He does not have a job himself, and they merely manage by growing and selling vegetables and things like that. I believe the woman also makes cassava bread and fried fish that she sells to travelers in the lorry park. However, I suspect that their main occupation is making 'omole,' you know, illicit gin; and I would not be surprised if they also drink the stuff. That is why I've been reluctant to go over there and join them. That brother of mine has never done well, as you know."

"But will you be able to live in Waterloo, a village twenty miles away from Freetown, having lived in Freetown for so long?" I asked. "All your friends are in Freetown. You would almost have to begin again."

"But what am I to do? My cousin here has made me understand that my staying here is only temporary. In any case, can you imagine me living here permanently after what I've been used to? At least, living with a brother would be better than living with a cousin. Their house is not much better than this one, but there is more space, and I won't feel as if I am living in a zoo. Besides, I'll be able to make and sell my coco-nut and ginger cakes there. Here there is hardly any space to do anything, and if you put your wares out in the street to sell, you can be sure that sooner or later someone will steal them. So I think I will have to go. Anyway, I'll let you know, before I go."

We only visited Annie once more at the Krootown Road house. It's not that we were being snobbish, but more for her sake than ours. We could see that she was really ashamed that we had found her living in such squalid surroundings, and we did not wish to increase her discomfort. As was customary when there was a death in one's circle of friends or in the family, Mr. T and I had given Annie some money, but we were sure that, with no one to support her, it would soon be finished. When she visited us later at this house at Murray Town, we gave her some more money. She'd come to tell us that she would be leaving for Waterloo at the end of that week.

"I have been very ill, Priscilla, that is why I haven't been to see you before now," she said.

"I am sorry to hear that," I replied. "What was the matter?" I'd asked the question although I was by no means surprised that she had fallen ill. After all she'd been put though following Eugene's death, it would have been more surprising if she'd continued to be hale and hearty.

"I had a severe bout of malaria," she said. "The doctor also said that I was suffering from severe exhaustion. I was as weak as a dog and hardly able to walk. You know that the area in which I now live is very unsanitary and very unhealthy. One must have the constitution of a giant to stay there. All the money I had went on medicines. As soon as I got better, I decided I would have to go and stay with my brother. Maybe the air at Waterloo will be better."

"I am sorry for your troubles, Annie," I said, "but go with God. God will keep you. Who knows," I said, trying to be facetious and raise her spirits, "maybe you'll find some handsome man at Waterloo who will appreciate your beauty and your excellent cooking."

"Please don't laugh at me," she said. "When the beans were raw they didn't fill the basket. Do you think they'll fill it when they are dry? What man will look at me now? Maybe some divorced man or some widower looking for someone to cook his food, clean his house, and wash his clothes. But after what happened to me at Eugene's house, I'm not sure I want to go through that sort of thing again. I will keep quiet in my brother's house, take an interest in my nieces and nephews, and make and sell my coco-nut cakes and ginger cakes. That way, I'll be able to keep soul and body together, and keep myself occupied. Perhaps village life will suit me. Town life has not been good for me. Freetown is a wicked place."

"I am sorry for what you have suffered, Annie," I said. "Josephine treated you monstrously. Eugene had treated you badly, but he had, to a certain extent, made up for it. There can be no excuse for the way Josephine treated you. There is even less excuse for the way she treated the body of the dead. She didn't behave like a human being, let alone a Christian. I can't understand how anyone can be so wicked."

"That is why I say there are wicked people in Freetown, my sister," Annie said. "What did I do to Josephine that she should treat me like that? After all, she was the one who stole my man, in the first place, and condemned me to so many years of loneliness and suffering. Can you imagine how the fortunes of my family would have turned out if Eugene had married me? That Jezebel stole my husband from me. Had I been as wicked as she is, I would have gone to some medicine man and got her killed. But I'm a Christian, and I believe in forgiveness. It wasn't I who told Eugene to kick her out of his house; it was her own bad behavior that led to that. And even after that, I hesitated for quite a long time before I agreed to join Eugene at Sanders Street. Nonetheless, Josephine blamed me for everything and humiliated me like that, treated me like a dog when Eugene died. Can you imagine how I felt when people came to sympathize with me and found me sitting outside like a stranger, while she was installed inside like the true and loyal wife? Still, it wouldn't have been so bad if she'd given Eugene a fitting funeral or allowed his friends to do so; but to go and bury him like a pauper, like a dog! But every morning I go out with cold water and pray to God to give her her just deserts. She thinks that because she is now prosperous and lives in a big mansion she is beyond God's reach. You wait! God will be the judge. Every evening, before I go to sleep, I pray to God to take my part, to take the part of the poor and innocent."

I then told Annie that I'd hardly seen Josephine after Eugene's burial. We'd met once or twice at a funeral or a wedding, but we'd only greeted each other. After the way in which she had behaved, relations between us were bound to be rather cold. We merely asked each other how we were doing. It was just as well that we now lived quite a long way from each other and weren't likely to meet often in the normal course of things.

As far as I know, her business continued to prosper, though she lived virtually alone in her big mansion on Circular Road. The way she had buried her husband was the talk of the town for several weeks. You would not believe it, but some people actually took her part. Some people actually said that she was justified in behaving like that because Eugene had treated her abominably. It would teach husbands, they said, to think twice before they drove their wives out of their houses to install their mistresses instead. As a man sows, they said, so let him reap. In fact, many saw Eugene's illness and shameful burial as God's punishment on him for the disgraceful way in which he had treated his wife. Of course, they did not know the full story, as some of us did, or they were just being bloody-minded.

So Annie left to join her brother in Waterloo. In a sense I was sad to see her go. The paths of the three of us, who had been such great friends at Sissy Dinah's establishment, had now completely diverged. Our fortunes had been so different. I would like to have thought that Annie would be heading for a better life in Waterloo, but from what I knew of her brother and his family, I had my doubts.

This brother had never done well in life. He'd played truant most of the time in school, and, without a firm male hand in the house, their mother had not been able to control him. He had taken to smoking cigarettes and worse things, and had drifted from one poorly paid job to the other. He'd hardly been able to bury his mother, the late Mrs. Macauley, when she died. Eugene had taken care of most of the expenses. To the best of my knowledge, he never married; he just kept on having children, one after the other, and by more than one woman, children he could hardly support. When he realized that he couldn't cope with life in Freetown, he had gone to Waterloo to live with the mother of some of his children, and it was rumored that their mainstay was the manufacture of illicit gin or 'omole,' as it is called. So it seemed as if he graduated from merely drinking alcohol to drinking 'omole'; and his woman drank it too. Such was the establishment into which Annie was now going. How could I be sure that the future held anything for her?

Anyway, some years passed.

Our life at Murray Town continued on its placid path. Our children continued to make great progress. Within a short time, we were able to celebrate their marriages, and, soon, grandchildren started to arrive. Our lot couldn't have been better. Mr. T and I were enjoying our retirement and were thankful for the way that God had blessed us.

I was in our bedroom one morning, dusting some furniture, when the young houseboy came up to me and said, "There's a woman downstairs who has come to see you, Ma. I asked her to sit in the parlor and wait." Who on Earth could it be, I thought, to come at this hour of the morning. Well, I walked downstairs into the parlor, and who do you think I saw there? It was Annie, of course. But she was a shadow of her former self. I barely recognized her. Even after the traumatic events following Eugene's death, she had retained some of her beauty and had remained rather plump. The woman who now rose to meet me was little more than skin and bones. Her face was long and haggard, and lots of wrinkles had started to appear. Those formerly beautiful dimples now looked more like sunken cheeks. She was wearing an old fawn dress that seemed to just hang on her body. On her head was a head-tie that looked like brown and blue, but could originally have been of another color. On her feet, there were embroidered slippers, but these were so old that one of her toes was showing.

"Oh Annie, how are you?" I asked her. "How's the body?" I preferred to use the traditional greeting rather than tell her that she looked ill and ask her what was the matter with her. I thought it wouldn't be polite to do so.

"Oh, my sister," she said, "you see me in a better condition than I've been in. Life has been very hard. Waterloo has turned out to be little better than Freetown. I am managing with my brother and his family, but the house is so small that I don't even have a room to myself. I have to share with two of the children. Besides, you will be surprised at the caliber of people who frequently come to the house. There's hardly any peace and quiet. Some of them come to drink, and you can imagine the language they use when they're drunk. Of course, I cannot complain, because it's not my house. It's not even my brother's house. So what can I do? And the woman he's with is so arrogant and insulting because she claims that the house belongs to her family. At times she treats me like a servant.

" 'Annie,' she'd say, 'I think you will have to go to market today, and do some shopping. I am so tired that I'm not good for anything.' At other times it's 'As you see me today, I'm not in the mood for cooking. Annie, you will have to cook today.' "

"But Annie," I said, "you must not take that kind of behavior from her. After all, you must be much older than she is. She ought to respect you for that, if for nothing else."

"I know," she replied. "But what can I do? Where can I go? I still manage to make my coco-nut and ginger cakes, and that helps me to keep soul and body together, but at times it's the money I make from that trade that I spend when I go shopping and that I use to cook and feed all of us. I don't make enough to go and rent my own place. My brother and his woman make some money out of the 'omole' that they sell, but it all goes on drinking. They seem to be drinking from morning to evening every day. Even the children have started drinking that stuff. You wouldn't believe it. It's terrible."

"If I were you," I said, "I would try to get out of that environment."

"It's easy for you to talk, Priscilla," she said. "Where should I go? Look at me! Look at the clothes I'm wearing! I don't make enough to buy myself decent clothes. In fact, the main reason why I've come to see you, Priscilla, is to beg you in the name of God and in remembrance of those times we've spent together, to give me some of your old clothes. You must have many that you no longer have any use for. Now that I have lost so much weight, they will fit me. They will look so much better on me than the raggedy things I am forced to wear. Please, Priscilla, I beg you in the name of God, help me! Nowadays I hardly go to church because I have nothing to wear."

Naturally, I was deeply touched by what Annie said and by that plaintive cry in her voice. I immediately went into my bedroom and selected two Sunday dresses that I'd had for years but no longer wore, and three old everyday dresses. I put them all in a bag for her.

"You can have these now," I said. "Later, when I have more time, I will look into some trunks and select some more. They'll all be in good condition, though some of them may have gone out of fashion. I daresay you won't mind that. Come and see us again in about three weeks, and by then I would have selected them."

"May God bless you my sister," she said, taking the bag of clothes. "You've always had a heart of gold. You are a true Christian. God will multiply your blessings and make sure that where these have come from, many more will go. God will continue to bless you and your husband and your family."

With that, she took her leave. Three weeks later, she came back, looking even more subdued and somber than she did the previous time. I had collected twelve dresses of various kinds that I put into a bundle for her. Once more, she thanked me profusely before putting the bundle on her head and leaving. As she walked down the street, I looked after her, sadly shaking my head and crying.

That was the last time I saw her alive. She died about a year later of bronchial pneumonia, so I was told. Surely, malnutrition and poor sanitation also had a lot to do with it.

Mr. T and I went to the funeral in Waterloo. In fact, we helped quite a lot with the funeral arrangements because the brother and his woman were in no position, financially and psychologically, to do so. We owed it to Annie to ensure that she at least had a decent funeral. Apparently, she had told her relatives that if anything happened to her, they should immediately contact Mr. T and me, even before they made any arrangements. It was just as well. She must have sensed that her relatives would be unable to do much, but that she could depend on us to help out and ensure that in death she was not put to shame.

The professional funeral people had just started business in Freetown at the time, and we conveyed the corpse to the funeral home for preparation. Mr. T ensured that Annie had a very good, solidly made coffin. Everyone commented on how decent the coffin was. We dressed Annie in a lovely blue lace shroud, embroidered with beads and flowers. She had a coronet of flowers on her head and a bouquet in her left hand. She looked like a bride going to the wedding she'd never had. The funeral services people were very good and did a most professional job in preparing the corpse. They succeeded in getting those dimples into her cheeks again, and were able to capture her original beauty, even though she must have been nearing sixty.

In the announcement, her relatives asked us to say that she was sixty, but I'm sure she was not yet sixty. It showed that they did not even know her exact age. I wonder how much else they didn't know about her, and what kind of relatives they were.

Do you know, as she lay in that coffin, she smiled radiantly; yes, she was actually smiling as radiantly as I'd often seen her smile in her youth.

And she seemed to be at perfect peace with herself, with the world, and with God. I've often heard people exclaim that death is beautiful, that death is sweet, when they're looking at their relatives gorgeously dressed in their well upholstered coffins. Well, I won't go to that extent, but as I looked at Annie, on that lovely February day, lying so contentedly and peacefully in her coffin, I couldn't help but think that, at times, death can reconcile us with the world and with God.

She seemed to be saying to us that, after all the troubles and tribulations, after all the suffering and disappoint-

ments, she was finally at rest and at peace, "safe in the arms of Jesus." Yes, this was truly "rest of the weary."

I cried a bit for the times we had all spent together, and I cried when I remembered the betrayal and the humiliation. But, the more I looked at Annie's corpse, the more I realized that this wasn't really an occasion for crying, for she seemed to be definitely at peace and to have gone to her rest.

She had made a number of friends both in Freetown and at Waterloo, and hundreds turned up for the funeral. We laid the corpse out in the schoolroom of the church, and a lovely funeral service followed, a service fitting the lovely personality of the deceased. The final hymn we sang at the graveside could not have been more appropriate:

> "Now the laborer's task is o'er,
> Now the battle day is past,
> Now upon the farther shore,
> Lands the voyager at last.
> Father, in thy gracious keeping,
> Leave we now thy servant sleeping."

And what about Josephine? She too died about two years later. Her business had prospered and she had acquired some property of her own. The mansion on Circular Road, where she still continued to live, now belonged to her siblings, as much as it did to her. I suppose, she felt she should have property that was hers and hers alone. So, she built a house somewhere in Lumley that she rented. Eugene's gratuity from the United Africa Company went to her, as the true and legal wife, and she ploughed it all into the business. But prosperous though she was, she had been living more or less alone, and she had no one to leave all that property to. She didn't remarry. Considering her reputation, who would marry her, even though she was wealthy? So, she continued to live in the house, husbandless and childless.

Then, suddenly, she fell ill. It was a matter of incredible irony that she too, like Eugene, suffered from cancer, cancer of the womb. Apparently it was discovered late, so there was little that could be done by way of surgery to help her. I remember the day I heard the news that she was seriously ill and had been admitted to one of the better nursing homes.

"I think I should go and visit her," I said to Mr. T. "We have not seen her for a very long time, and relations between us have been almost completely severed, but now that she's seriously ill, charity at least requires that I should go and visit her."

"Are you sure that she won't think that you are a false friend, who has come to crow over her now that she is ill?" asked Mr. T.

"Oh no, Mr. T," I replied. "Josephine knows me better than that. She has her faults, but she is a fairly good judge of character."

"In that case, go, and give her my best wishes."

So I went. I couldn't believe my eyes when I saw Josephine lying down on that hospital bed. Remember, she had always been stout? And, once her business started to prosper, she'd begun to look large and majestic. Now, she was nothing but skin and bones. She had completely shrunk. This cancer is a dreadful disease, I thought. I pray to God that they soon find a cure. It can reduce the most powerful person to mere shambles. Her eyes seemed to be shining, though, with an eerie and unearthly glow. In fact, they were the only part of Josephine that seemed alive. Her hands were wrinkled and looked more like the hands of an eighty year-old woman. Her breasts were flat and flabby on her chest.

"Priscilla my sister," she said to me in a very weak voice, "I am chewing pain; I'm actually chewing pain. When the pain starts, it's almost as though it's moving from my stomach into my mouth. The doctors have given me all

kinds of things to alleviate the pain, but it's still there. At times I can feel it coming on, almost like a tornado. Believe me, I'm actually eating pain. It is horrible."

"Take comfort my sister," I said. "Take surrur! God is in his heaven. He will do everything for the best."

"There it is," she suddenly shouted. "It's coming now! The pain is coming! God in heaven! It's coming. It's coming. Lord, have mercy! Lord have mercy! Lord help me!"

She writhed and twisted on the bed, and her shrunken features contorted in agony. She held up her right hand as if to ward off the pain, and continued to cry out "Lord, have mercy! Lord, have mercy!" Her voice went shrill. Then, it suddenly seemed that she couldn't shout anymore. She just lay gasping on the bed.

"She is really suffering," I told Mr. T when I returned home from the hospital. "I hope God will have mercy on her and cut her pain short. In this kind of situation, death can only be a relief."

But Josephine's agony was very prolonged. When the doctors saw that they couldn't do any more for her, they discharged her from the nursing home, and she returned home to the big mansion to die.

Her sister came from Ghana to help with the nursing, for a while. They hadn't been very close. To tell you the truth, Josephine hadn't been very close to anyone. However, when her sister learnt that Josephine was on the point of death and needed final nursing, she came to help out.

But Josephine's agony was prolonged, and though she was in great pain, death did not come easily or quickly. The sister had her own affairs in Ghana and couldn't stay indefinitely. So, she left, promising to return as soon as there was definite news. She arranged for a maid to look after Josephine, to clean her and cook whatever she needed to eat, and there was a male servant who did the heavier chores.

The sister had arranged, as well, for the making of a shroud. In the event of Josephine dying while she was away, it would be about a week before she could return to Freetown for the funeral. And then, it would be too late to start making such arrangements. The arrangements for something like a shroud should be made by close female relatives like a sister. So, she commissioned an elaborate shroud made, and left it with another female relative. I couldn't help feeling sad when I heard this. I wonder what Josephine would have thought if she heard they'd already made her shroud.

She is reported to have said to the sister when the latter was about to leave for Ghana, "So, you are going to leave me, you are going to leave me to this wicked Freetown!"

"I will be back very soon," replied the sister. "There are one or two matters that I have to go and arrange. I'll be back as soon as I can. But I leave you in the hands of God." So she left.

The maid she'd hired was not, I'm afraid, very conscientious. Perhaps she couldn't have been expected to be. She was a paid hand, not a close relative. Apparently, she had an eye open for whatever she could get out of the situation, and there were reports that several of Josephine's prized possessions, including trinkets, crockery and beautiful linen, went missing.

Josephine's business was closed soon after she fell ill, because the people who were hired to look after it were, similarly, unreliable; they were only out to line their own pockets.

After a while, so I heard, the maid didn't even go into Josephine's bedroom anymore. She'd cook the food, put it on a stool, and push the stool, at arm's length, close to Josephine's bed. She didn't take the food in herself, let alone feed Josephine. After Josephine had eaten what little she could eat, the maid pulled the stool out of the room.

As far as obeying the call of nature was concerned, Josephine had to manage, in whatever way she could, to reach a chamber pot, which the maid pulled out from time to time and emptied. The maid complained that Josephine stank, and, in her ignorance, probably thought that her illness was contagious. So she refused to go inside the room unless she absolutely had to.

When I visited Josephine one day toward the end, and went into the bedroom, I couldn't believe the stench that greeted my nostrils. The room already smelled like the chamber of death.

Tears came into my eyes, and I felt the poignancy of the situation even more when Josephine said, "Please Priscilla, I beg you, in the name of God, wash me. Please give me a bath. These people that they've left me with refuse to wash me, and I stink. Please wash me." I ordered the maid to heat some water and bring it to me in a bucket. I also asked for some scented soap and a sponge, and I gave Josephine a thorough washing, right there in her bedroom. I washed and combed her hair, and asked the maid to bring me clean clothes. After I'd finished, she said, "Thank you, Priscilla. The good Lord will bless you."

I could not but reflect on the reversal of fortune that can happen in human affairs. Who would have thought that the majestic Josephine would be reduced to this?

She died very shortly after that. It was reported that her dying groans could be heard from about fifty yards away. Her brother in the United Kingdom and her sister in Ghana came for the funeral as soon as they heard the news. By all accounts it should have been a very grand funeral. Josephine's family had been well known in Freetown, and she herself was a successful businesswoman and had a very large circle of acquaintances. She'd been a prominent member of the Annie Walsh Old Girls' Association and of the Young Women's Christian Association. The members should have turned up in droves for her funeral. After the separation from Eugene, she'd rejoined her parents' old church, St. George's Cathedral. Though that church is vast, it should still have been packed.

As God would have it, though, it rained very heavily on the August afternoon of the funeral. It seemed as though the heavens themselves opened up, and millions of gallons of rainwater poured on Freetown. It was impossible to have a long procession. The cortege drove as fast as possible from the house to the church, which was less than half full, and from the church to the cemetery for the interment. Only a handful of the members of Josephine's various associations were there. Of course, Mr. T and I were there. In spite of everything that had happened, we were loyal to the end. I went to the big house on Circular Road to take one final look at Josephine's corpse. The white lace shroud was elaborate, but the face was not in repose. It was quite obvious that she had died in agony. Try as hard as they could, those professionals at the funeral home could not simulate a look of peace.

I couldn't but compare that look with the look of serenity and peace on Annie's face as she lay in her coffin.

When we went back home after the funeral, Mr. T said to me, as though he was reading my thoughts, "this should be a lesson to us, to try and live as well as we can and to do all the good we can, because we don't know how we'll die." I could not agree with him more.

Now, I am the only one left of that trio of friends that laughed and joked and tried our best to enjoy life at Sissy Dinah's establishment. In those days, we couldn't have known much about what the future had in store for each of us, and how different our various fortunes would be. I was blessed with a worthy husband and several children. Mr. T and I enjoyed a very peaceful retirement. Our children turned out to be quite successful. They married and

had children of their own, and, in some cases, they've even given me some great grandchildren.

Some of my grandchildren are abroad. Some are still here in Sierra Leone. We have all been through tumultuous times, but we have survived in the end. Mr. T lived on till the grand old age of eighty, when he too passed away and was laid to rest with his ancestors. I am still here, in this magnificent house, which passed on to me after his death. Quietly, I await the day when it will please the almighty to summon me, so that I can finally join my Mr. T in the after-life.

Life has been good to me. I know that when that day comes, there will be hordes of children, grandchildren, great grandchildren, and friends and relatives to take me to my rest.

EPILOGUE

When we left Mrs. Thompson's house, the normally vivacious and talkative Kunle was very quiet for a while, and so was I.

Kunle, very carefully and deliberately, negotiated her way along Murray Town Road, Wilkinson Road, Congo Town Road, Ascension Town Road, Krootown Road, Adelaide Street, Campbell Street and on to Pa Demba Road. It was almost as though she was going out of her way to be polite to other drivers. As I've mentioned, she'd normally give as good as she got to those mad taxi and Poda Poda drivers. Now, she'd become overly courteous and even stopped for some of them saying, "After you!"

It seemed as though I was seeing a transformation. Was this the result of Mrs. Thompson's impact on her? Was she thinking of Mr. Thompson's words that we must be careful how we live and do all the good we can, for we do not know how we shall die?

"Didn't I tell you she was a very remarkable woman?" Kunle finally asked.

"Very remarkable," I said. "And what a memory! To think that at her age she can remember all those details!"

"And what tremendous zest she still has for life!" Kunle said. "She puts us all to shame with our whining and com-

225

plaining and bickering. She has given me so much material, material that I could use for many books, not just one."

"I am grateful to you for arranging for me to meet her. There are some people you meet, day after day, who never have an impact on your life. And then, you chance to meet someone, just once, who leaves such an indelible stamp, that no matter what you do or how long you live, you can never erase the impression. As far as I am concerned, Mrs. Priscilla Thompson is one such person."

Then, Kunle and I both resumed our pensive silence, as she drove me to my house and left me.